TRUTH OR DARE

Books by Fern Michaels:

Sweet Vengeance
Holly and Ivy
Fancy Dancer
No Safe Secret
Wishes for Christmas
About Face
Perfect Match
A Family Affair
Forget Me Not
The Blossom Sisters
Balancing Act
Tuesday's Child
Betrayal
Southern Comfort
To Taste the Wine
Sins of the Flesh
Sins of Omission
Return to Sender
Mr. and Miss Anonymous
Up Close and Personal
Fool Me Once
Picture Perfect
The Future Scrolls
Kentucky Sunrise
Kentucky Heat
Kentucky Rich
Plain Jane
Charming Lily
What You Wish For
The Guest List
Listen to Your Heart
Celebration
Yesterday
Finders Keepers
Annie's Rainbow

Sara's Song
Vegas Sunrise
Vegas Heat
Vegas Rich
Whitefire
Wish List
Dear Emily
Christmas at Timberwoods

The Sisterhood Novels:

Need to Know
Crash and Burn
Point Blank
In Plain Sight
Eyes Only
Kiss and Tell
Blindsided
Gotcha!
Home Free
Déjà Vu
Cross Roads
Game Over
Deadly Deals
Vanishing Act
Razor Sharp
Under the Radar
Final Justice
Collateral Damage
Fast Track
Hokus Pokus
Hide and Seek
Free Fall
Lethal Justice
Sweet Revenge

Books by Fern Michaels (Continued):

The Jury
Vendetta
Payback
Weekend Warriors

The Men of the Sisterhood Novels:

Truth or Dare
High Stakes
Fast and Loose
Double Down

The Godmothers Series:

Getaway (E-Novella Exclusive)
Spirited Away (E-Novella Exclusive)
Hideaway (E-Novella Exclusive)
Classified
Breaking News
Deadline
Late Edition
Exclusive
The Scoop

E-Book Exclusives:

Desperate Measures
Seasons of Her Life
To Have and To Hold
Serendipity

Captive Innocence
Captive Embraces
Captive Passions
Captive Secrets
Captive Splendors
Cinders to Satin
For All Their Lives
Texas Heat
Texas Rich
Texas Fury
Texas Sunrise

Anthologies:

Mistletoe Magic
Winter Wishes
The Most Wonderful Time
When the Snow Falls
Secret Santa
A Winter Wonderland
I'll Be Home for Christmas
Making Spirits Bright
Holiday Magic
Snow Angels
Silver Bells
Comfort and Joy
Sugar and Spice
Let it Snow
A Gift of Joy
Five Golden Rings
Deck the Halls
Jingle All the Way

FERN MICHAELS

TRUTH OR DARE

KENSINGTON PUBLISHING CORP.
http://www.kensingtonbooks.com

KENSINGTON BOOKS are published by

Kensington Publishing Corp.
119 West 40th Street
New York, NY 10018

All Kensington titles, imprints and distributed lines are available at special quantity discounts for bulk purchases for sales promotion, premiums, fund-raising, educational or institutional use.

Special book excerpts or customized printings can also be created to fit specific needs. For details, write or phone the office of the Kensington Special Sales Manager: Kensington Publishing Corp., 119 West 40th Street, New York, NY, 10018. Attn. Special Sales Department. Phone: 1-800-221-2647.

Kensington and the K logo Reg. U.S. Pat. & TM Off.

Library of Congress Control Number: 2017955129

ISBN-13: 978-1-4967-0322-4
ISBN-10: 1-4967-0322-7
First Kensington Hardcover Edition: April 2018

10 9 8 7 6 5 4 3 2 1

Printed in the United States of America

I would like to dedicate this book to the memory of the real Demetri Pappas.

Rest in peace, Demetri Pappas, rest in peace.

Prologue

It was an enormous truck. White in color, with brilliant decals of fruit and vegetables stenciled over the wide side panels. In the center of the panel was large, vivid red lettering proclaiming that the truck was owned by B. M. Produce; then in smaller letters it read, "Fresh produce today and every day." At the very bottom, at the back end of the huge truck was ID for the company's business license.

There were four such trucks in the United States. One in Charleston, South Carolina; one in Falls Church, Virginia; one in Denver, Colorado; and one in San Diego, California. The company also owned twenty-four other trucks the size of a school minibus. Six each were allocated to the four geographical areas of the company that housed the bigger trucks.

The four large trucks were used for transporting produce. The twenty-four smaller trucks were used for promotional purposes to ensure that B. M. Produce became a household name. The only thing the smaller trucks did was roam the streets and towns so that people would see the trucks with the colorful decals and come to recognize the name of the company. The trucks patrolled the areas from six in the morning till eight o'clock at night.

The drivers were paid well for doing the cushy job.

B. M. Produce had been in business for seventeen years. To date, each and every employee had been hired seventeen years ago, when the company started. Not one employee had left the company, and no new ones had been hired.

The main headquarters for B. M. Produce was in San Diego, California, where the company was run by a man named Ortiz Ozay. He set up the driving schedules for the four big main trucks. He was the man responsible for the intricate locking mechanisms on the rear doors of each truck for special deliveries so that not even the drivers could open the doors.

The drivers called Ozay the traveling man because once a month, like clockwork, he would visit the other three locations to check on how things were going. At least that's what they were told.

In order to work, and keep working, for B. M. Produce each employee had to agree never to ask questions and to mind their own business and also agree not to talk to anyone about the company.

The employees agreed because who was interested in hearing about a load of overripe melons, stinky cabbage, and rotting lettuce?

None of the employees had ever seen the inside of the trucks they drove. If they had, they would have seen benches anchored to the floor and piles and piles of sleeping bags. They would have gagged at the sharp ammonia smell of urine and the fetid odor of human feces.

Because . . . B. M. Produce wasn't really in the business of transporting fruits and vegetables at all.

B. M. Produce was in the business of trafficking little blond-haired ten-year-old girls.

Chapter One

Demetri Pappas, doctor of veterinary medicine, dropped to his haunches to stare at his patient. There was a protocol to these visits that both doctor and patient adhered to every six months. The doctor spoke in Greek first, then back in English to see if his patient remembered his earlier teachings before having gone to live with Jack Emery.

Cyrus yipped, then yipped again.

"Fetch me the tennis ball. When you bring it to me, drop it into my hand." It was all said in Greek. Cyrus rose to his feet, all 160 magnificent pounds of pure dog. He raced to the end of the room, pawed through the toys, and found the tennis ball, not the red plastic ball, not the yellow rubber ball but the green tennis ball, and then carried it in his mouth back to where Dr. Pappas waited. He dropped the ball into his hands, offered up another yip, and smacked his paw into the doctor's open palm. He waited for the praise he knew was coming. No treat, however; Dr. Pappas was stingy with his treats, and Cyrus knew it.

"Well done, Cyrus. That was our last test. And you passed each one. Jack is going to be very proud of you. Go along, Cyrus, you have ten minutes to visit your old friends out in the yard. Ten minutes." This order was also given in rapid-fire Greek. Cyrus trotted off, allowing the doctor to home in on Joseph Espinosa, who was watching the scene play out in dumbfound amazement.

"Cyrus understands Greek?" He might as well have said, "Cyrus just returned from the moon," by the expression on his face.

"But of course. All my dogs understand my language. Every animal I breed is extraordinary, as you can see by Cyrus. His intelligence is superior to that of some humans. His stamina is equal to that of several men. He knows right from wrong. He is loyal to me and to his master, in this case, Jack Emery. He would and will kill for either one of us if he sensed our lives were in danger. He understands that children need to be protected at all times, at all costs. Cyrus graduated canine school at the top of his class of five."

"Uh-huh," was all Espinosa could think of to say.

"So, tell me, Mr. Espinosa, how is Jack and why did you bring Cyrus today?"

"Root canal. Jack had already canceled it twice, and the doctor told him no more, and the tooth was bothering him. Jack said he called to clear it with you."

"Yes, my assistant took the call. My checkups are mandatory, and I suffer no cancelations. Jack knows this, and that is why you're here. In other words, Mr. Espinosa, I run a tight ship."

"Uh-huh," Espinosa said again.

Espinosa watched as the doctor took a beef-flavored stick from a jar on the counter and slipped it into a plastic sleeve that he then placed in the cylinder that was Cyrus's report. A ritual. The doctor looked down at his watch just as Cyrus sauntered through the door. He looked around, then trotted over to the doctor, and waited for the doctor to tie the cylinder to his collar.

"Do not remove this cylinder, Mr. Espinosa. That is for

Jack to do. It's part of our ritual. In addition to my warning, be advised that if you were to try to take off the cylinder Cyrus *would* take off your hand."

"Uh-huh," Espinosa said.

"This visit is now over. Cyrus, it was lovely seeing you again. We'll meet again in six months. Take care of your master and anyone else who needs your help. Let's have a hug, and then you can be on your way."

Espinosa watched as Cyrus stood on his hind legs and wrapped his front paws around the roly-poly doctor. Then he nuzzled the man under the chin. He let loose with two sharp yips, turned, and headed for the door. He didn't look back. Espinosa scurried to keep up with the prancing dog.

Outside, the compound was quiet. Espinosa wondered how many dogs were housed here. He asked Cyrus, not expecting an answer. Cyrus barked seven times. So much for being stupid. Seven dogs at fifty grand a pop was some serious money. He could hardly wrap his mind around a dog, any dog, being worth fifty grand. Except maybe Cooper. *Cooper. Don't go there*, he warned himself.

Once inside the shiny black Silverado, Cyrus settled himself, buckled his seat belt, and went to sleep.

Espinosa tooled along the winding country road that would take him back to the District and the BOLO Building, admiring the trees on either side bursting with fall color. Jack would be waiting to pick up Cyrus, he let his mind wander. He was supposed to meet up with Ted and Maggie after lunch to do a photo shoot with some gung ho new congressman who loved getting his picture in the papers. He hated puff assignments, as did Ted and Maggie. But those puff assignments paid the bills.

He sniffed and smiled. Alexis had used his truck a few days ago to pick up some beauty supplies, and the scent still lingered. He liked the powdery floral scent, whatever it was. Lilacs, maybe. He missed Alexis, and she'd only been gone for thirty-six hours. The girls were on a mission that, according to Alexis, was so hush-hush she couldn't even tell him where she was going, much less tell him what it was about.

Espinosa looked at the clock on the dashboard. He had made good time on the way out to Reston and was making good time on his return. His thoughts turned to how pleased Jack was going to be with Cyrus's stellar report.

It happened all at once. A flash out of the corner of his eye, a streak, movement of some kind. A deer? Cyrus's bloodcurdling bark, the dog's seat belt clicking open. Espinosa almost lost control of the Silverado. He took his foot off the gas pedal, slowed, and steered the big truck to the shoulder of the road. Cyrus pawed the window, then pressed the door handle. The door flew open, and he was out like he'd been shot from a cannon, sprinting, and then airborne down the embankment. He was lost to sight before Espinosa even got out of the truck.

Espinosa plowed through the brush, and before he knew what was happening, he lost his footing and rolled down the embankment, Cyrus's ear-pounding barks almost splitting his eardrums. He shook his head to clear it and then did a mental check to see if he'd broken or sprained anything. Other than a sore rear end, he thought he was okay. He opened his eyes wide, not sure he was seeing what he was seeing as Cyrus continued to bark relentlessly.

Three little kids, filthy dirty in equally filthy dirty clothing, clustered together, their frightened eyes on Cyrus. Espinosa swallowed hard. He came from a huge family of eleven siblings. He knew a thing or two about kids. First things first. "Cyrus, shut the hell up, or I'm going to call Dr. Pappas. I see them. I know what to do. Chill, okay?"

Either the threat of calling the doctor or Espinosa's calm tone or the big dog's just getting tired worked because he stopped barking. The fur on the nape of his neck stood straight up, his ears went flat against his head just as his tail dropped between his legs. Warrior pose.

Espinosa struggled to take a deep breath, the doctor's words ringing in his ears that dogs like Cyrus knew to protect children. Surely, the monster dog wouldn't turn on him. Or would he?

"Like I said, Cyrus, I know what to do. Just let me do it, okay?" He waited. Cyrus yipped and advanced a few steps, the children cowering against each other.

"Okay, kids, listen up. My name is Joseph. This is Cyrus. He means you no harm. I won't hurt you. How did you get here? Are you lost? Tell me where you live, and I'll take you home. Are you hungry?" When there was no response to his questions, Espinosa wondered why there were no tears. He estimated the age of the oldest girl going by how tall she was to be maybe seven, the other girl, almost as tall, six or so. Maybe they were twins. The little guy looked to be four, perhaps five years old. He was missing a shoe and a sock.

Espinosa tried wheedling. "Come on, tell me your names so I can take you home." The sudden thought that maybe they didn't want to go home hit him. Maybe they had run away from abusive parents. He corrected that thought. These kids, from what he could see by the layers of dirt and the condition of their clothes, looked to have been on the run for a while. All three were skinny and scrawny. They looked alike. Siblings.

Cyrus barked. *Do something already.*

Espinosa pondered the situation. How was he going to get all three kids to the top of the embankment without them cutting and running? Cyrus, of course. They were afraid of him. Cyrus could herd them to the top, and then he would secure them in the backseat of the Silverado and head for the BOLO Building. He'd send out a call for an emergency meeting. A *dire* emergency meeting.

"Okay, listen up, everyone. This is what we're going to do." Espinosa spoke directly at Cyrus, whom he knew would understand. "You herd them to the top of the embankment. You watch, and I'll put them in the truck one by one. I'll call Jack and the others to meet up at the BOLO Building, and we'll work things out there. Right now, these kids are just too damn scared to do anything. Let's do it, big guy."

Cyrus barked. *At last, a plan.*

It took some doing, but they finally got the three kids into the back of the truck. All three were crying now as they clung to one another. Cyrus never took his eyes off them, even for a second.

Espinosa turned on the engine, then called the team. He ended each call with, *I'm forty minutes out. I repeat, this is a dire emergency.* After he ended the last call, to Abner Tookus, he put the truck in gear and headed down the road.

Chapter Two

Sir Charles Martin smacked his hands together before he scooped out a blend of his special rub for the prime rib he was preparing for his and Ferg's dinner. He was so looking forward to eating it hours from now and sharing it with Fergus, who was keeping himself busy shelling fresh peas from the garden. "I don't know about you, Ferg, but I'm starting to feel like we're bachelors again. I see more of you these days than I do of my wife. That's not necessarily a bad thing," he added hastily.

"I hear you, mate. Anytime you have enough of me, just let me know, and I'll head on down the road to rattle around alone in that big farmhouse. Is it my imagination, or are the girls busier than we are? They just finished a mission, they graced us with their presence, and then three days later they were gone again. Ah, don't pay any attention to me, I just hate not having anything to do. Sometimes, I talk to myself just to hear my own voice."

"Well, the garden is flourishing under your care. The dogs are loving that we're here all day and giving them our attention. I'm thinking if there are any leftovers from dinner I'd fix us a shepherd's pie for tomorrow's lunch. What do you think, Ferg?"

"I think that means an extra hour on the treadmill."

"There is that," Charles agreed as he washed and dried his hands. His special encrypted phone took that moment to buzz like an angry bee. An incoming text. A second later, Fergus's phone gave off three cheery notes. Both men looked at one another. Lady reared up and looked at both men.

"It would appear that our services are required at the BOLO Building. Take note, Ferg, of the word *dire*."

Fergus was already covering the bowl of emerald green peas he had just shelled and putting them in the refrigerator. He held the door open so Charles could slide the roasting pan holding the prime rib onto the big shelf.

Preparing dinner early in the morning was something Charles liked to do so that when nothing else was pending he could putz around with his memoirs, the very ones he knew he would never publish.

Quick as a wink, the kitchen was cleaned, the coffeepot was turned off, and the aprons were hung on the door of the pantry. "Ten minutes to change our shirts, grab our gear, and call Marcus to come sit the dogs. Hustle, Ferg."

Twelve minutes later, Charles backed the Land Rover from its parking space and whizzed through the open gates.

"Feels good to know we're needed, doesn't it, Ferg?"

"I have to admit I do like the adrenaline rush. I hope everyone can make it."

"You know the first rule, Fergus—we drop whatever we're doing, and no matter where we are we show up. No one to date has broken that rule."

In the District, Maggie had just hung her backpack over the back of her chair when her cell phone chirped to life. She looked down just as Ted Robinson fished his own chirping phone out of his pocket.

"Oh, boy, here we go! Hey, Caruso, you're up!" he yelled across the room. "You get the congressman and his social-climbing life. Do a good job." He was rewarded with a loud moan.

"*Dire!* Did you see that, Ted?" Maggie whispered, her eyes wide in anticipation of what "dire" meant. "Do you think it has something to do with Cyrus? Oh, God, if something happened to that dog, Jack will go nuclear."

"Not Cyrus. See the last few words. *Cyrus is fine.*"

"I missed that. Okay, okay, let's go. Are we taking the van or your car?"

"Caruso needs the van. We'll take my car. Did Dennis check in this morning?"

"Nope. Haven't seen him. He likes to go to Dings before coming to work. If he's there, he's right across the street from the BOLO, so he'll beat us there. What *are* you waiting for, Ted?" Maggie called out on her way to the elevator.

Ted scrambled to his feet. "I'm trying to come to terms with the word *dire*," he muttered to himself. "I didn't know Espinosa even knew the word. What the hell . . ."

"We'll know soon enough," Maggie said, punching the button of the elevator that would take them to the lower-level parking basement. "I'm excited. It's been a while since we had a case. The girls are busy as all get out. They're off right now, but it was so hush hush they wouldn't even tell me. Do you believe *that*?" she asked, outrage ringing in her voice.

Ted did believe it, but he wouldn't admit it for all the tea in China. "Have you heard from Abner lately? I called him yesterday and asked him to meet for lunch, but he said he was up to his eyeballs in something to do with some black ops and cybercrime at the CIA. That stuff is all Greek to me anyway. He said he could make lunch tomorrow. Want to join us?"

"Sure, why not. But only if we are not otherwise engaged. Remember the word *dire*, Ted." Ted nodded to show he understood as he slipped behind the wheel of his BMW. His thoughts turned to Dennis and wondering whether if he was at Dings he would bring some bagels to the meeting. Ted had been in such a rush this morning that he hadn't had time to eat his usual bowl of Cheerios.

As a matter of fact, Dennis West was at Dings, sitting outside at his favorite bistro table and scarfing down a bacon, cheese, and egg sandwich on a bagel. This was his favorite time of day, early morning, his favorite breakfast, and he got to spend some time doing one of his favorite things, people watching. Today was going to be run of the mill, so he was in no hurry to head for the *Post*. For some reason, news was sparse in the summer months. Despite the pleasure he took in watching people, what he really liked was action; he thrived on it. What he liked even more was being in the middle of said action.

Dennis finished his coffee and was about to head back inside for a refill when his phone announced an incoming text. He read it, blinked, then read it again. Holy crap! Action was about to go down, and here he was, sitting just across the street. If he left now, he'd be the first one to hit the BOLO Building. Or . . . he could refill his coffee and order a dozen bagels to take with him the moment he saw the first member of the team arrive. *Yeah, yeah*, he decided, *that's what I'll do*.

A dire emergency meeting. From Joe Espinosa. Of all people. Cyrus was fine. What did that mean? He got up and headed inside, where he got his coffee refill and a dozen bagels in a sack that had handles on it. "Throw in some strawberry cream cheese and butter," he instructed, knowing how much Abner loved strawberry cream cheese.

At the same moment that Dennis was thinking about Abner Tookus inside Dings, that very person was about to enter a secure conference room at the CIA, also known as

The Farm. Years earlier, he'd been recruited by the head man, whose *real* name he still did not know. Nor did he care. He had agreed to "help" for an outrageous sum of money with several other caveats. He could wear whatever he wanted, he could work whenever he wanted, and he answered to no one save himself and the man with no real name. The last condition was necessary so that he could quit or walk away at any time and his departure would not be with any reprisals. Should there be a reprisal, even the hint of one, Abner let it be known that he and his secret band of hackers would cripple the infamous agency.

So far, everything had worked just fine.

So far.

Abner, dressed in his paint-stained jeans with holes in the knees and high-top Keds with ragged shoelaces, stood in direct contrast to the men in Hugo Boss and Brooks Brothers suits sitting around the table. He stood in the open doorway, his gaze sweeping the room.

Today, Abner was wearing a bright red T-shirt that said, "EAT GRASS," and in smaller letters, "YOU'LL LIVE LONGER." He had no idea if eating grass would let a person live longer or not. He'd purchased the shirt off a street vendor for fifty cents, knowing he had gotten one hell of a bargain. He wore a watch that was as big as a mini alarm clock that did everything but tell time. Abner loved it because people stared at it wondering what it was. Every so often, it gave off a few earsplitting notes to the "Star Spangled Banner." Abner, you see, had a wicked sense of humor.

Abner turned the knob on the door and breezed through, waiving airily at all the buttoned-up suits sitting at a highly polished egg-shaped conference table. His boss, whose name he still didn't know or want to know, was behind him.

Abner figured the empty chair was for him. He plopped down, looked around at the occupants, and said, "Hit me." Confusion took over.

Abner sighed. "Tell me how I can help you. Why are we here? What is it you want from me? Is there a spokesperson here, or am I supposed to guess what this is all about? Who are you, anyway?"

"I don't like your flip attitude, young man, nor your mode of dress," a jowly, bald-headed man said. "This is the CIA! We're authorized to be here and to ask questions." Abner raised his eyebrows but said nothing.

A man at the far end of the table, a man who could have passed for the jowly bald-headed man's twin, shouted, "We'd like to see a report of some kind to justify the exorbitant amount of money this agency is paying you. You aren't even on the books. And we want to know exactly what it is you *do*."

"If I'm not on the books, that means I don't exist. That would mean I'm a ghost. So what are we doing here? I could be a volunteer, for all you know." Abner looked around at the well-fed, extremely well-dressed men with their gold Rolexes. If there was one thing he hated more than broccoli and people who harmed animals, it was men like the ones he was looking at.

"We don't need a snow job, young man. And you would be wise to curb your tongue," a skinny, stringy man with bulging eyes said. "My esteemed colleague asked you a perfectly legitimate question, so please answer it in a civil manner."

"You need to take that up with someone else. What I do here is confidential, and only one other set of eyes sees it." Abner leaned forward, hands folded on the shiny table, the small alarm-clock watch scratching the smooth surface. The sound was loud in the room. "Do any of you sitting at this table know anything about cybercrime other than what you read or see on the news? Are any of you aware of the dark side of the Internet, the underbelly of it? That's where I live and dwell to keep your asses safe as well as the asses of your assets out in the field." The shocked expressions gave Abner his answer. "Do you know what malware is? If I told you my computer was air-gapped, would you know what it meant? Or how about algorithms? Do you know what they are? Broadband?" In his eyes, these men were just a bunch of stuffed suits impressed with their own incompetence.

"Now see here, young fella . . ." a bewhiskered, white-haired gentleman started to bluster.

This is going nowhere fast, Abner thought. "Listen up, dudes, and try this on for size. Tonight, when I go home, all I have to do is log onto my computer, press a few keys, and I can wipe out your identities. Tomorrow morning, you'll be shopping at Goodwill and standing in line at a soup kitchen. I can do that. Just ask the gentleman standing behind me."

Abner was about to clarify his little speech when his cell phone, which was on vibrate, buzzed in the pocket of his ragged jeans. He pulled it out, looked at the text message, and stood up. "Meeting's over, boys. I gotta go!"

Abner's boss snapped to attention. "Wait! You can't leave now! This meeting has been on the books for months. You can't just walk out of here with no explanation."

"Yes, I can. Watch me walk out the door. Read my contract! The one that doesn't exist. I'm a ghost, remember?"

The clamor in the room rose to a full crescendo as Abner pushed back his chair.

"But . . . when will you be back?" his boss asked.

"I don't know. Maybe soon. Maybe never," Abner called over his shoulder.

"You're fired!" someone shouted from the conference room.

Abner stopped for a second. "Now you're sounding like Donald Trump. Try this on for size. I. Quit! See you at Goodwill. By the way, that's where I bought the jeans I'm wearing."

As he walked through the doorway, Abner muttered to himself, "Sometimes I just crack myself up."

Man, did that feel good, Abner thought as he raced out of the building and down a long walkway that took him to where his SUV was parked. *Dire*. "Dire" meant serious. Deadly serious when it came from Joe Espinosa.

The clock on the dashboard said it was 8:20.

The last person to receive Espinosa's text was Jack Emery, who was sitting in the dental chair in Bruno Sabatini's office undergoing a root canal. Actually, it was his second treatment, which, to Dr. Sabatini's dismay, Jack had already postponed three times.

His mouth wide open, Jack was ripe for his good friend's tirade about missed appointments, gum disease, toothless people, and a whole host of other horrible things that were going to go wrong because Jack kept postponing his dental appointments.

Long years of familiarity allowed both men to talk "guy talk" when no one else was around. Other times, Jack showed respect to the doctor and vice versa.

"I love it when I have you at my mercy and you can't do a damn thing. If there was a way for me to strap you into this chair, I'd do it in a heartbeat. I have a good mind to yank this damn tooth right out of your mouth. Like right now, Jack."

Jack gurgled something that sounded like, *I'll kick your ass all the way to the Canadian border if you do that.*

Undeterred by the garbled threat, Dr. Sabatini turned to the counter for something he needed. Jack's encrypted cell phone took that moment to vibrate in his pocket. Who would call him here? Everyone knew Dr. Sabatini didn't abide phones in his office and was known for snatching them up and putting them under lock and key. Many a patient had learned the hard way that even begging didn't help. Rules were rules.

The moment Dr. Sabatini turned back toward him, Jack was reading Espinosa's text. Dire. But Cyrus was all right. What the hell. Dr. Sabatini made a move to grab the phone.

Jack, a murderous expression on his face, stiff-armed the dentist. "Listen, Bruno, let's cut the shit here," Jack said in a voice Dr. Sabatini had never heard before. "I have an emergency. Do something to the tooth and do it quick. I have to leave. I'll come back tomorrow, I swear." He ripped at the paper collar around his neck and waited for whatever magic potion Sabatini was going to put on the tooth, then the cap.

"Done."

"Listen, Bruno . . ."

"Go! I get it, Jack. What I just did for you is temporary. Get back here tomorrow, or you are going to be in a world of pain. Are you listening to me?"

"Yeah. See you."

In the waiting room, Harry looked up from a dog-eared copy of *Field and Stream*. Why he was even looking at it he had no idea since he didn't fish or hunt. Jack rushed right by him. "Did you get the text?"

"No. The sign said to turn off all phones. You know me, I always obey the rules. What text?"

"From Espinosa. We're to meet at the BOLO Building. He said it was *dire*. Dire, Harry. It's not Cyrus—he said he's fine. Some kind of dire emergency."

Harry was Jack's transportation this day, which meant he'd driven him on his Ducati. He unlocked it, settled himself, then waited for Jack to do the same. Then he drove, hell-bent for leather, low over the handlebars, Jack's arms wrapped around his waist.

Seventeen minutes later, none the worse for wear, Harry slowed and approached the massive iron gates that controlled entry to the alley behind the BOLO Building. He slid off, hung up his helmet, and waited for Jack, who was staring down the alley at something. Harry looked to see what was so interesting. "Is that . . . ?"

"Sure as hell looks like it to me," Jack mumbled, aware that his mouth was now throbbing.

"But how . . . ?"

"Retina scanner," was Jack's response.

Harry bent close, let the scanner see his eye, stepped back to wait for the hydraulics to open the door. He blinked, then blinked again at what he was seeing. Julie Wyatt and Cooper stared back at him and Jack. Cooper barked a greeting.

"How did you get in here?" Jack asked.

"Cooper let us in," Julie said in a brittle voice. "He woke me up at two o'clock this morning. He didn't bark or touch me or anything like that. I just woke up, and he was sitting by my bed. I think his warm breath is what woke me. He was packed and ready to go, his gear by the door. I . . . I was going to get dressed, but he was having none of that, and he herded me to the door. I didn't even brush my teeth, for God's sake. He wanted to leave right then, that minute. In case you haven't noticed, I'm still in my pajamas and slippers. I drove all night. He knew exactly what to do when we got here. We were the first ones here. Others are back in the offices and kitchens. I think all your friends are here except Joseph and your dog."

She was breathless when she finished her spiel, her dark brown eyes full of fear. "Something around here is wrong, and he needs to be here. Did you hear me?" she cried shrilly. "*Needs* is the key word. Oh, God, I am never going to understand this dog. I love him, but I don't understand him." Fat tears rolled down her cheeks. She swiped at them.

Jack looked at Harry.

Harry looked at Jack.

Both men stared at Julie Wyatt, who was still dressed in her pajamas and slippers and was wringing her hands, her bed hair all tousled. Her eyes were getting wilder by the moment.

"I'm going home," she said in the same brittle voice. "I brought him, so you can bring him home. When he's ready. No questions, please. I'm out of here."

Cooper scampered over to Julie, who bent over to hug the strange, mystical dog with tears in her eyes. Cooper licked at her tears, yipped softly, then walked her to the door. She waved, her gait unsteady.

"What the hell?" Jack said. He sat down on the floor, his back to the wall. Cooper sauntered over and looked Jack straight in the eye. Not knowing what else to do, Jack simply nodded as he ruffled the dog's ears.

Chapter Three

The team eyeballed Cooper, who, after a soft whoop by way of a greeting, walked over to the monster door and lay down. He closed his eyes, but everyone knew that the strange dog wasn't sleeping.

Cooper was waiting.

For what, no one knew.

Jack massaged his throbbing cheek. When Harry handed him four aspirin, he reached for them greedily. He chewed them dry; then Harry handed him a green leaf of some sort from the plastic bag he always carried in his pocket. Harry was a health-food nut.

"What is it?" Jack asked, suspicion ringing in his voice. Harry ignored the question.

"Just bite down on it. It will take the edge off the pain. You need to head back to the dentist. There are a lot of hours between now and next morning, and the pain will just get worse."

Jack nodded, knowing that Harry was right. Harry with the perfect teeth with nary a cavity, as in ever. Sometimes he hated Harry and his glistening pearly whites.

"Does anyone have a clue as to why we're all here?" Fergus asked. "I get the part about no matter where we are or what we're doing, we drop everything if a call goes out to meet. But we're all here except for the person who called the meeting." Cooper yipped to show he'd heard Fergus's last comment. Fergus immediately corrected his last statement. "And one unexpected four-legged guest we're always happy to see." Cooper yipped again to show that he accepted the correction.

"Are we just going to stand here in the hall or go to the conference room and talk about . . . something?" Abner asked.

"You got something to say?" Ted asked.

"As a matter of fact, I do. I just quit my job at the CIA." A chorus of "whys" hit the air.

"I hate working for stupid, buttoned-up suits who can't find their ass even with a road map and a flashlight. I was just about ready to walk out when Espinosa's text came through."

"Wow! What are you going to do now?" Dennis asked.

Abner laughed. "Count my money and tally up all the beachfront properties I own." The team laughed, knowing Abner's penchant for buying up beachfront properties for his future retirement. "And I plan to keep my eye on all those suits. One false move and . . ." He flexed his fingers, then rolled his eyes to show what he could do to the suits if they came after him in any way. The team nodded. They understood perfectly what Abner Tookus was capable of with a computer and his magic fingers.

Cooper stirred. Then he got up and walked to the door just as the red light over the door turned green. The hiss of the hydraulics sounded like a thunderclap in the quiet building.

Eyes bulged, jaws dropped when Cyrus bounded into the room, the cylinder the vet had attached to his collar swinging back and forth as fast as his tail. He started to bark, loud, then louder as Espinosa tried to herd the three squalling kids, who were dragging their feet, to the center of the room. Espinosa himself looked like he'd just gone ten rounds with Godzilla and lost all ten.

The group stared, shocked speechless at what they were seeing. Cyrus barked relentlessly. The kids wailed louder as they clung to one another as if their lives depended on one another. Jack's tooth beat like a bongo drum.

Ted let loose with a loud, shrill whistle that made everyone in the room cringe. Cyrus howled, and the kids sobbed and shrieked even louder.

Cooper moved. First to Cyrus. The two dogs stared at one another. Cyrus clamped his mouth tight and stood at attention. Cooper walked over to the crying children and looked up at them. He pawed first one, then the other, and finally the little boy. The wailing and crying stopped immediately.

Espinosa came out of his trance and started to babble. "We were on our way home, and I caught a flash of something out of the corner of my eye on the side of the road. There was barely any traffic, so I knew it was something. Cyrus started to howl and unbuckled his seat belt. I pulled to the shoulder, and you know Cyrus, he knows how to open the door. He was out like he was shot from a cannon. He was over the rail and down the ravine before I could turn off the engine and get out. I followed him—actually I lost my footing and rolled down the hill." He pointed to the kids and said, "And there they were!"

Maggie's maternal instinct, which she had no idea she had, rose to the fore. She swooped forward and gathered the trembling children close. "They're so little. And so dirty. We have to do something. Right now, they are scared out of their wits. You're all *men*!" she said, as if that explained the current circumstance. "Let's all calm down. I'll take them to the bathroom and get them cleaned up. Dennis, go to that children's specialty store across the street and get some new clothes for them. Take a picture of them for the size before you go. Shoes, too. The place is a specialty children's boutique, so they'll have everything. It's where the rich people shop. Buy three sets of everything from the skin out. We have two girls here, so get something pretty. Why are you still standing here? I told you to *go*!

"The rest of you do something constructive like maybe calling Dings and ordering some food for these kids. What! What! Do I have to do everything? Move it, people!"

The people moved, even the dogs, at Maggie's tone. Cyrus followed Jack to the conference room, as did the others. Cooper followed Maggie and the kids to the bathroom. She heard Espinosa say the kids hadn't said one word, so he had no clue if they were runaways, kidnap victims, or simply lost.

"Figures it would be up to me," Maggie muttered as she ushered the kids down the hall into the bathroom. She fixed a steely eye on Cooper and said in a voice that had cowed many a man, "I don't know what your *schtick* is, but it had better be good. You're here, so that means you want to help. No one is going to hurt these kids. You must know that, or you wouldn't be here. I'm running with that, Cooper. So, start doing whatever it is you do, and let's get this show on the road. I need information. The reason I need information is because I'm a reporter. We want to help, but we need to know who these kids are. You can't talk, so it's up to them."

Cooper cocked his head to the side as though he was weighing Maggie's words. Then he circled the kids, stopping at each one and licking dirty hands before he walked over to the linen closet, where the towels were, and lay down.

"Right! Right! I'm on my own here. I see that. Okay then. Listen up, kids, we're going to get cleaned up here. Do you want showers or a bath?"

Cooper barked once. A gentle bark. "A shower please,"

the older girl said. "My sister likes a bath, and Andy likes a shower. I can take him in with me and wash him down."

Maggie almost blacked out. She looked at Cooper and nodded her thanks. *Don't you worry, Mr. Cooper, I'm going to figure you out at some point.* Maggie absolutely believed that the strange dog grinned at her.

"Good! Good!" Maggie said cheerfully as she smacked her hands together. "By the time we're all finished in here, Dennis will be back with some nice new clean clothes and shoes. Then we're going to get you something to eat. Let's think of it as a picnic inside. Okay, then," she said, turning on the tap in the oversize tub. "I'm going to sit over here so you can all strip down, and I won't look. Be sure to clean your ears good, wash your hair twice. There is some really nice shampoo in there that's mine. It smells like strawberries. Use it all up, I don't care. The soap smells like lilies. When you get out, you're all going to brush your teeth. That's if I can find some new toothbrushes."

Maggie turned off the tap just as the middle sibling stripped off the last of her clothes, showing no modesty. "Need any help?" The little girl shook her head. In what she hoped was a motherly sounding voice, Maggie said, "After the first wash, I'll let the water out, then fill the tub again. Do you want me to help you wash your hair?" The little girl nodded. Maggie dived right in, scrubbing and rubbing and rinsing. She blinked at the dirt filling the tub. She let it out and started to fill it again. "I'm thinking maybe we're going to need three tubs full of water," she said, and giggled. "How did your hair get so dirty?" she asked casually.

"We slept on the ground. Carrie tried to pick all the leaves and sticks out."

Aha. "So your sister's name is Carrie. What's your name?"

The little girl looked over at Cooper, who was watching her. "Emily."

"I told you that my name is Maggie. What's the little guy's name?"

"Andy."

"Is Andy your brother?"

"Uh-huh."

"Okay, your hair is nice and clean now. You start washing, and I'm going to look for some toothbrushes. Don't get out till I come back, okay?" What a stupid order that was. Like Cooper was going to let that happen.

Maggie beelined for the door and called to Ted, "Quick, I need toothbrushes and toothpaste. There is a drugstore two doors up from Dings. I know their names now, and they're brother and sisters. Cooper got them to cooperate. I need to know how he does that, Ted," she said fretfully.

"That's for another time. Three toothbrushes coming up." A second later, he was gone.

Maggie yelled again, "Hey! Somebody! I need a trash bag to put the kids' clothes in."

Charles appeared out of nowhere, a large black plastic bag in hand. He held it out.

"They're talking, Charles. Tell the others. I have names now. Just the first names, but it's a start. It was all Cooper's doing. Suddenly, I feel like a mother."

Charles smiled. "That's a good thing. The children need a woman at their side right now. And you called it right when you said the all-male team was intimidating them, not to mention Cyrus and Cooper. That dog confounds the life out of me."

"Yeah, me too. But things seem to work for the better when he's around. He has this . . . this . . . mystical way about him. He just looks at you, and you . . . you do what he's thinking. Did I express that right, Charles?" Maggie dithered.

"As well as I could, my dear. I think we should just accept he's on our side and let it go at that. I know that goes against everything you as a reporter live and breathe by, but from where I'm standing, it seems to be the way to go."

Maggie nodded. "I need to get back in there. They seem like such sweet little kids. Their parents must be worried sick. I think they've been on the run for a while from the condition of their clothes, especially their underwear."

Charles nodded. "Food is on the way, and here comes Ted with the toothbrushes."

Ted was breathless as he handed over the drugstore package. "Dennis is on the way; I saw him coming up the street. He has two helpers from the store. He must have bought it out."

Maggie stood on her tiptoes and kissed Ted on the cheek. "Thanks, honey." She whirled around and entered the bathroom.

Charles grinned from ear to ear. "Honey?"

Ted laughed. "When was the last time someone called you honey, Charles?"

"The truth is, Ted, I don't ever recall anyone calling me honey." Both men were smiling when they made their way inside the conference room.

Back in the BOLO's oversize bathroom with the heated tile floor, the children huddled in the thick, plush towels wrapped around them. Maggie made sure the towels were secure, then towel dried their hair and combed it. The girls had curly hair; the little boy had a wave to his.

"One at a time, brush your teeth. Three times. Each. Carrie, you go first, then Emily, and Andy last." The children obeyed. When they were finished, the toothpaste tube was empty. "Remember which one is yours for the next time," Maggie said, lining the toothbrushes up on the counter.

"You said the next time. Are we staying here?" Carrie asked in a jittery voice. Cooper barked.

"Just for a little while until we figure things out. First we have to get you dressed; and then you have to eat. After that, we're all going to talk and decide what to do."

A knock sounded on the door. It was Dennis, loaded down with shopping bags and boxes of shoes. "Do you need any help? I had the salesgirl mark the bags for the biggest size, the middle size, and then the little boy's. I can help with the boy."

"Sure, that will help. What's this bag?"

Dennis flushed bright pink. "It was some stuff on the counter, you know how they put stuff out that you didn't mean to buy but you pick up at the last second. Hair ribbons, barrettes, some bracelets, and a key chain with a truck on it for the little guy."

"They'll love it. Thanks, Dennis." She waited as Dennis scooped up the little boy under one arm and took him to the kitchen, where he dressed him from the skin out. He handed him the key chain and smiled when the little boy's eyes lit up. "I need a key. Thanks, mister."

"You're welcome. And I think I have a key right here," Dennis said, removing a key to his bike rack and sliding it onto the key chain.

The team sat around the large table in the kitchen while they waited for Maggie and the kids. Jack massaged his aching cheek as Cyrus pawed at him. "Ah, jeez, Cyrus, I'm sorry. With all this going on, I forgot about your checkup." He unclipped the leather cylinder on the dog's collar and made a production out of reading it aloud to everyone in the room. "A-1 all the way! Nice going, big guy. And your retention of the Greek commands is stellar! And . . . ," Jack paused dramatically, "he gave you a gold star! That makes four in a row. We'll frame this when we get back to the farm and hang it up with the other three. I'm proud of you, Cyrus!" Jack hugged the big dog close and whispered in his ear. Cyrus danced away, his tail swinging so hard, the others thought of it as a weapon. "And a special thanks from all of us for finding those kids!"

Cyrus made the rounds getting a treat from everyone. His job done, he took his place on the carpet in front of the stove. He dropped his head onto his paws and closed his eyes.

The team sat silently, staring at the open doorway and willing Maggie to appear with the kids. The front doorbell rang. Dings' food delivery. Dennis rushed to the door and returned with two shopping bags full of Styrofoam containers. The bill stapled to the shopping bags said there were scrambled eggs, sausage, toast points, jam, butter, fruit bowls, orange juice, and milk. In another bag the bill said there were pancakes, waffles, syrup, butter, and crispy bacon.

"Do you think three little kids can eat all of this?" Dennis asked dubiously.

"Depends on how long it's been since they've eaten. Or what they've eaten," Charles said just as Maggie ushered the three kids into the kitchen. The gang stared at the kids in their clean new outfits, their faces shiny clean, the girls' hair tied into ponytails with colorful ribbons.

"Time to eat!" Fergus shouted.

Fergus set out the food and motioned to the gang to head on out.

"You kids eat all you want. Cyrus and Cooper will stay with you. When you're finished, they'll come for us and we'll all have a nice talk. Okay?" Charles said.

Three small heads bobbed up and down, their eyes on the feast in front of them.

"Andy isn't real good with a fork yet. Is it okay if he uses his fingers? Manners are important, but he doesn't understand that yet," Carrie said, never taking her eyes off the food in front of her.

"Absolutely! Today, manners do not count," Charles said as he walked out of the room.

In the conference room, the gang all looked at one another, their eyes full of questions. And then they all started talking at once.

Charles rubbed at the stubble on his chin. He held up his hand for silence. The room was so quiet, the movement of his fingers against his chin sounded like sandpaper being rubbed on a piece of wood. "I have no clue what we're dealing with. They're beautiful children, but then, all children are beautiful. There have been no Amber Alerts that I'm aware of, so that more or less takes kidnapping off the table. Where are the parents? Are the children from around here? I watch the news constantly and constantly get updates. There have been no reports of missing children. Three missing children, not one, not two, but three."

"Maybe they're from another state and were being transported somewhere and somehow they managed to get loose and ran away. Who would report them missing without incriminating themselves?" Espinosa said.

"Which brings us back to the parents," Abner said. "I'm checking all the databases I know of. I'll put the word out to my colleagues and see what they come up with. Now, I have to warn you. If this is something like child trafficking, then we're talking about the underbelly of the Internet, that black hole reserved for the lowest of the low."

"Get on it, Abner," Charles said.

From that point on, everyone in the room had an opinion, each one different, but in the end it came back to, where are the parents? At last, they simply gave up and stared at one another until Cyrus appeared in the doorway.

Finally.

The troop headed for the kitchen, stunned to see that it was neat and tidy, all the Styrofoam boxes closed and stacked on the kitchen counter. The plastic silverware had been rinsed and dried, the shopping bags folded neatly in a pile. The table was clear of crumbs. Carrie and Emily sat at the table, their hands folded. Andy lay curled up next to Cooper and was sound asleep.

"Andy always takes a nap after he eats a lot," Carrie said.

"That's fine," Maggie said. "Are you guys ready to talk?" Two heads bobbed up and down. The room went quiet as Charles leaned forward. "Where are your parents, Carrie?"

"I don't know. When we woke up, Aunt Betty was there. She told us to get dressed and go with her. Then she lost us."

"Where did she lose you?"

"At the mall," Emily said. "She bought us some ice cream and said to wait till she got back. She had to get her ear fixed.

"Aunt Betty has a hearing aid, and she wanted to get it fixed. We waited, but she never came back. Andy started to cry. Then Carrie started to cry. I didn't know what to do. Then two men came up to us and said Aunt Betty said we were to go with them."

"When did that happen? How many days ago?" Charles asked.

"I don't know. Lots of days. We missed school."

"Before the flags," Emily said.

"The holiday with the parade," Carrie said.

"I think she means Memorial Day, and they were still in school. School doesn't let out till the middle of June. Oh my God, these kids have been on the loose for several months," Maggie said as she fought the urge to hug the two little girls.

"Where did you live all that time?" Charles asked.

"With all the other kids. Then they left, and more kids came. No one picked us."

"No one wanted us 'cause we're mixed up," Emily said. "They didn't like our pictures. That's what they said, right, Carrie?" Carrie nodded.

"Oh, crap, I see where this is going already," Harry hissed in Jack's ear.

"Do you know where the place is that you lived in?"

Both girls shook their heads. "It was full of big boxes and it smelled funny. Not stinky, something else. Like church at Christmas."

"Incense," Maggie said.

"I don't know what that is," Carrie said.

"What's your last name?"

"Bannon."

"Do you know your mother's and dad's names?"

"Mommy and Daddy," Emily said.

"Their other names. Like what did your daddy call your mommy?" Maggie asked.

"Sweetie pie." Emily giggled. "Mommy called Daddy her hunk of love. It always made him laugh."

"Do you know your address and phone number?" Jack asked.

Carrie looked offended at the question. "I'm seven years old. Mommy made me learn it. Emily gets confused. We lived at one-eleven Apple Avenue in Arlington. I don't know the phone number because it was in my cell phone. I just pressed the number one for Mommy and the number two for Daddy. The people took it away. Emily didn't have a phone. Mommy was going to get her one on her birthday."

"I'm on it, I'm on it!" Ted said.

"Me too," Maggie said.

"Do you know Aunt Betty's last name?"

"Smith. She's Daddy's aunt. She doesn't hear good. We have to talk real loud. And we have to help her walk, too, because she has a cane. Sometimes she drops it, and we have to pick it up. She's old. Daddy said we have to look after her."

Ted groaned at the name Smith.

"Do you know where Aunt Betty lives?" Charles asked.

"With all the old people. They play games and sing, but they don't dance. Daddy said they would fall down if they danced. Aunt Betty lives fifteen minutes from our house if there is no traffic."

"That's a help," Charles said as he zeroed in on Ted to make sure he was getting everything the little girl said. He nodded that he was on that, too.

"Do you know where your parents work, Carrie?" Charles asked.

"It's a secret," Emily chirped. "You can't tell a secret."

Carrie nodded. "Mommy said if people know what they do, we could get hurt. That's why it's a secret."

"I'm going to take a wild guess here and ask you if your parents carry guns," Jack said, fixing his gaze on the little girl. Her eyes almost popped out of her head at the question. She turned to look down at her new shoes and said loudly, "No!" It was a lie, and everyone in the room knew it, even Emily, who squirmed on the chair. It was also obvious to everyone in the room that lying did not come naturally to the two little girls. Jack let it go and gave a slight shake of his head to indicate that Charles should continue.

"Law enforcement of some kind," Maggie hissed to Ted, who nodded.

"That should be a breeze, locating Sweetie Pie and Hunk of Love Bannon," Ted said, tongue in cheek. "That's right up there with Betty Smith with a hearing aid and cane."

"Tell us about the place you lived in before you got away. How many children were there with you?"

"Sometimes a lot. Sometimes just us and three more. People kept taking our pictures. They dressed up some of the girls in real pretty dresses. Then the girls left and didn't come back. The monster lady was real mean to me and Emily. Sometimes, she wouldn't give us food. Then the Hammer Man would slap us. He was mean, too."

"Tell them about Funny Eyes, Carrie," Emily said.

Carrie put her fingers to the corner of her eyes and pulled the skin back. "Kind of like him," she said, pointing to Harry. "When Andy cried, Funny Eyes would tell him stories. If the Hammer Man saw him do that, he would kick him and call him a half . . . a halfwit."

"How did you get away?"

"Funny Eyes helped us. A big truck came with lots of kids. Lots and lots of kids. He said they wouldn't miss us for over an hour, so we should run fast. That's what we did. We cried because we knew they were going to kick him for helping us. Sometimes so bad he couldn't walk; then he had to crawl. Then they'd whip him like a dog and call him names."

Emily started to cry. Carrie put her arms around her sister and crooned in her ear. "Funny Eyes will be okay. Stop crying now. You're a big girl, and big girls don't cry," she said, her own eyes filling with tears.

"Son of a bitch," Jack muttered under his breath.

"How many days ago did you leave? Do you know? How many times did it get dark at night?" Charles asked softly.

"Seven. Every day we counted so we would remember. Seven," she repeated.

"What did you eat? Where did you hide?" Dennis asked, his expression one of disbelief that three little kids could survive on their own with no help for a full week.

"Funny Eyes gave us some apples when we left. We got some food out of trash cans. It rained, so we drank the rainwater. We were trying to find a policeman when you found us."

"You're safe now. We're going to do our best to find your parents and the people who took you away. For now, we're going to keep you here. How would you all like to watch some television while us grown-ups make a plan?

"*Dora the Explorer*?" Emily asked hopefully.

Charles smiled. "*Dora the Explorer* it is."

Chapter Four

Maggie settled the kids in front of the TV in the main office before she returned to the guys in the conference room. The team looked at her expectantly. "They're fine. I think the girls will both be asleep in about fifteen minutes. The good news is they aren't as scared as they were when they got here. They trust us now. So, let's get to it and find out what's going on and how best to help them. For as little and as young as they are, I have to say, they have guts. I'm not sure I could have done what they did when I was their age."

The others concurred. "It's a good thing it's summer. I hate to think what would have happened to them if it were winter with them on the loose," Charles said solemnly.

"Can we get to it? I need to head back to the dentist. My mouth is killing me," Jack said, his face a mask of misery.

"Never mind getting to it. Come on, we're going right now to the dentist," Harry said, getting up and hauling Jack to his feet. He looked at the others. "You can clue us in when we get back." No one disagreed.

Cyrus was waiting at the door. "Sorry, bud, you can't go," Harry said.

Cyrus backed up a step and showed his teeth, and magnificent teeth they were. Harry held up his hands, palms outward. "Um . . . obviously, I misspoke. Cyrus?" He started to explain as though he were explaining the situation to his daughter, Lily. Cyrus ignored him and simply waited for Harry to finally give up and open the door.

"Since Cyrus is coming, we need to go in your car, Jack. Where are the keys?" Jack handed them over.

Thirty minutes later, Jack, Harry, and Cyrus exited the elevator on the eighth floor, where Dr. Bruno Sabatini was waiting for them. "What took you so long?" He grinned. He eyed the massive dog and took a step back.

"He's a good guy, Cyrus. Stay with Harry. That's an order," Jack mumbled. He turned to Dr. Sabatini. "You hurt me, and you're toast."

Bruno Sabatini clapped his hands gleefully. "Let's get to it then."

Cyrus sat in the open doorway. He never once took his eyes off the dentist and what he was doing to his master, to the dentist's chagrin.

Ninety minutes later, Jack sat up, woozy but still with it. He wobbled out to the waiting room, Cyrus at his side. To his dismay, he had to lean on Harry. He waved airily as Harry escorted him out to the elevator. The dentist ran after them, a pill bottle in hand.

"Tell him to take one every twelve hours and to finish the bottle. He's groggy right now, and he should sleep around the clock. I want to see him a week from today. Any problems, call me either here or at home. Even if it's the middle of the night. Jack has both numbers."

"How you doing, hot shot?" Harry asked, as the elevator door slid shut.

"I've been better. Like I'm really going to sleep around the clock." Harry grinned, and Cyrus barked. They piled into the car, Jack in the back, Cyrus in the front passenger seat. Jack was asleep the minute he buckled up. Cyrus barked his approval.

Back at the BOLO Building, Harry called Ted to come and help get Jack inside. He was deadweight, and the two men actually had to carry him. A debate followed as to where to put him. Maggie made the final decision to put blankets down on the floor so the cots could be saved for the children. "He'll be fine," was her final assessment when she covered Jack with a light blanket. Cyrus took up his position near the door.

Back in the conference room, Abner was reading off his computer. "Here's the thing, guys. I learned a lot at the CIA. The main thing is everyone has an alias. For security purposes, of course. I'm going to go out on a limb here and say if the kids' parents work for some top secret government agency, they probably use aliases. Meaning Bannon probably is not their legal name. Going with first names, Sweetie Pie and Hunk of Love is not going to help us track them down."

Ted raised his hand as if he were in the third grade. "Can't you and your . . . ah . . . club hack into the records? What about that guy Phil something or other? We're going to need real names."

Abner pretended to pout. He responded as though Ted really were in the third grade. "Well, of course I can, *Teddie*. And I don't need any help. I can do it on my own; it's just going to take some time to figure out which agency the parents work for so I can hit the right database. This is the government we're dealing with, so bear that in mind."

Properly chastised, Ted returned to his laptop.

"I think we should pack up and head out to the farm. Our quarters here are too cramped, and we're going to need all the equipment we have at our disposal in the war room. This place is good for conferences, quick meetings, and the like," Charles said.

"What about the kids?" Dennis asked.

"They'll be safer at the farm and have actual beds to sleep in, plus all the dogs to keep them busy. And we can cook nourishing food for them opposed to takeout and having them eat on the fly," Charles responded.

The group batted Charles's idea around for a few moments before they finally decided it was the way to go.

It took a half hour before everyone was settled as comfortably as possible in the parade of vehicles that would travel to the farm. Maggie was right—the kids were sound asleep and had to be carried to the cars. It took Ted and Espinosa both to drag Jack to his own car, with Cyrus's hot breath on them every step of the way. Cooper eyed these goings-on before he marched over to Maggie's car, where the children slept in the backseat. He pawed the passenger door until it opened, then settled himself for the ride to the farm.

"Guess that settles who is going to ride with me," Maggie mumbled under her breath.

The normal sixty-minute commute to Pinewood took a full ninety minutes, given the heavy rain that started to fall before the caravan made it to the Interstate. Another hour was used up settling the kids in beds, with Cooper standing guard.

Ted and Espinosa huffed and puffed as they literally dragged Jack as far as the family room and somehow got him settled on the couch. He never opened his eyes. Cyrus took up his position in front of the sofa. He looked up at the wheezing duo, yipped as if to say, "I have it covered, you can go now."

"Damn, that guy weighs more than I thought. And he didn't even bat an eye—he's out cold," Ted said.

"Wait till he wakes up here and wonders how he got here. They must have given him some kind of super-duper deluxe painkillers to knock him out like that. Even when he wakes up, he's going to be out of it for a day or so," Espinosa said.

"Come on, the gang is waiting for us. We need to get moving. I sure could use a good cup of coffee right now. How about you, Espinosa?"

"I smell it brewing, so that has to mean everyone is in the kitchen. They're waiting for us. I hope we can help those kids. It must be awful for them that they don't know where their parents are. They've been through a lot, and now, when they wake up, it's a whole other ball game. I'm not sure I could ever be a parent. I don't know how my parents raised eleven of us kids. What about you, Ted? Could you handle parenthood?" Espinosa asked fretfully.

"I don't know. I think if you have the right partner, and you're both on the same parenting page, it's possible. I'd probably be one of those helicopter parents who hover over the kids twenty-four/seven. You know, eyes glued to them every minute. But that's not good. Why are we talking about this? We don't have kids, and it doesn't look as if there are any in either of our immediate futures."

"Everything okay?" Charles asked. "Grab your coffee, boys, and let's get to work. I think with all the dogs here, especially Cyrus and Cooper, it's safe to go down to the war room and commence work. Lady will stand guard with her pups here in the kitchen."

Chairs scraped back, and laptops snapped shut as the parade moved forward. Charles was the last in line because he had treats to hand out. A treat for doing nothing was something Lady took seriously. It meant she was in charge of her unruly brood and the house they all lived in.

As always, the minute the lights came on in the war room, so did the free-hanging monster TV showing Lady Justice in all her glory. The team saluted, then took their seats at the special table while Charles and Fergus moved to the dais and the banks of computers that would have rivaled those at NASA.

The gang chattered, their voices low so as not to disturb Charles and Fergus.

"Have you come up with anything yet, Abner?" Maggie asked.

Deep into what he was doing, Abner shook his head.

"I think Espinosa and I should go check out the Bannon house," said Ted. "Joe can take pictures of everything. We can show them to the kids to see their reaction. As we all know, no one is perfect. We might pick up some clues. If nothing else, their backgrounds."

"I can take on Aunt Betty. Older people like me for some reason, and I have a rapport with them," Dennis said. "There can't be that many senior housing compounds within a fifteen-minute radius of the Bannon household."

"What about me?" Maggie snapped. "Don't think for one minute that I'm doing babysitting duty. Charles and Fergus can do that. I'm going with Ted and Espinosa. Besides, we're a team."

And that was the end of that.

"I don't know if this is a good idea or not," Harry said, "but I can call some of the law-enforcement agencies that train with me. They like to talk. Brag, actually. Just last month, I took on a special rush class of three guys from Homeland Security. It was some kind of special hush-hush assignment that they couldn't talk about but did anyway. Jack and I know this one guy at the DEA who's pretty far up the totem pole. He likes to show off how important he is. He might have some intel he can share. For a price. Meaning dinner and really good wine. That kind of thing. Jack and I both know scores of agents at the CIA and FBI. I'll throw out some bait and see what happens. When Jack comes back to the land of the living, he can dig right in."

"There's always Jack Sparrow," Fergus said, taking his place at the table, his arms full of printouts. "Just think about the man's Rolodex! He was director of the FBI for a good many years. He also knows where all the bodies are buried."

"I just sent him a text," Charles said, taking his place at the table. "Now, boys and one girl, tell me what you all came up with while I was printing out the materials here in my hand. One at a time, please."

"It's a little late in the day to head on out," said Joe. "I'm all for going home and starting out fresh in the morning. I'll see what if anything I can dig up this evening and apprise you early tomorrow. I did a Google Map house search, and it appears the Bannons live or lived in a very nice residential neighborhood. The big question is will the neighbors be watching three strangers break into a house and not do anything?"

"What about the kids' school?" Ted asked. "I can't find a trace anywhere of any missing children within a fifty-mile radius of the kids' home. I'm working on day-care centers now for the little guy. So far nothing. I'm all for heading home and starting fresh in the morning."

Dennis agreed.

"I should go home to do some rescheduling. Choa can handle my classes tomorrow, and I can come back out and get Jack up and running. That leaves Abner here with you and Fergus," Harry said, addressing Charles. "I think you guys are in good hands with seven dogs here to watch over things."

"I'm staying," Abner muttered. "I can do what I'm doing here just as well as at home. If Jack wakes up, I can hold his hand," he said, grinning, his fingers tapping fast and furious. "And before any of you ask, I have my . . . ah . . . colleagues on this, and that includes Phil. Backup only."

"I guess that pretty much covers it all then," Charles said. "Everyone report in in the morning. Don't any of you do anything that will bring attention to yourselves. We're dealing with children here, remember that. In the meantime, when they wake up, Ferg and I can take another shot at seeing if we can get any more information out of them. It's just that they're so young. And scared. I'm sure their parents drilled information into their heads about talking to strangers and all that goes with it. Schools do that now, too, I'm told. Am I wrong, or am I not remembering correctly that the older girl, Carrie, had a cell phone?"

"No, you heard right," Ted said. "Carrie said the people took it from her. I'm on that, too. She also said there were only two numbers she could call by pressing the number one and the number two. Mom and Dad. She doesn't know who her parents' carrier is. I have calls into some friends who have friends who work at various providers. If I come up blank, Abner will have to hack into the records."

"On my list of things to do," Abner mumbled.

"All right then, we're outta here," Maggie said, getting up and gathering all her gear and paperwork. "Wish us luck."

Ninety minutes later, the trio from the *Post* pulled to the curb outside Maggie's house in Georgetown. "If you guys want to come in, it's okay. I can make some sandwiches, and we can keep on working or we can hit the sack." Then she lowered her voice to a harsh whisper and said, "Unless you guys are up for a little night trip to one-eleven Apple

Avenue in Arlington." She held her breath waiting to see what Ted and Espinosa would say.

Ted shifted into reverse, inched out from the parking space, did a lightning U-turn, and they were off. "I love the way you think, Maggie," he cackled happily.

"We could get caught, you know that, right?"

"Absolutely I know that. The neighborhood probably has one of those Neighborhood Watch groups that does nothing but spy on their neighbors. We'll park a few blocks away and go on foot. Just three people out for a nightly stroll before turning in. We'll go in from the back—I have my lock-picking kit," Ted said, excitement ringing in his voice.

"What if there's an alarm system that's activated?" Espinosa asked nervously.

"Then we use that gizmo Avery Snowden gave us. In ten seconds, it can figure out the code and dismantle it. I have it in my backpack."

"What if it's a silent alarm?" Espinosa persisted.

"Then, my friends, we're screwed," Ted said cheerfully. "Right now, this rain is in our favor. No one is out walking around; people looking out their windows see only rain. I'm going on the theory here that the Bannons walked away on their own for whatever reason but left things just the way they would if they were going away for the weekend. Timers. Outside lights come on at a certain time. One light or two goes on at another time. That kind of thing."

Espinosa wasn't about to give up. "What about mail piling up and trash pickup. How is that explained?"

"Post office holds the mail, it's that simple. As to the trash, the Bannons are neat and tidy, and there is no trash or their story to the neighborhood is a family crisis of some kind, and you'll see us when you see us," Maggie snapped. "Whatever it is, we'll deal with it when and *if* it happens. Now shut up, Joe, before I smack you. If you're that worried, you can stay in the car."

Espinosa mumbled something that sounded like, *Smart-ass*, then went silent.

Twenty minutes later, Ted did a slow drive-by all the way down Apple Avenue. "Looks like half-acre lots. Nice space between the houses. No dogs will be outside barking. It's late, but there are still some lights on in people's houses. Okay, roll down your windows and tell me what you see. The house should be the third one on the right."

"Lamppost gaslight by the mailbox. The numerals one-one-one are those stick-on tapes. There's dim light inside coming from somewhere, and I think there's a light in the back, or else it's the neighbor's light. When you do the return, I'll be looking at it from another angle. We might have to go in by the front door if it is the Bannons' light in the back. It looks pretty bright even from here and through the rain. Turn around," Maggie ordered.

Ted obliged and drove to the end of the street, then turned around and inched his way down the road. There were no other cars in sight, and there were no other cars on the street. "Everyone parks in their own driveway. I wish it were that way in Georgetown," Maggie groused. "Crapola. It is the Bannons' backyard light. Let's get to it. Park down at the very end, and we'll run back. We're lucky there's no light by the front door. Be sure you have your picklock in hand when we get there."

Ted hated it when Maggie gave him orders. What did she think he was going to do, stand in the middle of the road so everyone could see him as he looked for his picklock? He didn't say a word, just slammed on his brakes and grinned when Maggie almost landed in his lap.

"That wasn't funny, Ted," Maggie yelped.

"Yeah it was. It shut you up for a few seconds."

"Can you two bill and coo later? Let's do this and get it over with," Espinosa said as he climbed out of the car and sprinted forward without waiting for his colleagues. Maggie was next out, followed by Ted. They all arrived at 111 at the same time, and Ted raced up the steps and got to work. "Run-of-the-mill lock. Five seconds and we're in. Hurry up!"

In they were. The trio stood stock-still, waiting for their eyes to adjust to the semidarkness. To their surprise, there was no alarm system. In each room there was a small night-light plugged into a wall socket. The lights gave off virtually no illumination but did reveal what was on the floor, so no one tripped over anything. In the kitchen, there was a light over the gas range and a clock whose numbers read 0000. "Let's spread out. Espinosa, take the upstairs. I'll start here in the kitchen and work my way to the front of the house. Ted, you take the garage and the basement. Move, guys. If you discover anything, give a soft whistle."

Maggie watched Ted as he prepared to head to the basement. "Hey, watch your head there!" she warned the lanky reporter before she set to work. First, she went through the cabinets. Service for six of everything. Family plus one guest, and if more guests showed up, they got the paper plates. Pantry. Nothing unusual and not well stocked. Staples mostly. She moved things but discovered nothing. The utility closet gave up nothing other than a broom, a dustpan, a mop, and a bucket along with a bag of what looked like cleaning rags. A shelf held two boxes of trash bags, a bottle of some kind of floor cleaner called Finish. Nothing.

The laundry room held a washer and dryer, both front loaders. Two cabinets overhead contained detergent, fabric sheets, and two bottles of bleach. All lined up neatly. An ironing board was set up in the far corner, with a steam iron resting on a metallic pad. A portable drying rack sat next to the ironing board with four purple hangers. There was no laundry basket; nor were there any clothes in the washer or the dryer. Nothing here.

Maggie made her way back to the kitchen to check the refrigerator. A six-pack of Dasani water sat on one shelf. Four bottles of green tea sat next to the water bottles. A four-pack of peach yogurt that had yet to expire sat alone on the top shelf next to a can of Reddi-wip. There were no eggs, milk, juice, or cheese. No dried or wilted fruit or vegetables in the bins, like in her own refrigerator back in Georgetown. This refrigerator had been cleaned out in preparation for leaving, an indication, at least to Maggie, that the Bannons planned on returning or that they wanted whoever checked the house to think that.

There were two small cactus plants in little cardboard containers on the windowsill. Cactuses could virtually live forever without water. Probably a project Carrie brought home from school.

Maggie moved to the front of the house and was no more successful than she had been in the kitchen and laundry room. All neat and tidy. One lone picture on the mantel of the three children standing next to a carousel at some amusement park. No photo albums on the coffee table. No pictures of the parents. No prints on the walls.

This little night visit was a total bust as far as she could tell. She frowned. Something was bothering her. Something different. Odd. What? She couldn't come up with a thing, and she did have a sharp eye. Or as Ted often said, "Maggie has an eagle eye, she doesn't miss a thing." Well, whatever it was, she was missing it. She hated when that happened because it made her crazy.

Ted appeared out of nowhere. He shook his head in disgust. "I didn't find a thing. Anyone could live here. There's no junk in the garage or basement. Crazy-ass staircase going down to the basement. I almost killed myself. No overflow of any kind. No cars, of course. A lawn mower and a leaf blower that looked barely used. Mr. Bannon is not someone who tinkers in the garage. No little jars of nails or screws that every home owner has. No cans of paint on the shelves. Strangers with no ties to anything live here would be my assessment."

"What about the basement?" Maggie asked.

"That was the basement, weren't you listening? Totally empty except for the furnace. There are four small windows with wire mesh nailed across them. That's nothing out of the ordinary; most people do that to avoid break-ins. The main reason probably being that crazy-killer staircase. And the lights were burned out. I had to use my flashlight," Ted said.

Espinosa joined them. He threw his hands up in the air. "Nothing. Clothes. Not a lot. Three changes each from what I can tell. Suitcases in the closet in the master bathroom. No excesses of any kind. Two bars of soap, three extra rolls of bathroom tissue. Six bath towels, six hand towels, six washcloths. One extra tube of toothpaste. No extra toothbrushes. One bottle of Aleve in the medicine cabinet. One bottle of baby aspirin, for the kids, I guess. Two boxes of Band-Aids. Peroxide and alcohol. Shampoo and hand lotion. One can of shaving cream. No meds of any kind. A big fat nothing."

"That tells me their departure was planned. There is no trace, no clue as to where they went. They must have been called to go on an assignment, and they called Aunt Betty to pick up the kids, which we already know she did. That's where everything stops. I wonder if they had a cleaning lady or if the kids had a babysitter," Maggie mused.

"I think it's weird there is no landline. They obviously relied on cell phones. There is no computer, printer, or fax machine. I thought everyone had a computer in their house. One TV. None in the kids' rooms. A cheap model, two hundred and fifty dollars tops. My bad," Ted said.

"So now what?" Espinosa asked.

"Maybe we missed something," Maggie said. "Hidden safe, false wall, something under the floorboards, that kind of thing. I hate thinking this was a bust. There has to be *something*. Something we missed."

"Give it up, Maggie. This is a cookie-cutter house, not a custom-made one where all those things you mentioned could be installed. The Bannons just existed here, nothing more. It's all a screen."

Maggie's shoulders slumped. She hated to admit defeat. "Hey, we could go to the post office tomorrow and see if we can collect their mail. Yeah, yeah, that's a federal offense. It was just a thought," she said, at the look of horror on her partners' faces.

"What was in the desk?" Ted asked.

"Just receipts for household bills. Canceled checks. All the same: electric, water, taxes, insurance. The checking account is in Wells Fargo and in both names. Allison and Steven Bannon. This address. The last bank statement shows a balance of $656.23. One monthly cash deposit of $1,000. That's it. Wherever they deposit their paychecks, it isn't in this account. These people are pros. Special agents of some kind would be my guess," Maggie said. "Everything appears to be geared to a quick getaway and leaving very little behind and easily replaced at their next location."

"We should go," Espinosa said. Maggie nodded.

In the car on the way back to Georgetown, the trio was silent. When Ted pulled to the curb, Maggie got out and walked to her door. Ted drove away to drop off Espinosa.

Hero, Maggie's rescue cat jumped up into her arms to greet her. He purred as Maggie crooned to the contented cat. "I know there was something there, Hero. My gut says it's there, and I missed it. I missed it. Me! Do you believe that?"

Maggie headed to the kitchen, poured herself a glass of wine, and got out some tuna for Hero.

"Sooner or later, I'll figure it out. You know why, Hero? Because I am an investigative reporter."

Hero stopped eating long enough to raise his head and offer up a meow to show he was on her side.

Chapter Five

It was early, and the sun had yet to crawl toward the horizon, when Charles Martin slid a tray of sticky buns into the oven. Fergus clapped his hands in anticipation as he scooped out the seeds from a delicious-looking melon. The table was set for three, as Abner had spent the night.

"It smells good in here. Cinnamon, right?" Abner said as he took his place at the table. He was freshly showered and shaved. He wore the same messy clothes, but as he put it, "I'm clean, and I smell good."

"Did you get any sleep?" Charles asked. "Ferg and I took turns taking catnaps."

"Two hours. I don't require much sleep," Abner said. "I finally cracked the code, and I now know who the kids' parents really are. It's a good thing I'm an honest man," Abner said, tongue in cheek. "I could sell this information to our enemies and make a fortune for myself." When there was no response from Fergus or Charles, he hastened on. "Not that I would ever do that. I simply took what information I needed, closed all the doors I opened, and backstopped everything. Phil went behind me to make sure I covered all my tracks. Trust me when I tell you no one will ever know that file was penetrated. We are good to go, gentlemen."

"So what did you find out?" Fergus asked as he held out a generous slice of melon.

"Allison and Steven Bannon are the names the kids' parents go by at the moment. They are special agents of the CIA, which assigns them to various agencies with no real home base other than The Farm at Langley. From what I could gather, they work on a three-year assignment, then move to another location and work for another agency. Before this gig, which is only twenty-two months old, they were assigned to the DEA and lived in Gilbert, Arizona. One could call them floaters, for want of a better term. They go where their special talents are needed. They are at the top of the heap. The best of the best. The rarity here is that they are husband and wife. Originally, they were partners that . . . ahhh, came together. They got married and had kids. A small war broke out, and they were going to be split up. The couple fought it and won. They are the only husband and wife team for any of the alphabet agencies. I guess the powers that be recognized their value and unique talents, and finally agreed to keep them together rather than lose them. And the money invested in their training also has to be taken into consideration. It's expensive to train a covert agent."

Charles removed the tray of sticky buns from the oven and set it on the counter. "From everything I've read over the years about the agencies, that is the one thing that is verboten. No romantic entanglements. Emotions interfere with the job at hand. I'm impressed. The Bannons must be an incredibly special couple would be my opinion."

Using a spatula, he removed the sticky buns one by one, the cinnamon syrup and butter drizzling down the sides. He placed the platter in the middle of the table. A dozen sticky buns. Abner would eat ten, Fergus and Charles one each.

"Who are they in real life?" Fergus asked.

"As far as I could tell, that information had been scrubbed from the database. Whatever their real names, she is thirty-nine and he is forty-one. Both were recruited by the CIA right out of college. Five years later, they were partnered up. From that point on, I guess, you could say the rest is history, which brings us to the here and now."

"Ah, yes, the here and now. The only problem with that is we do not know where they are. Did Aunt Betty show up in either of their background information?" Fergus asked.

"No. Nothing was said about relatives on either the mother's or the father's side. At least none of record. I think this Betty, whoever she is, is just another agent who works for one of the agencies. Remember now, being the best of the best means you carry a lot of clout, so if the Bannons, to use the name the kids go by, need help with those kids, they get it via Betty or someone like Betty. I think that would apply to babysitters also," Abner said as he shoveled his fifth sticky bun into his mouth.

"So, we know that they are CIA agents. But we still have no names. What do we do now? They're gone, and we have their kids. Do they even know that? And where is Betty?" Charles looked at Fergus and Abner as if they had the magic answer when his cell phone chirped to life. He held up his hand and mouthed the name Maggie. He turned the phone to speaker mode and set it in the middle of the table so the others could hear.

Maggie quickly recounted the night's events, ending with, "The place was scrubbed. It's so sterile, you could eat off the floor. The Bannons are gone, that's the bottom line. I do want to say, though, something is niggling at me, something I either saw or felt that wasn't right. That doesn't mean I'm right—it's just . . . I don't know, call it a gut feeling that I missed something. We're going back as soon as we catch some breakfast and prowl the neighborhood, talk to the neighbors, and see if we can shake the tree. Dennis is on his way to some senior housing complex. He said he'll check in later. Did any of you come up with anything during the night?"

Charles motioned to Abner to speak up, which he did.

"Wow, Maggie, that's really good work. Do you think you'll be able to find out which agency they're working for now?"

"That's my job for today. I'll find it."

"Be careful when you go out to the neighborhood, Maggie. There might be other agents living there as backup, or, as the agency calls them, 'minders.' In other words, the Bannons' backup team."

"We'll keep it in mind. I'll check back before we leave the area."

The call ended. The three men looked at one another. Abner stuffed the tenth sticky bun in his mouth, nodded to the others, and left the kitchen for the war room, leaving Fergus and Charles to tidy up the kitchen.

"We are talking child trafficking, right, Charles?"

"That would be my guess. I hate to grill the children because they're so young, and they have been traumatized. They'll probably have to undergo years of therapy as they grow and mature. I don't know about you, Ferg, but I'm ready to blame the parents here. Considering their professions, their dedication to their careers, they never should have brought children into their world. I'm all for love and family, but look where their children are. It's just pure dumb luck that they ended up with us. Think about the other side of that coin. Just think about *that*!" Charles said angrily as he got up from the table.

"I am thinking about that, mate, and I'm with you. For now, let's just be grateful the children are safe with us. I wonder if the parents even know they've gone missing. For all we know, they might be totally clueless. Which doesn't say much for their parenting skills. What do we do now?"

"Wait for the kiddies to wake up. Make them some breakfast and hope we can get some information out of them without scaring them half to death. I was wondering, Ferg. Do you think we should call in Avery?"

"I don't see how it could hurt. If you plan on asking him to come out here to the farm, ask him to bring one of his female operatives with him. The children react differently to a female presence, a motherly type if he has someone like that on his payroll."

While Fergus cleared the table and cleared off the counter, Charles called the old spy and gave him the current rundown, asking about the availability of a motherly female operative to relate to the children. "We think it's child trafficking, Avery. You're usually up on all of that. What if anything have you heard coming out from the dark side?"

Rarely if ever did Charles hear any kind of emotion in the old spy's voice, but he was hearing it now. So was Fergus, who stopped rattling the dishes in the sink as he, too, listened.

The fine hairs on the back of Charles's neck moved. He waited. Fergus inched closer to the table.

"Where have you been of late, Sir Charles? Aren't you keeping up with the news? I know you and the ladies have been busy, but you do need to come up for air now and again. What you just told me works into a child-trafficking gang that is so monstrous the different agencies can't keep up with them. They nail one person, and three more sprout up to take their place. And those they manage to catch are just hired bodies to do the transportation. They get paid and head off into the sunset or to the next call. They get paid by the head. In other words, by the child. It's a *big* ring, Sir Charles. It sounds to me like you fell into the inside track by pure dumb luck. I'll be out there as soon as I can clear my decks.

"And I know the perfect operative to bring with me. I use her constantly because she's the grandmotherly type, and no one gives her a second glance. Children love her. Sit tight, I'll be there before you know it."

Charles bit down on his lower lip, a frown building on his brow. "As Jack would say, I didn't see that coming. I Don't remember seeing or hearing anything in regard to child trafficking. What about you, Ferg?" Fergus shook his head as he hung the dish towel on the handle of the oven door.

"We watch the news every night. How did that get past us? Jack or Ted and Maggie would have said something."

Abner appeared in the doorway and said, "I'm checking the center for missing and exploited children right now, and from what I can tell, these three particular kids are not on that list. I've looked at Polly Klaas's and John Walsh's Web sites. Thousands of kids, but so far, not our three. Something needs to be done about this!" he said, jabbing his finger at what was on his computer screen. "I just had to come up here and tell you that, and to see if Jack was up and mobile."

Charles shared Avery Snowden's news. "Avery's on his way and should arrive soon."

"Did I hear my name mentioned just now?" Jack said as he shuffled into the kitchen and headed straight for the coffeepot.

"You did hear that right. Drink your coffee and we'll bring you up to speed. You look terrible, by the way. How do you feel?" Charles asked.

"I've felt better. The pain is gone, so that's all I care about. I feel sluggish, but I think a shower and shave will have me back up and running shortly. Any new news?"

Jack listened and didn't say a word until Cyrus reminded him it was time to go out. Fergus opened the door, and the big dog scooted out. His only comment was, "What the hell is Snowden talking about? There hasn't been anything on the news. I keep the cable news on twenty-four/seven. I'd remember something that serious. He is in the United States, isn't he?"

"I would assume so since he said he would be here shortly. Take your coffee and head upstairs and take your shower. I want you alert when he gets here."

Cyrus bounded into the room and waited for his treat before he galloped after Jack.

Charles threw his hands in the air just as Harry roared into the courtyard on his Ducati.

"I'm thinking you might need to start cooking again, mate." Fergus guffawed.

"I'm thinking you're wrong. Harry is a no-breakfast guy, and Jack won't want anything. Trust me. A fresh pot of coffee will do. You might want to boil some water in case Harry wants tea."

Fergus muttered something under his breath that Charles couldn't hear. He shrugged as Harry flopped down across the table from Charles. He waited, his gaze expectant.

"Jack is taking a shower. He's sluggish but pain free. I'll bring you both up to date when he joins us. Avery is on his way out here. The children are still sleeping. There was activity last night. Would you like some toast, tea, some melon?"

"Tea is fine."

The little group talked about everything and nothing as they waited for the others to join them. The bottom line was there were no rules when it came to finding the other missing children that had been warehoused with Carrie and her siblings.

"What I'm not understanding is where are the parents of those children? Are they orphans, kids in foster care whose caretakers just do it for the money and not report the kids if they go missing? What about the schools? Or are the kids homeschooled? Carrie said they were young like her and Emily but that Andy was the youngest. Most of them, if not all, are girls, at least according to Carrie. Sold to perverts and dirty old men," Abner snarled. "I'd just like to get my hands on one of them for five minutes. Five minutes!" he bellowed.

"We don't need five *minutes*. Put me in a room with them, and all I need is five *seconds*," Harry said.

"I hope it comes to that. Scum of the earth is what those sickos are," Abner said before he went back to what he was doing.

Jack entered the kitchen just as the huge outside gates to Pinewood opened to admit Avery Snowden and his motherly operative.

Introductions were made before Cyrus escorted Margie Chambers to the second floor via the staircase off the back kitchen. He returned almost immediately to take up his position next to Jack, who was drinking coffee.

"Let's get to it!" Avery said.

Ten minutes later, everyone looked at everyone else, their expressions helplessly blank.

"We have the inside track, so to speak," Charles said. "But the kids are young and are not big on remembering details. We shouldn't expect much of anything from them further."

"That's what Margie is for. She used to be a teacher in her other life. She'll have the kids draw from memory. She brought all the tools of her trade with her. That's where the information will come from. Margie knows her business," Snowden said.

Just then the phone in the center of the table rang. It was Maggie, alerting them that she, Ted, and Espinosa were heading back out to Apple Avenue to talk to the neighbors about the Bannons. She finished up with, "Dennis sent a text earlier saying he thinks he's onto something. He left half an hour ago to check out a senior development where he thinks Aunt Betty resides. He said he checked at least fifty locations last night, and none of them seemed like a place that someone like Aunt Betty would fit in. And, the ones he checked out do not allow small children except on Sunday afternoons. The Granite Hill Gardens development is geared to people fifty and over. He says it's just a gut feeling, but he's going to run with it."

"How is he going to find someone named Betty with no last name? How many houses or apartments are there in Granite Hill Gardens, did he say?" Jack asked.

"He didn't say, Jack. Dennis is resourceful, you know that. If Aunt Betty lives there, he'll find her. Okay, I'll report in when we're heading back."

"I suggest we retire to the war room. I'll leave cereal out for the kiddies and some fruit. Miss Margie can handle that and whatever else she plans. Anyone have any questions?" When none were forthcoming, Charles settled a box of corn flakes and bananas on the counter along with three bowls and spoons. He led the parade out to the secret staircase that would take them down to the war room.

Fergus turned on the overhead light. As one, the men saluted Lady Justice, then took their seats at the table. "Seems like everyone has a job but me and Harry. What do you want us to do, Charles?"

"Harry said you both have contacts with some of the agencies, people who like to . . . um . . . brag about how important they are. If you think you can worm something out of them that will help us, go for it. Or you might want to arrange a face-to-face. I always find people are more forthcoming when there is an actual dialogue going on. Your call, boys."

Jack looked at Harry, who shrugged. "I say we head to

the dojo, get the names and numbers, then go to the BOLO Building and work from there. We'll have to take my car since Cyrus will be with us unless you want to take the cycle and meet me there."

"I'll meet you there." Cyrus raced to the steps that would take him out to the main floor, where he saw the children eating their breakfast. When no one paid any attention to him, he threw back his head and howled at this strange event. Cooper yipped as much as to say, *Get over yourself.*

In the car, Cyrus buckled up and settled down for the long ride into the District.

The ride into town was uneventful. Jack, his thoughts racing, with every possibility under the sun concerning the children working its way through his mind, kept his eyes on Harry, who was directly ahead of him.

Ninety minutes later, the hydraulics of the gate hissed to life. Cyrus bounded forward to the kitchen, where the treats were, and waited. Jack dutifully handed one out. "Let's work here at the kitchen table, Harry." Harry nodded to show he was okay with that; phone calls could be made from anywhere. The real trick was going to be getting the braggarts to agree to a face-to-face.

"Piece of cake, Harry. Those guys are so scared of you, they'll do whatever you want them to do." Harry beamed at the compliment.

It only took half an hour to nail down four fifteen-minute meetings starting at a quarter till twelve.

"Now what do we do until it's time to leave?" Harry grumbled.

"We could head out to Apple Avenue to see if Maggie and the guys need any help. Or we can sit here and twiddle our thumbs."

"Let's go!" Harry said, jumping to his feet.

Outside, Jack voiced a question that was bothering him.

"Harry, do you really think Snowden's operative is going to get anything out of the kids that will help us?"

"She looked pretty capable to me. I'd say yes. Back in the day, Lily was like that. She could draw the story better than she could verbalize it. Yoko thinks she's a genius. The truth is, all kids do that. I read up on it."

"Well then, okay."

Back at Pinewood, Miss Margie, as Margie told the kids to call her, moved her charges to the dining room, where she unpacked the large canvas bag she'd brought with her. "We're going to draw this morning. Your pictures don't have to be perfect. That means there is no right or wrong. I'll say something, then you draw it. Here is the first thing I want you to remember and draw for me. When Aunt Betty lost you, draw me a picture of the place the people took you to. Draw as many stick figures as you can remember. Can you do that?"

The girls set to work, while Andy fidgeted in his chair. "I don't want to color."

"Because he can't stay in the lines," Emily chirped.

"Oh, Andy, I don't care about staying in the lines. That's not important to me. I just want you to color for me. Pick whatever color you want, and if you want to draw something different, that's okay, too."

The little boy reached for a purple crayon. He opened his sketch pad and set to work. "Mommy likes purple," he said as he started to scribble on his pad.

"Use as many pages as you need. Tell me the whole story," Margie said playfully.

The game was on as the children rushed to fill the pages for Miss Margie's approval and the promise of hanging the best on the refrigerator along with a huge gold star.

Margie watched the children carefully. There was almost a frenzy to the way Carrie and Emily were drawing.

Andy, on the other hand, seemed intent only on covering the entire paper in front of him with his purple crayon.

Thirty minutes passed, and the girls were still going full bore, flipping the pages in the sketch pad to a clean sheet. A sick feeling settled in the pit of Margie's stomach.

Another fifteen minutes went by before Margie called a halt. "That's enough for now. Let's go outside and take a walk. Maybe we can pick some flowers for Sir Charles to put on the table when he serves lunch."

Andy hopped off his chair and ran to the door, where Cooper was waiting for him. The strange, mystical dog allowed the little boy to hug him and tickle his ears.

"Do you have a dog or pet at home, Andy?"

"No. Daddy said we aren't old enough to take . . . to take care of them. Emily had a goldfish, but it went to sleep on top of the water."

"Uh-huh. Let's not go there, Andy. Come along, children, it's a beautiful day outside."

Carrie remained in her chair. "I'll stay here so no one takes our pictures. You should never leave anything behind; you have to keep it safe."

"There's no one here who will take your pictures, Carrie. We can close and lock the door when we leave. Will that work for you?"

"Mommy would say no, that's not all right," Emily said. Carrie's head bobbed up and down.

"I promise nothing will happen to your drawings. No one will see them. Come along now. Watch, I'm locking the door, and I'm putting the key in my pocket. If you like, we can ask Cooper to stay here and guard the room. Will that work for you?"

"I guess so," Carrie said.

Cooper seemed to know what he was supposed to do without being told. He stretched out across the doorway and closed his eyes.

Outside, as Margie steered her little group down a flower-bordered path, stopping as Andy pulled off flower heads with no regard to the stem, she asked questions in a tone of voice that was neither harsh nor threatening. "Tell me what Aunt Betty looks like. You go first, Emily."

"Sometimes she's pretty. She has lots of clothes. In two closets. When she picks us up, she wears her white hair. She has brown hair, too."

"Red!" Andy chimed in. "Curly like mine."

"Do you know where she lives? Like the numbers on her house or mailbox?" All three children shook their heads.

Andy stopped on the path. "She lives in a house."

"Wonderful!" Margie said, putting as much enthusiasm in her voice as she could.

"Why does your Aunt Betty have a lot of clothes? Does she like to get dressed up?"

"We're not supposed to talk about Aunt Betty," Carrie said.

"Oh, I didn't know that, Carrie. I'm sorry. I just thought if we could find her, it would make it easier for us to find your mom and dad."

Carrie made a face. "She lost us. She left us at the mall, and those people took us."

"Maybe someone took your Aunt Betty the way they took you, and that's why she lost you. I bet that's what happened."

"No one can steal Aunt Betty. She has a gun in her purse," Emily said, disgust at Margie's suggestion written all over her little face.

"I want to go home," Andy started to wail as he plopped down on the path.

Margie dropped to her knees beside the little boy. "And we all want to take you home, but we don't know where you live. We thought Aunt Betty could help us. Do you know anyone at all who can help us find your parents? What do they do? What's their job, do you know?"

"It's secret," Emily said.

"We don't know, our parents never talk about it to us," Carrie said.

"Can we go back now? I'm thirsty," Andy blubbered.

"Of course we can, little man," Margie said cheerfully. "Come along, girls."

Margie used up ten minutes in the kitchen pouring glasses of orange juice for the kids while she looked for a small vase to put the flowers in.

"Ready?"

The kids remained silent as they trudged behind Margie back to the dining room, where she made a big production of opening the lock and motioning for Cooper to lead the way, which he did. She made another production out of rummaging in her carryall for the big gold stars she planned to attach to the kids' artwork.

"Who wants to go first?" No one responded. "Well, then, since you're the oldest, I guess you go first, Carrie. Tell me what your drawings mean."

Carrie fidgeted in her seat. She finally sucked in her breath and opened her sketch pad. She held it up for Margie to see. "What does it mean, Carrie?"

"This is the place the men took us after Aunt Betty lost us."

"What are all these squares?"

"Boxes. Some are pretty and shiny. Some have blankets in them."

"How many? You have six here. Were there more?"

Carrie flipped the page. There were squares covering the entire page. "That's a lot of boxes," Margie said. "Were there other children there when you got there?"

Carrie flipped to another page. Nine stick figures clustered together, each with a number over the stick figure's head. "So that means twelve kids, counting you three, right?"

Carrie's head bobbed up and down as she flipped another page.

"Is this outside where you were?" Carrie nodded.

"It smelled bad. You had to hold your nose," Emily said.

"What is it?"

"A place to cook. The monster lady told us if we didn't stop crying, she would cook us in it. We tried not to cry," Emily said.

A wild idea ripped through Margie's mind, but she said nothing. "What's on the next page?"

"Jars with flowers and letters. Big fat candles."

"Where did you kids sleep?"

Emily opened her sketch pad. "We slept in the box. They let Andy sleep with me because he wouldn't stop crying." She flipped the page. "This is the Princess Queen!

"She was the only one who got the pretty dress. And that crown on her head. She got picked first. No one wanted Carrie and me because we . . . why didn't they want us, Carrie?"

" 'Cause we're mixed up. The monster lady said someone would pick us sooner or later if the price was right."

Margie swallowed hard. "Well, now, that didn't happen, did it? You are safe and sound, and we're going to find your parents and take you to them. Think, Carrie, you too, Emily, when they took you from the mall, how long were you in the van? Was it a long time or did it just take a little while?"

Carrie's face puckered up. "I can tell time but not real good. I think one hour. I looked at my phone before they took it away from me."

"That's real good, Carrie." Margie looked at the watch on her wrist. "I'm going to see what the gentlemen have in store for us for lunch. I'd like you to keep drawing, any-thing you think will help us find your parents and your Aunt Betty."

"She's not our real aunt," Emily said. "Uncle John isn't our real uncle either. They're . . . what is it, Carrie?"

"Pretend," Carrie said, glaring at her sister. "And you aren't supposed to tell that to anyone."

"I don't care. I just want to go home. I hate it here. I want Mommy and Daddy. I want to go home," Emily wailed.

Margie did her best to comfort the little girl. "How does ice cream sound for dessert?" she asked as she tried to dis-tract the child.

"Strawberry?"

"Let me see what I can do. In the meantime, you kids keep drawing me pictures, okay? Even if you think it's not important, draw it anyway. Cooper will watch over you while I'm getting lunch."

Margie Chambers stood in the middle of the spacious kitchen and raised her eyes upward. She knew where the kids had been taken. Now she had to tell her boss. She pressed the number 2 on her cell and waited. "Come up to the kitchen. I think I know where the kids were held. I'm making them lunch right now."

"Where?" Snowden barked.

"I'll tell you when you get up here."

Chapter Six

Allison Bannon, aka too many aliases to remember, stared at the red numerals on the tiny bedside clock— 3:10. The bed was lumpy, and yet, somehow, it was almost comfortable. Steven Bannon, her husband, her partner, her teammate, snored lightly next to her. The sound annoyed her. Steven annoyed her. He'd annoyed her for years now, and it was time she started thinking about doing something about it. Everything in this screwed-up life she was leading annoyed her. She hugged her arms to her chest as a lone tear rolled down her cheek. She didn't bother to move to wipe it away because if she did that, she knew a waterfall would start. Besides, special government agents didn't cry. Special government agents were tough. Almost inhuman, with no emotions.

I can't do this anymore. I don't want to do this anymore. I want a life. Fifteen years serving the United States government on American and foreign soil is enough. She wanted *out*, and she wanted out *now*.

All she had to do was slip out of the lumpy bed; pull on her boots, because she always slept in her clothes for a quick getaway; and walk out the door. That's all she had to do. Steven would never know she was gone till he woke in the morning. She'd leave it up to him to make up some story to tell the other three men on the five-person team she was leaving behind. He'd find her, though, because he knew exactly where she would go. And then there would be a huge blowout between them, with their handler stepping in. Well, not this time. This time, she was really done. And she didn't give a good rat's ass about anyone or anything except her kids.

For a week now, she'd tried through all the channels set up with her handler to get some face time with her kids, all to no avail. She was given one excuse after another as to why that couldn't happen. Steven didn't seem the least bit concerned, but she was having none of it. She'd tried calling Betty, Andrea, and all the other agents, supposedly substitute parents, who looked after her kids, but every single call went straight to voice mail. Eight days had passed since that initial conversation, and nothing had happened. She was now on her last nerve.

Allison moved then, just slightly, waited to see if Steven would wake, but he just continued to snore. She moved again, stood up, pulled on her boots, reached under her pillow for her Sig Sauer, and stuck it in the back of her jeans. The rest of her arsenal was in her backpack, which weighed thirty-eight pounds. It held her life, her very survival. Steven had an identical backpack, as did the other members of her team. Between the five of them, they called the packs their L&D packs, which meant live or die.

Allison was almost to the door when she heard her husband ask her where she was going. Answer or not? She sucked in her breath, wondering if this was going to escalate to something ugly they'd both regret. The answer was yes.

"I'm going to find my kids. I'm done, Steven. You're in charge now. That's what you've always wanted. Well, now you have it." Without another word, Allison was out the door and headed to the Jeep they'd arrived in the night before.

Steven was right behind her, pulling on his boots as he hobbled after her. "You can't walk off a mission like you're going out for a loaf of bread."

"Is that what you think? Watch me. Try to stop me, and I *will* shoot you. You know I will, Steven. So stop right there."

"What the hell has gotten into you, Ally? We're so close now. We almost . . ."

"Almost! Almost! Almost isn't good enough anymore. We've been chasing the Karas brothers and their child-trafficking organization for three years, and we're no closer to finding them than we were three years ago, when we started out. Something's wrong here, and I don't like what I'm smelling. Someone in this little team is not who he seems to be. I think it's you, you son of a bitch! You're a traitor. Right now, I don't even care about that. All I care about is my kids. Those goddamn people have my kids, I know it. I know it!" Allison screamed in the quiet night. "And I'm going to get them back. Me. Just me. Run along now and report to Luka. And when you talk to him, tell him if he gets in my way, I'll shoot him, too."

Allison knew she had the advantage because Steven had to go back into the rattrap rental for his backpack. She hopped into the Jeep and tore out of the parking lot burning rubber. She didn't look back. Let Steven and the team find their own way from here on. From this point on, she was going solo and would depend on no one but herself.

As she drove through the dark, quiet night, she reviewed her life with the Agency. Fifteen years she'd given them. And they lost her kids, something they promised would never happen. And no one was doing a thing to find them. All they were doing was lying to her. For all she knew, they were on some boat waiting to be sold to the highest bidder for things she didn't even want to think about.

It had been so glamorous in the beginning, when she'd been recruited right out of college. The life of a dangerous spy. It was right up there with all the stars in the sky. Mata Hari, slinky gowns, speeding cars. *Action!* She took to the training like a seal to water. She excelled, graduating at the top of every class. There was nothing she couldn't ace. She could fieldstrip a weapon in the dark with her eyes closed. She was the best sniper to come out of Langley, also known as The Farm. The prestigious CIA. She was the fastest on the field and outdid her instructors every single time, earning her the title of the Bionic Woman after the famous character in an old television series. She was the best of the best, and no one had ever had the audacity to challenge that claim.

Allison slowed when she saw neon lights ahead on the road. She stopped. She needed gas and some coffee. And a new supply of burner phones. She was in and out and back on the road in twenty minutes.

Ten miles down the road, she saw a turnoff that would take her to a strip mall set far back from the road. Across the road from the ratty mall was a run-down trailer park. She had to ditch the Jeep and see if she could hot-wire a stolen vehicle. No sense letting her handlers follow all the GPS trackers they had on everything she owned.

Allison headed straight for the trailer park and drove around till she found what she was looking for. An old Bronco with a lot of leaves and debris on the hood. Whoever owned it obviously didn't drive it much. She stashed the Jeep in the far corner but not before she ripped off the trackers, knowing she was probably missing a few of them. She tossed them as far as she could and hoped for the best. In the next aisle, she noticed a tarp covering a car. She ripped it off and settled it over the Jeep. At least it wouldn't show up like a beacon in the night. It would allow for a small head start but not by much.

There was no need to hot-wire the Bronco. The key was in the ignition. *Trusting lot, these trailer owners*, she thought. And the gas tank was full.

Allison let her thoughts go to her children. To all the mistakes she'd made when she put her career ahead of her family. She deeply regretted each and every one of them. Nothing she'd accomplished could ever take the place of missing the kids' first tottering steps, the loss of their first tooth, the gold star on a spelling paper, the warm hugs and kisses, the sweet, innocent baby smell. Nothing.

Tears leaked from her eyes and rolled down her cheeks.

Allison knew she needed a plan. She needed to find a place to hide out for a day or so to get her wits together. She was smart enough to know she was going to get one shot at what she was trying to do, and if she flubbed it, her kids would be lost to her forever. Well, that was not going to happen.

The sun was starting to creep toward the horizon when Allison saw a sign advertising a mom-and-pop rest stop. They'd take cash and ask no questions, and hopefully it would be a clean place where she could catch a few hours' rest and take a long, hot shower and put on some clean clothes. Then she'd make a plan.

The inn was a cozy little place with just eight rooms. She signed in, paid cash, took the key, and walked around the corner to her new digs. The room was just as she hoped it would be. Clean, nice soap, comfortable bed. Four hours, and she should be up and clicking on all cylinders. For now, it was the only plan on the agenda.

Allison did everything she promised herself. She washed her hair, stood under the shower until the water ran cold, brushed her teeth three times before she crawled naked between the cool sheets. She set her internal clock to wake up in four hours. She woke with one minute to spare, feeling like she could take on the world.

She ordered a fried egg on a bagel and a huge pot of coffee from the limited menu next to the phone. She couldn't ever remember anything tasting so good.

A plan. She was smart enough to know by now that Steven had notified Luka, and the hunt for her would be on. They'd sanction her. Agent gone rogue. Armed and dangerous. In other words, if necessary, shoot to wound. With no results, that order would change to STK, shoot to kill. Her people didn't mess around.

Allison sat down at the little desk under the window. She pulled a blank sheet of paper toward her. She reached for a pen. She had known that this day would come at some point and had taken steps toward this moment. She had the next best thing to a photographic memory and didn't trust herself to put anything in writing or on a computer. But right now, she wanted to see her short list of people she knew she could count on, a short list of people who would have her back. She needed to see it in black and white. With her own eyes. What the eye saw, you could never take away.

1. Lizzie Fox.
2. Harry Wong.
3. Ethan Franz.

Three people! Just three people she could depend on. Pretty damn sad, she thought.

Lizzie Fox had her POA, power of attorney, and as such had set up a safe haven for her if she ever had to take it on the run. Harry Wong had turned her into the lethal person the powers that be had ordered. And Ethan Franz controlled her money, and there was plenty of money, enough to last her and her family through ten lifetimes. Better not to think about where all that money came from right now. No one knew about the money except Lizzie and Ethan and herself. Technically, she supposed she'd stolen it, but the truth was, she had found it. By accident. On a drug bust eight years ago. Ten teams of agents had scoured the three acres where the bust went down. Two weeks later, they closed the case, and the money was forgotten, all $57 million of unmarked money that had already been laundered. It had bothered her that the money had never been found, so six weeks later she went back to the area and plopped herself down and let her memory go to work. There had been one squirrely dude whom she'd watched because she thought he was the one who would give it up, but he hadn't. But his eyes gave him away.

First rule of thumb: If you want to hide something, hide it in plain sight. Uh-huh. She remembered how she'd let her eyes do the same dance the squirrely dude had performed; and then she saw it. Six straggly pine shoots each no more than a foot high. And there wasn't a pine tree to be seen for miles. She stared at them for a long time before she started digging with her bare hands. In the end, she'd had to use a shovel and dig down five feet before she found four trash bags full of shrink-wrapped money.

She remembered staring at the money for well over an hour. She was a federal agent, an officer of the law that she'd sworn to uphold. If she put it back, it would just rot in the ground. The case was closed. The drug dealers would be in jail for the rest of their natural lives. They weren't going to talk, not now.

Finders keepers.

She'd lugged the bags back to her SUV, shoved them in the cargo hold, and drove a hundred miles out of her way to a small town outside Memphis, Tennessee, where she rented a storage unit for a five-year contract that she paid for up front in cash. She'd renewed the contract once for a second five-year term. And she'd never touched a penny of the money. Technically, that is. She'd faithfully sent Ethan

Franz $150,000 twice a month for the last ten years to invest for her.

Her plan, if you could call it a plan, was to retire on her investments, which were now beyond the robust stage, and somehow figure out a way to return the original $57 million to the government. There was a lot to be said for being an entrepreneur.

No, money was not a problem.

Allison put a check mark next to Lizzie Fox's name. Then she plugged in one of the new burner phones and waited. It took her less than three minutes to program the phone; then she dialed the special cell-phone number Lizzie had given her so many years ago. It rang three times before the call was answered.

Allison cleared her throat. "Lizzie, do you know who this is?"

"Tea Pope," was the immediate response. Allison had the crazy thought that Lizzie was just sitting there waiting for her call.

Allison closed her eyes at the sound of her birth name. "Today, I go by Allison Bannon. I need your help."

"Talk to me," Lizzie said softly.

Allison laid it all out quick and fast. "I need a car, a clean one. Paperwork should all be in the name of Doris Brown. Use the address of the safe house. Right now, I am right outside of Delaware. I need you to call Ethan and have him activate the Doris Brown bank account. Twenty thousand should do it for now. I'm driving a stolen Bronco I need to get rid of. Do you know anyone who can take it off my hands and make it disappear?"

"I do," Lizzie said. "Where are you going to go, Allison?"

"To find my kids. I'll do whatever I have to do to get them. If . . . if something goes wrong, you know what to do, right?"

"I do, Allison. What about Steven?"

"We're done. We've been done for years now. He's never gotten over the fact that I was made team leader, and he's my second. I stopped trusting him a long time ago. I believe he's a traitor. I knew there was a mole in the nest, but I never thought it was my husband. I was wrong, Lizzie. The rest of the team, they're all rock solid. I can't worry about them now. Call me when you have me set up. We good, Lizzie?"

"We're good, Allison. Listen, if you get in a bind, I know some very good people who will be only too glad to help you. You know one of them already, Harry Wong. Promise me you'll ask for help if you need it."

"I promise. Thanks, Lizzie."

Allison found herself doodling on the paper in front of her. She drew circles, then arrows, then more circles around Harry Wong's name. For some reason, it didn't surprise her in the least that Lizzie Fox knew Harry Wong.

Nothing to do now but wait.

The clock in the Pinewood hallway struck twelve. Twelve o'clock meant lunchtime. Jack Emery wasn't hungry, and his mouth was still tender, so he settled for his fourth or fifth cup of coffee, he couldn't remember which. He sat down at the table and was surprised to see Cooper come through the door right on Harry's heels. The strange, mystical dog ambled over to Jack the way he always did for a soft tickle to the sweet spot between his eyes just long enough for a thought to enter Jack's head. Jack didn't disappoint him. Satisfied that his job was done, Cooper ambled back out of the room.

"A little TLC." Harry guffawed.

"Who is Tea Pope?"

"What?"

"You heard me. Who is Tea Pope?"

Harry smacked at his forehead. In a strangled-sounding voice, he demanded that Jack tell him where he had come up with that name. Jack shrugged. "It just popped into my head. Why? Who is she, Harry? An old girlfriend, what?"

"Just like that, you came up with her name. Out of the blue? Why?"

"I just said I don't know. I was petting Cooper and then I . . . Oh, shit! He put that thought in my head. He's done it before. Son of a bitch! Okay, okay, who is she?"

"She was the best student I ever had. She's the one in the center of the wall of pictures at the dojo. She has the center spot because no one ever came close to her. She's in a class all by herself. She's her own weapon. Black belt. Honors. The truth is, and I hate to say it out loud, but the woman is a killing machine. That's what her superiors wanted, and that's what they got. All one hundred and fifteen pounds of her. They called her the Bionic Woman, and not because she had artificial parts or anything. It was just that she was . . . hell, I don't know what she was, but she was something special."

"What happened to her?"

"I have no clue. I never saw or heard from her again after she graduated. I did ask around for a little while, but no one would admit they knew her or even that there was such a person as Tea Pope."

"Better than you, Harry?" Jack asked curiously. He fully expected his old friend to deny it, but he didn't. He watched as Harry thought about the question. "No, not better, but if it came to a contest, we'd both be bloodied and battered. She's my match. What does it mean, Jack?"

"Damned if I know. Obviously, Cooper seems to think we need to know about her. Here's a stretch. Maybe she's the kids' mother. That would make some kind of sense, don't you think?"

"Well, I'm suddenly thinking we should find her. Where's Abner?" Harry asked.

"Down in the war room," Jack said, and descended the secret staircase that took them down to the war room, where Abner was toiling over his laptop.

"We need you to stop what you're doing, Abner, and hack into something and find a Langley recruit named Tea Pope."

"Why?"

"Because Cooper told us to do that. Is that good enough for you?" Jack snapped.

Abner shrugged, then rolled his eyes. "I didn't come across that name yesterday, when I hacked into the files. Right, right, okay, I'll try again. Just so you know, if they erased her true identity, then it's probably gone for good."

Jack stood in the center of the room listening to what was going on. Everyone was talking on top of everyone else and answering each other at the same time. In a cockamamy way he understood it all because they were so attuned to each other. He listened as Maggie said her team drew a blank back on Apple Avenue, no one knew the Bannons, and they were never part of the neighborhood and even in broad daylight no one would be able to point to them as the Bannons.

Dennis echoed Maggie's report with one exception, Betty, who minded the Bannons' kids, lived in a residence where there was top-notch security with no chances of breaking and entering and questions were frowned on. He said security copied down his license-plate number and watched until he drove through the security gates.

And then the room went silent with a shrill whistle from Avery Snowden. He motioned for everyone to take their seats, and that included Charles and Fergus. When he had everyone's attention, he got right down to it.

"I believe this child-trafficking ring is headed up by the Karas brothers. They are untouchable. They have their own private army. They're Armenian. At least we think they are. Hell, when it comes right down to it, they could be any nationality. They came on the scene about seventeen years ago. They just materialized out of thin air. They would have you believe they are international playboys. Unlimited monies. They're known the world over. No agency has ever come even close to bringing any kind of charges for anything against them. And yet everyone on the dark side knows they are behind all the human trafficking that goes on in the world. You talk, you die. It's that simple. I am willing to stake my life and my reputation that they are behind what is going on. And as much as I hate to admit it, we are no match for the Karas brothers. We'd need a private army to get within ten miles of either one of them."

"Well, if we can't get to them, then let's make them come to us. Or, let's come up with a plan that would exclude them. We plan something, then allude to the fact that people of their ilk are not fit to attend. Something to do with children. Not that we would actually use children, we're just going to allude to it. Hundreds of children, hundreds of young women, the kind of women sickos salivate over."

"The *Post* can kick it off. Even though Annie isn't here, she won't have a problem with us using her name to arrange something like this," Maggie said.

"Where are the Karas brothers now? Do you know, Avery?" Ted asked.

Snowden shrugged. "Check Page Six or TMZ. They love getting their names in the paper. Time! We're going to need time."

"We have the kids, they're safe for now. So, we do have

time. Social media is instant. Mention Annie's name, and the news is all over it in an instant. A banner headline in the *Post* will make it happen. The brothers will be aware of it within an hour. Black tie, invitation only."

"In the meantime, we go straight to the top of every organization to have their top people in the wings. It might work," Charles said. "It just might work," he repeated.

Chapter Seven

Jack was the first to arrive at Myra and Charles's Pine-wood farm. He'd simply cut across the field in his farm truck, saving himself seven miles and twenty minutes in the heavy downpour that had started an hour earlier. The time was six o'clock. He shrugged out of his rain slicker and hung it on the rack near the door before heading to the laundry room for a towel to dry off Cyrus.

"Smells good in here," he called over his shoulder. Cyrus yipped to show that he, too, agreed. He did love pancakes as much as his master did. Not to mention the strip of bacon and one sausage link that always found their way to his plate.

"Can you eat solid food, Jack?" Charles asked.

"Yep. I'm good to go. Take your time, I'll have some coffee while you guys finish your breakfast. Where is everyone?"

"Avery is down in the war room. Abner is upstairs sleeping. Margie has the kids out in the barn. That lady is the best thing to happen to those children. They've bonded with her. She has their whole day mapped out. In the barn. All the animals, the barn cats, and there's a new litter of kittens. Avery tells me she has a theory, and he's working on it because, as he said, it actually makes sense. The important thing is the kids are safe."

"Agreed. The others are coming this morning, right? I know I'm early, but when Nikki is away, I hate being alone in the house with just Cyrus. It just feels . . . empty."

"No one has called in to say otherwise. I expect they'll be here within the hour. We need to work on a plan. I'm especially intrigued by the Karas brothers. Avery promised a profile when we get down to work. I hate to admit this, but I had never heard of them."

Jack waved his hand in the air. "Me neither. But then, I'm not up on all that society stuff and who attends what and when. It's all I can do to keep up with Annie and what she does. Maggie will probably have the skinny on it all when she gets here."

Fergus cleared the table as Charles stirred a monster bowl full of pancake batter. "How many, Jack?"

"Six for me and six for Cyrus. Today is his day to get three scrambled eggs, so just add them to his plate. By the way, where's Cooper?"

Charles lowered his head and looked over the top of his glasses at Jack. "Now, where do you think he is? In the barn with the kiddies. He never leaves their side; you know that." Jack shrugged. Cyrus looked up at his master as much as to say, *I knew that.*

"I didn't know Abner stayed the night," Jack said.

"He did. That young man is exhausted. He went to bed around four, at least we assume he went to bed then, because that's when Fergus and I retired. I told him I didn't want to see his face until eight o'clock this morning. I think I heard the shower running, so I assume he will be down shortly. He did tell us one thing. He was able to find the birth name of Tea Pope's husband before they were erased from the files. His name was/is Simon Spinelli. I'm not sure how those agencies do things in regard to the children. They go by the name Bannon, and that appears to be the name they've used since birth. The parents go by different names according to whatever mission or job they're on, but the kids, mostly for school purposes, I assume, go by Bannon. This is just a theory on my part. Abner is the expert."

"Did someone just mention my name?" Abner asked as he sauntered into the kitchen. "Ah, pancakes, my favorite!"

"How many?" Charles asked.

"Eight, ten, a dozen. I'm starved."

"How do you do that? You eat like a stevedore and never gain an ounce," Jack said as he eyed the computer hacker's lanky frame. Abner shrugged as he poured himself a cup of coffee.

"I don't eat lunch," he offered by way of explanation. "Nor do I snack."

Cyrus reared up, as did Lady and her pups. They all ran to the kitchen door.

Ted, Espinosa, and Maggie were running through the rain. Jack held the door open while Abner ran to the laundry room for towels.

"All this rain is going to be good for your garden, Charles," Ted mumbled as he handed out the towels.

"Well, I hate it!" Maggie grumbled. "It makes my hair frizz up. In fifteen minutes, I'm going to look like a firethorn bush. First one who laughs at me gets it right in the snoot! So what's up? Talk to me," she barked.

"I have nothing to report," Jack said. "Abner has some news, but I don't see it helping us in any way. Just something to add to the Bannons' dossier. I'm not making light of it, I'm just saying I don't see how it can help us." He dug into his pancakes with gusto as Abner reported his limited news.

Charles tested Cyrus's food and set it down. He adjusted the griddle and started to pour out batter for the latecomers' breakfast.

Dennis arrived, with Harry right behind him. Both were soaking wet by the time they raced into the kitchen. More towels were called for.

"Looks like you have laundry duty today, Ferg," Charles quipped. "And no shortcuts; you wash them, then you dry them, no just drying them.

Cyrus looked up at Charles and beelined for his space next to Jack. Just because he knew how to fold towels didn't mean he was going to do it. Jack grinned as he patted Cyrus on the head.

"Anything we need to know?" Dennis asked.

"Kids are in the barn with Margie and Cooper. Avery is in the war room. We're all here. Abner found out the birth name of the kids' father, but that's all," Jack said.

Harry sat down at the table, shook his head at the offer of pancakes, and reached for the cup of tea Fergus had placed in front of him. "I might have something, and I might not. Choa, my right-hand man at the dojo, checked in with me late last night. He said some woman called the dojo nine times yesterday. *Nine times!* His English is limited to yes and no. So when the woman asked for me, he just kept saying no. She didn't leave a name. I wrote out my cell-phone number for him to give her in case she calls back today. It's probably some senator's wife who wants to learn a little self-defense without anyone's knowing. I get those calls all the time. Other than that, nothing."

"Well, crap!" Jack exclaimed as he pulled his cell phone out of his pocket. "I forgot I turned it off. I was wondering why no one was calling me. Oh! Shit, shit, shit! Guess who called me seven times, and I missed all seven calls! Lizzie Fox!"

Everyone stopped eating to stare at Jack. No one said a word until Harry said, "Maybe it was Lizzie calling me yesterday, and when she couldn't get me, she called you or vice versa. But then Lizzie would have called Charles or Maggie or someone. Doesn't make sense."

"Well, what are you waiting for, Jack, a bus? Call Lizzie," Maggie snapped irritably as she worked at smoothing down her frizzy hair.

"There's a little matter of the time difference, Maggie. Lizzie is three hours behind us and is probably still asleep. Or she's taking little Jack to school. Let's give her another half hour. It's like Harry said, if it was some kind of emergency, Lizzie would have called one of you guys when she couldn't get me."

"I just got goose bumps," Dennis said. "When I get goose bumps, something always happens. And it's never good."

"And you felt the need to share that with us . . . why?" Ted growled.

"To alert everyone to possible trouble coming our way," Dennis growled in return.

"I think we're already in trouble," Espinosa mumbled.

Cyrus reared up, as did Lady and her pups, just as Avery Snowden stepped into the kitchen and Harry's cell phone rang and Jack's cell buzzed like a horde of angry bees. Both men stepped out of the way to take their calls as Avery headed to the coffeepot. The silence in the room was deafening as the gang struggled to hear whatever they could, which wasn't much as both men appeared to be listening to the person on the other end of the phone and contributing nothing to the conversation.

Then Jack explained in detail to Lizzie about his root canal and his phone's being shut off and what was going on at the farm. Lizzie listened, then got right to the point of her call. "Listen to me, Jack. I am going to do something I never thought I would do as in ever. I don't know how I'm going to live with myself after this, but when it comes to children I . . . Just listen, okay, and judge me later. Years ago, a young woman came to me, her name at the time is not what it is today. She works for the government. For want of a better term, she's the agency's superspy. They literally created her into this . . . this . . . machine. They invested millions of dollars training her, turning her into, like I said, this superspy. If they could have, they would have drained all emotion from her, but that didn't happen. She had me set up a safe house for her, take care of her finances for the day when she said she would need it. She came by a lot of money in a nefarious way, but that's not important right now. Out of the blue, she called me yesterday and asked me to help her. I had already done everything she asked, so it was just a matter of making some phone calls.

"She's a rogue agent now, Jack. She's on the run. She has kids and a husband. A husband she thinks swung to the other side. Rivalry there. Someone snatched her kids, and her people are not helping her, so she went rogue. This woman . . . Jack, she's one of a kind. I gave her your number and Harry's. Here's the kicker, Jack. Harry trained her. She said she'd call you guys. You need to help her. You can talk now, Jack."

Jack had followed Lizzie's words at warp speed. He knew exactly who she was talking about. "We have the kids. It all fits now. Espinosa found them two days ago. They're right here at Pinewood. Long story, but the main thing is they're safe. If we have to, we can call Pearl Barnes and put them temporarily in her underground. Just assure her they're safe. Call her and tell her. And, Lizzie, I would have done exactly what you just did by calling me. Sometimes the rules just have to be broken. I'll get back to you."

Jack clicked off, shoved the phone in his pocket, and stared at Harry, who looked like he'd just seen a ghost or was talking to said ghost. If his eyes grew any rounder, they'd be marbles.

He waited.

They all waited.

"That was . . . that was . . ."

"Tea Pope. Your star pupil. The one whose picture hangs in the center of your dojo wall," Jack said.

"How . . . how do you know that, Jack?" Harry whispered.

"That was Lizzie on the phone. Your star pupil just happens to know Lizzie, and she contacted her and Lizzie told her to call us, that we could help her. Did you tell her we have her kids safe and sound?"

"I did, and she cried. I swear to God, Jack, I never for a moment thought that young woman had an ounce of empathy for anyone or any thing. She cried. No, she damn well bawled. That's a difference. We need to go downstairs and get to work. She's going to call me again in two hours. Right now, she is in Tennessee. We have to find a way to get to her. She only uses a burner phone for one call, then ditches it, so we can't call her back. She has to call us. She's what they call a rogue now. Shoot to wound, and if that doesn't get her then it's STK. She wants to see her kids before that happens. She said they'll show her no mercy no matter how much they have invested in her."

"Harry's right," Abner said. "I know how those guys at the CIA work. Right now, she's on American soil, so the FBI and Homeland Security are on her ass, and don't think for a minute that every other agent who is available, no matter what the alphabet says on their jackets, isn't on it with them. She's marked. We have to get her to safety."

"Then let's go," Jack said.

Charles looked around at his kitchen, winced, then shrugged and followed his lads, and one lassie, with a last minute warning to Lady to watch over things.

As always when entering the war room, they all saluted

Lady Justice, who was on the big screen hanging from the ceiling. Everyone took their seat.

Charles held up his hand. "The children are safe, and so is Ms. Pope for the moment, so let's give the floor over to Avery, who has been toiling down here all night long. Maggie will go next with her plan. What do you have for us, Avery?"

"The Karas brothers. And it isn't all that much. As I had originally mentioned they came 'to be' around seventeen years ago. That's not a definite, give or take a few years on either side. For the most part that information was erroneous. They appeared out of nowhere twenty-three years ago. That was the first mention I found of them anywhere. They have more money than God, and no one knows where it came from or how they got it. They do not work. As in having jobs. One can't even say they live off their investments because I couldn't find any investments to track. No clue where monies are stashed. They're considered international playboys. Their names are Ryland and Roland. Ages are iffy. Midforties is the best I could come up with. Nationality-wise, they could be anything. One report said Armenian. But if you look at their pictures they could be Greek, Italian, Spanish. I just don't know, and I cannot confirm.

"They eased their way into international society by donating vast, and I mean vast, sums of money anonymously, and being coy about it but still managing to leak it that they were the ones doing the donating. When questioned they just smiled but would not confirm or deny. They were in demand. Look at the screen. This is the last sighting of them, taken last year at some black tie event in England."

Lady Justice faded to a gray screen to be replaced with two very handsome men, which made Maggie whistle appreciatively. "Hunks. Both of them." Ted scowled at her exuberance.

"They started out traveling with a small group back in the day. That group increased as the years wore on. Think in terms of an army. A gun-toting army. Not that the normal person would view it that way. These guys dress the part of top-notch security: clean-cut, military bearing, specially tailored suits to hide the shoulder rigs.

"The Karas brothers own property all over the world. At each location, there is top-notch security. Think in terms of a fortress. The cars they travel in are the same kind only better than the ones our president travels in."

"Someone must know something," Jack said.

"For sure. But in that kind of life, you talk, you die. It's said they pay their people more than Wall Street bankers earn in a year and we all know how hefty those sums are," Snowden said as he looked down at his scribbled notes.

"Earlier, you said it was rumored that the brothers were involved in slave trafficking. If no one talks, how did that rumor start?" Charles asked.

"I can't help you out on that, mate. I simply do not know. The dark side of the Net, I would assume. It was said. Period."

"Rumors have to come from somewhere. There has to be a starting point," Dennis said.

"The best I can come up with, and don't think I haven't been on this twenty-four/seven, is the many trips they take abroad. Their passports read like a three-inch travel log. White women are in high demand. As much as I hate saying this out loud, I'm still going to say it. A seven- to twelve-year-old girl goes for millions. That's as in plural. A young woman of say twenty-one goes for half that. It's all over the world. Do the math."

"Where are the scumbags right now? Do you know?" Ted asked.

"As a matter of fact, I do know. They blew into Atlanta, Georgia, a week ago today and took over three whole floors of the Ritz-Carlton in Buckhead. Their security, or army if you prefer that word, are with them. They also have their own waitstaff, who prepare their food and take care of all their needs, with them. I haven't been able to figure out yet why they're there. Nothing social is going on. A stopover? Atlanta is not that far from Washington, D.C. I do know that there is a fleet of eight armored SUVs parked in front. Guests have complained. The hotel grants a lot of freebies to the complainers."

"What about women?" Maggie asked.

"No attachments that I could ferret out. There is no background on them. It's like they were hatched from an egg and took on life. There simply is no backstory to be found. I don't even know if they're twins or who is the older and who is the younger. I'm telling you, it's just a blank slate."

The gang looked at one another. If Avery Snowden said it was a tabula rasa, then it was a blank slate. All eyes turned to Abner Tookus.

"You want me to get in touch with Philonias Needle-meyer. That's what you want me to do, right?"

"Well, yeah," Maggie drawled as she continued to work at her hair, which seemed to be growing outward at the rate of an inch a minute. In the end, she dug around in her backpack for a scarf and wrapped it around her unruly curls.

"Where is their home base? What country? Who do they pay allegiance to?" Dennis demanded.

Snowden shrugged. "They live in the wind. There is no home base. They do own property all over the world, and they pay the taxes or some dummy shell company does on the properties. If you're asking about taxes like you pay here in the States, nada. It's like I said, they hatched from an egg, then became invisible, not literally, but financially. They are under the eye of every law-enforcement agency in the world, yet no one can touch them. In essence, and speaking in the official sense, they haven't done anything wrong. They live the high life, but so do millions of other people. They constantly give away money, tons of money. No one wants that well to dry up. They charm the ladies and bullshit the gents. What's the harm in that?"

"This isn't making one damn bit of sense," Jack said. "If all that you said is so, how did they even get a wink in regard to child trafficking or slave trafficking or whatever the hell we're calling it these days?"

Snowden threw his hands in the air and risked a glance at Charles as much as to say, *Sorry, Sir Charles, I failed you.* "I simply do not know is both the short and the long answer," he responded miserably.

Fergus spoke for the first time. "Always follow the money trail. I'll give my old stomping grounds, Scotland Yard, a call. I still have some clout there and I'll see what I can come up with. Charles, you call MI6. Jack, you call Jack Sparrow and see if he knows anything or has heard any rumors while he was running things at the Bureau."

Maggie chewed on her thumbnail. "I never ever heard of the Karas brothers. Not a whisper. Now, you see, that's not normal. Do they go by any other names? Do they stay away from D.C.? I'm just not getting this. Ted, are you getting it? Dennis? Espinosa? Hatched from an egg, my ass," she exploded. "They had a life somewhere. We need to find that place and go from there."

All three men shook their heads. If Maggie wasn't getting it, then they would all be wise to agree with her. No one wanted to upstage Maggie because the consequences were always too seriously negative, as they had come to learn over the years.

Harry swallowed the last of the tea in his cup, propped his elbows on the table, and stared across the table at Avery Snowden. "You said something about your operative having a theory about where the kids were, something they obviously shared with her. What is it?"

Snowden sat up a little straighter, squared his shoulders, and said, "This is her theory, not mine; just remember that. She thinks the kids were held at a mortuary. Hence the *boxes*. To a kid, a casket or a coffin, whatever you want to call them, would be a big box. The older girl said Andy slept with her so that would kind of bear out the casket business.

"The monster lady that one of the girls referred to said if she didn't behave she'd cook her in something outdoors that the kids said smelled terrible. Margie thinks it was a crematorium. And the kids did say the place smelled like church. Incense and candle wax. After the first blush, it doesn't sound so lame if you think about it.

"What could be more perfect? Who is going to look for missing kids at a funeral parlor? It's so far under the radar, it hardly bears thinking about it. And Carrie, the older girl, described the soft pillows and blankets. It might be a stretch, but there you have it. I don't think it's worth a second thought, but you did ask."

"Whoa! Whoa!" Espinosa barked. He stood up and started to wave his arms about. "No, no, it's worth more than a second thought. Listen to me, everyone. Like *now* would be good!"

"What the hell!" Jack exploded.

"Ha! Yeah, well, Mr. Attorney, your dog was a witness to what I'm going to tell you, so listen up. On the way back from the vet's, and I'm sorry I didn't see it on the way in, but I wanted to make sure I didn't miss the turnoff. To the vet's, that is. Anyway, I'd say at the halfway mark, there was a fork in the road, and I took the wrong one. Cyrus didn't bark or anything, so I just assumed I was going in the right direction. I was wrong. Two miles, maybe two and a half down the road, there was this . . . almost like an oasis. Buildings and something that looked like a giant igloo. Lots of green grass. Everything was top notch, neat and tidy. Paved parking lot and *six* hearses all lined up behind each other. There were several other vehicles in the parking lot, but I just got the hell out of there. It got all creepy. In my turnaround, I got a good look at the giant igloo. I guess that's where they . . . you know . . . crisp them up and put them in a jar.

"When we got to the end of the road, there was a sign that said, LAST STOP BEFORE HEAVEN. I got out to look at it to be sure it said what it said. Don't ask me why, I just did. The sign was weather beaten from the elements. I think the kid was right, and that's where they ran away from. From that road, it's maybe five miles to where Cyrus spotted them. Five miles. Plus they had to cover the two to three on the road I was on before they hit the highway. Little kids like that get tired, so we're talking about eight miles. It makes sense if you think about it."

Jack looked down at Cyrus. "Is that how you see it, buddy?" Cyrus yipped.

Maggie was on her feet and struggling with her backpack. Ted, Espinosa, and Dennis were doing the same thing.

There was no need to ask where they were going—everyone knew. "Take a lot of pictures *after* you talk to the people who own the joint!" Jack yelled.

Harry looked over at Jack. "That totally creeps me out. Little kids sleeping in coffins. When we find those bastards, they're *mine*. You hear me, Jack, they're mine."

"I hear you, Harry."

Chapter Eight

The Karas brothers stared at each other across an impeccably set table for two as they waited to be served the lunch they had ordered from the five-star chef who traveled with them all over the world.

The Karas brothers were, as a matter of fact, twins, with Ryland, to Roland's chagrin, being two minutes older. Though they were not identical twins, they looked enough alike so that people knew they were related when meeting them for the first time.

Soft classical music played from somewhere in the luxurious suite the two men shared. Shared because they shared everything, even their space, with Ryland listening to his beloved classical music and Roland reading nonstop. Except for their sleeping arrangements, they were never more than a few feet apart.

The brothers were movie-star handsome, and both were elegant dressers. They paid fortunes for hairstyles, manicures and pedicures, and gym privileges. They'd been referred to as "good catches." The terms *studly*, *ripped*, and *rich* were constantly used when they were being referred to. Invitations to particular events along with pleas for donations from various charities arrived by the truckload the moment some gossip columnist announced their arrival in a particular city.

They always attended at least one event and donated to at least half of the favorite charities of the people whose pleas for their contribution found their way to their hands.

Ryland looked down at the jumbo prawns, which had been marinated in a lime citrus marinade before being grilled. A vegetable rice medley was a side dish that was not only delicious but colorful. Another side dish that both men loved was braised brussels sprouts with vinegar and bacon bits. They loved the dish so much it was a staple on their daily menu.

There was no one in the dining room, something else the brothers always insisted on. Members of their personal security team stood outside every door leading into the dining room. Even so, the brothers spoke in different languages, sometimes English, or some other exotic dialect, or else they'd resort to sign language. In addition to these rules, the suite along with all the other rooms they'd rented were swept daily for possible listening devices.

The brothers' manners were impeccable even in private. They were the kind of men whom you would never see leaning against a bar, swigging a bottle of beer, or chomping down on a burger or, God forbid, a hot dog. Under no circumstances would they attend a barbecue or a clambake, much less a beach party or NASCAR competition.

Only the best of the best in *everything* was good enough for the Karas brothers.

"You're sure, Roland, that there has been no mention of the three children? It's coming up on ten days. Children can't survive on their own for that long. Even I know that. That has to mean someone rescued them, and we're in danger? I want to hear you tell me that is not possible,"

Ryland said, deferring to his brother's computer expertise along with his penchant for the written word.

"Not a word. But there is other news. I was just informed before we sat down here at the table that Mrs. Bannon has gone rogue. Every agency in this country is on the hunt. Mr. Bannon has also gone to ground, or he is being detained by his own people for reasons unknown to us at the moment. Mrs. Bannon has a twenty-four-hour head start on our people. I'm being told that she is on the hunt for her children because she is a *mother*. That is something neither you nor I know anything about since we never knew a mother. We must assume there is a very strong bond that we will never understand, so we need to bear that in mind. We must find those children.

"D.C. was a mistake. I wish you had listened to me when I told you that the FBI was going to get involved. With five hundred children gone missing in the first three months of the year in one area, it had to happen."

Roland pierced one of the jumbo prawns and stared at it. His brother watched as he tried to make up his mind to either eat it or drop it back on his plate. The prawn dropped to his plate. "We need to leave here right now. I'm still wondering why you wanted to come here in the first place."

"A diversion. You know people watch us every second of every single day. Why does there have to be a particular reason for us to visit Atlanta? I could have chosen Newark, Delaware, but who goes to Newark, Delaware? No one I know. People flock to Atlanta for many reasons. Women like to shop. They have a great baseball team. And it's not that far from Washington, D.C."

Roland swirled the prawn around on his plate as he absorbed his brother's words. "No, we are not going back to D.C. That would be the biggest mistake of our lives. We have to leave the country. Like now, Ryland. That means immediately. I keep telling you that my gut is churning, and you keep ignoring me. Damnation, I wish you'd read more and listen less to all that soothing music you live for."

Ryland ignored his brother's remark. "Before you can ask, our people are on the way and will sanitize the facility. The bogus owners, the Obermans, left for a forced vacation last evening. No one is there. But, then, you already know that. Sometimes you worry like an old grandmother. The cleanup crew will sanitize the facility. A notice will appear in the local newspapers announcing the Obermans' retirement, and in a month or so, the facility will go up for sale. Last night, I told you that the chain of funeral homes would be going up for sale, not all at one time. It was part of the plan, and you agreed to it, brother."

"And you don't worry enough, Ryland. Yes, yes, I do enough worrying for both of us according to you. Until we became aware of the Bannon team, I never lost a night's sleep. Now, I barely sleep. I repeat, D.C. was a mistake. We have never made mistakes before. You need to listen to me, Ryland."

Ryland looked at the Rolex on his wrist. It was just noon. Then he looked at his empty plate, then over at his brother's plate. A small worm of fear scurried around inside his stomach. Maybe he did need to pay more attention to Roland's concerns. It was true, they'd never made a mistake before. Suddenly, he didn't like what he was feeling.

Ryland's cell phone chirped inside his trouser pocket. He withdrew it, clicked it on, and listened. Roland saw the sudden alarm on his brother's face. Unflappable Ryland! Roland swallowed hard as he listened to his brother's end of the conversation.

"Four people! Yes, I understand what you're saying. They were already there when you arrived. You were a fool to announce yourself. They *saw* you! You're saying they actually laid eyes on you! You know what that means! It doesn't matter that you pretended to be a . . . what is the word . . .

customer for the death of a loved one. Whoever those people are, they are not fools. A ten-man cleanup crew doesn't just show up out of nowhere to . . . make final arrangements. I can guarantee none of you looked like grieving mourners, and don't try to con me. Where are you now?"

At a Best Western down the road was the response.

"I need details. Vehicle, license plate. How many people? Ages? Armed? Do not go near the facility until I give you the go-ahead to do so. Now, tell me what you have. Oh, you already checked it all out. Tell me what you have."

When Ryland ended the call, he stared down at his empty plate for a full minute before he spoke. "I bow to you, my brother. This is what I just heard from the cleanup crew. There are four people at the facility. They appear to have arrived in one vehicle, a van that is registered to a newspaper in the District, the *Post.*

"They must be reporters, but our men did not question them. They pretended to be a customer or whatever you call a person who wants to either bury or cremate a family member. The team leader said the woman of the group was in charge and told them the place was temporarily closed and to go someplace else. She also said they were waiting for the local authorities to show up. I think it's safe to say our people panicked. They left and are at a Best Western a few miles down the road. We need to leave here right now."

"I hate saying this, Ryland, but I did say it was a mistake to snatch the Bannon children. You disagreed, and now here we are. That means we made *two* mistakes. Are you listening to me, Ryland? *Two!* Do you want to try for three? Three is the charm, as you well know."

"Yes, here we are. But we're leaving right now."

It wasn't like the brothers had to pack up tons of luggage or files the way most people like them who traveled with an entourage such as theirs. Other people took care of those details. The suites in use would be sanitized, all luggage and file cases would be carried personally out of the hotel by their own people. The hotel would be paid for the full week through a shell company even though they had a week to go on their reservation. All the brothers had to do was put on their jackets, pick up their briefcases, and walk out the door. Everything else would be taken care of by their minions.

Roland walked over to the window, parted the sheer curtains, and looked down at the highway that ran along the side of the hotel. There was a walkway for guests to use to get to the Lenox Mall, which was across the highway. The people, some single, some looking like families, appeared to him to be like big ants hurrying to find bargains at the giant mall. He wondered briefly what it would be like to be one of those people he considered *ordinary*.

Roland Karas lived a secret life in his mind. A life where he lived in a small house in a tree-lined neighborhood, possibly a building that would be considered a cottage. The people would be ordinary, a mix, so to speak. Some would be elderly, some young, some middle aged, some single. There would be children, dogs, and cats. The cottage where he lived would have a fireplace in a brick-lined room because he loved brick walls. Soft carpets because he liked to go barefoot. The cottage would have soft, comfortable furniture; a large-screen TV he would rarely watch; scads of electrical outlets; a gourmet kitchen because he loved to putter in the kitchen trying out new foods and recipes, most of which were inedible, but despite which he continued to try. The rest of the house would have rooms full of books from floor to ceiling. The rooms would have custom-made oak bookshelves because oak was a hardwood and books were weighty. The only exception would be his bedroom, for all he wanted in that room was a space that a monk would love. It was such a waste of time to sleep when he could be reading one of his beloved books.

The cottage would have a fenced-in backyard with flowers everywhere and a big shade tree with a chair under it, where he could sit and read and feel the spiky grass tickle his bare feet. *Ordinary.*

It was never going to happen, and he knew it, but still, as long as he kept the fantasy in his head, it *would* be possible if only in his dreams. No one could take away a person's dreams. No one, not even Ryland.

"What are you doing, brother?" Ryland asked as he slipped into his jacket.

"Thinking."

"About what? I'm ready. What are you seeing out that window?" Ryland asked.

"Nothing out of the ordinary," Roland lied. "Have you decided where we are going? Do not say D.C., because if you do, you will go alone. We need to get as far away as we can, and that means out of the country."

Ryland offered up a nervous laugh. "What? All because of one female agent who has gone rogue? Are you actually going to stand there, look me in the eye, and tell me you are afraid of Mrs. Allison Bannon, superspook, superagent, super government weapon?"

"No. I'm not afraid of that person at all. Look at me, Ryland, and listen to me very carefully. I am afraid of Allison Bannon who is the mother of the three children you decided to have kidnapped. And if I'm afraid of her, then you need to be afraid, too.

"Neither one of us knows a thing about motherhood. Or, I should say, you don't, but I do because I read. There is no stronger bond, no force in the world that will win out over motherhood if her cubs are in danger. She, yes, she, one lone woman, will come after us. She'll find us, too. You see, that's the thing about mothers. They will do anything, and I mean *anything*, to protect their cubs. No stone will be left unturned. You, more so than I, cannot conceive of that, but it's true nonetheless."

Ryland forced a blustery laugh. "Are you serious, Roland? Surely not. You cannot seriously believe one lone woman on the run from her own government is going to be able to seek us out and take us out. I believe that is the right term. One lone woman! That is never going to happen. Her own people will find her first and deal with her. We might hear about it later on or not. It simply is not going to happen."

Roland licked at his lips and nodded. "Not just a woman, Ryland. *A mother*. Therein lies the difference. Remember, we already made *two* mistakes, and she's made none. She's on the hunt. She's been so well trained, even her own people won't be able to locate her. You need to believe what I'm telling you. Well, I think I'm ready," he said, shrugging into one of his favorite Armani jackets. In his dreams, where he was an *ordinary* person, he would be slipping into a worn denim jacket with leather patches on the elbows. Cost was probably $49 opposed to the $5,000 spent for the Armani jacket he was putting on. *Ordinary*.

Ryland stopped at the door before he opened it to stare at his handsome brother. "You really believe all that stuff you just said, don't you?"

Roland nodded. "This is not going to end well, Ryland."

In the car on the way to Hartsfield-Jackson Atlanta International Airport, Ryland looked over at his brother, and said, "Tell me everything you know about motherhood."

"I never heard of this place before," Maggie said as she hopped out of the van and looked around. "It's part of a chain. I looked it up, and there are hundreds of them, independently owned, of course. It's like an oasis in the middle of a desert. There must be some kind of underground sprinkling system to account for all this lush grass and landscaping. For miles and miles, all you can see is scrubland. And not that far from the District, too. Last Stop before Heaven. I gotta say, for a funeral home, it's aptly named."

"Looks deserted," Dennis said uneasily. "Who is going to pick the lock? It's a given this place is buttoned up. It looks . . . *dead*."

"You had to say that, didn't you," Ted squeaked. "I guess I am since I have my own lock-picking kit."

Espinosa moved then to take as many pictures as fast as he could, so they could leave. He did not like funeral homes. He wondered if anyone really liked funeral homes. Probably only the morticians. The thought of being married to one sent chills up his spine. He continued to click his camera in a frenzy.

"Make it snappy, Ted. I want to get this over with," Maggie said as she chewed on her thumbnail, which was already bitten down to the quick.

"Okay, got it! Who wants to go first?" Ted shoved the lock-picking kit into his backpack and stepped back.

"You're all a bunch of wusses. I'll go. The place is empty. No boogeymen here," Maggie said.

"Think about all those spirits that might have come through here. It is the last stop before heaven. Maybe they weren't ready to head on . . . up there and are still hanging around. I bet there are hundreds of them inside," Dennis mumbled.

"One more word out of you, and you're going to be the last customer to walk through these doors," Ted shot back.

Maggie turned to lock the door, then slid the dead bolt at the very top. "Do you all notice this place is . . . like for handicapped? There are no stairs, just ramps. Strange, don't you think?"

Her response was a chorus of nos.

"Well, I think it's strange, and that's all that matters. So, should we split up or stay together?"

"This place gives me the creeps, I say we stay together," Dennis said, inching closer to Ted, who didn't object. Espinosa continued to click away as the foursome walked up the ramp into what looked like a receiving room for mourners. The scent of incense and dead flowers permeated the air.

Maggie led the parade. They switched on lights as they went along. "Chapel. Four pews. Religious statues, empty, of course. Leave the door open. We might need to check this out again. This floor must be what they consider the public area, where the bereaved come. The rooms off to the side with all that heavy velvet must be the . . . You know, where they . . ."

"Put the dead bodies on display," Ted barked. "We get it. The two on the left have coffins in them. The room on the right has six. This is a huge place. We need to split up, or we'll be here all day."

"Maybe this is the room where they . . . you know . . . get them ready for viewing. Or . . . this is the area for . . . prospective . . . what's the word, customer, guest . . . what?" Maggie babbled.

Espinosa stopped clicking long enough to scowl at Maggie.

"Oh jeez, oh jeez," Dennis yelped. "Okay, okay, I'll go down to the next level. It looks like office space," he said as he pressed a light switch. Two things happened simultaneously. The room was flooded with blinding white light, and somber, spine-chilling music bounced off the walls. Startled, he adjusted the switch. The lighting turned dim, and the music became a mournful dirge. He soldiered on, calling out his findings as he checked out the suite of rooms. "Eli and Ethel Oberman are the owners of this . . . this place. The license is hanging on the wall. Looks fake to me if anyone wants my opinion. There is no raised seal. A license has to have a raised seal. Why didn't they take it with them? It's bogus, I'm sure of it. File drawers are full of folders, the records of all the deceased. Hundreds of them."

Maggie tuned out her colleague as she made her way to the rear of the first floor. The plaque on the door said, STORAGE. She opened the door to see row after row of coffins. She turned on the light and gasped. *Boxes* was her first thought. The kids were right. This is where they were kept and probably slept. She suddenly felt sick to her stomach. "Espinosa, get in here! *Now!*"

Espinosa skidded to a stop in the doorway, his gaze raking the rows of coffins of every shape, size, and color. "Oh crap!"

"Take some close-ups. The . . . the . . . bedding is mussed." Maggie swallowed hard. The vision of little kids sleeping in what was in front of her was almost more than she could bear. Tears pooled in her eyes. She felt a gentle hand on her shoulder. Ted. Ted was always there for her. She bit down on her lower lip. She needed to toughen up. She really did need to do that.

"If it's any consolation, Maggie, little kids wouldn't have any conception of what this place was to them. They said they slept in boxes. These are just boxes. That's how you have to think of it."

Maggie hiccuped. "This place is in the middle of nowhere. Where's the damn cemetery? I didn't see one driving in."

"Just because this is a mortuary doesn't mean there's a cemetery that goes with it. That's an ordinance thing towns work with. I'm not an authority, I'm just guessing here," Ted said soothingly as he kept a tight grip on Maggie's shoulder.

Maggie almost jumped out of her skin when she heard Dennis let loose with a bloodcurdling yelp. "You need to come see this. There must be close to a thousand of those jars! Those are ashes! People! What's left of them. Look, they have names on them. They fry . . . burn . . . roast, crisp them in that big brick thing in the back, then . . . then they bring them in here and line them up. Look! That big one has a lightning bolt on it. Who does that?" he dithered.

"Either my hearing is accclerating, or someone is ringing the doorbell. Do you hear it?" Espinosa asked as he lowered his camera to tilt his head to the side. "It is the doorbell."

"Oh, shit!" Ted muttered. "What should we do?"

"Well, we lit this place up like a Christmas morning, so whoever it is knows someone is in here. If we stay here, maybe they'll go away. I locked the door and slid the dead bolt at the top, so even if someone has a key, they can't get in. Let's finish with this room, check out the basement where they . . . where they . . ."

"Where they what?" Dennis demanded.

"Drain the deceased's blood and embalm them," Espinosa shot back.

"I don't think we need to go down there," Maggie finally decided as the doorbell continued to ring.

"If we go to the front, stay close; I think we can make it to that hallway where all those coffins are. The room on the right with the six coffins will give us a view of the front door and those two side panels. We'll be able to see who it is being so damn insistent," Ted said.

"This feels like a conga line," Dennis said as he grabbed hold of Ted's belt and allowed himself to be dragged forward.

"Okay, we're here, now what do we do? The bell is still ringing. They must be desperate, whoever they are," Maggie said as she stared down at the bronze coffin in front of her. She frowned when she saw the small brass plate near the gold-plated handles. Agnes Twitt.

"You guys ever hear of a casket line called Agnes Twitt?" Maggie asked. "Springfield I've heard of. Pricey. Top of the line. I just saw a commercial for them on TV a few weeks ago. Creeped me out."

Ted turned around so fast he almost knocked Maggie off her feet, the force making her fall back against the coffin, causing it to hit the wall and the lid fly open, then careen around and roll down the ramp toward the front door, where it came to a full stop with Agnes Twitt bouncing up and back in her nest of pillows.

"Holy shit!" Ted, Dennis, and Espinosa said in unison. Maggie, her eyes glazed, tottered down the ramp to stare at Agnes Twitt, then at the men on the other side of the door. "What . . . what just happened?" she managed to squeak as she stared at Agnes Twitt and the string of pearls that were caught in one of her ears.

"We're closed! Can't you read the sign?" Ted bellowed, so the men on the other side of the door could hear him.

"Our grandfather just died. We need to bring him here. We wish him to be cremated. This is his wish. Our family's wish. He wanted this place," the man closest to the window shouted.

"Sorry, mister, the owners left town. There is no one here to help you."

"Then what is that person doing in the casket behind you?" the voice on the other side bellowed just as loud as Ted had bellowed. "Why are you here if the place is closed?"

"That's . . . that's Agnes. She's waiting for pickup. Why

else do you think she's here by the door? You need to leave now. We're just here to help out temporarily. We have our orders. Besides this place is expensive. See this casket, it's bronze, and it costs $25,000. Top-of-the-line Springfield. You can get it cheaper somewhere else," Ted said in a jittery voice.

"Tell him the bedding is silk and cashmere," Maggie hissed. Ted looked at her like she'd sprouted a second head.

"Just the cover and pillows cost a fortune because they're silk and cashmere. It was what . . . what Agnes wanted," Ted managed to gasp, his eyes wide as saucers as he stared first at Agnes Twitt, then the men at the door. He wondered who would fix the pearls around her neck.

"Money is no object," came the retort. "We want to send our grandfather off with the best."

"Well, buddy, that ain't gonna happen because . . . because it ain't gonna happen. Now, skedaddle, or I'm calling the police," Ted said with as much authority as he could muster in his voice, considering the circumstances. "We're closed. We are out of business. Read the sign. You . . . you have our condolences on the death of your grandfather."

Maggie, Espinosa, and Dennis bobbed their heads up and down to show that the men outside had their condolences as well.

Cursing, the men turned to leave. The four intrepid reporters pressed themselves up against the two side windows to watch as the gaggle of men trailed back to two mud-caked pickup trucks. They watched until they lost sight of the trucks.

As one, they turned around to stare at Agnes Twitt and her pearls, which were askew.

"We're really sorry about this, Agnes. Wherever you are, think about this. If Ted hadn't jostled me, you'd be in that room maybe forever. Everything happens for a reason—we all know that. Oh, God! Do you think there are other bodies in those other coffins?" Maggie babbled as she stared down at Agnes Twitt.

"Did you take a picture of Agnes?"

"Yes. I. Did!" Espinosa responded.

"Good, because no one is going to believe this. Come on, we need to check the rest of those . . . those boxes, then make some calls," Maggie said.

"What about Agnes?" Dennis asked.

"Seriously, Dennis? We can't take her back up. She has to stay here. Move!"

Back in the room, it was left to Ted to raise the tops of the coffins. "This is Alfred Saddlebury. Looks like he's been here a while. He's not looking so good. And this one is Chester Mason. He looks kind of fresh, like he was just done recently. And this one is Sasha Yakodowsky. Too much rouge for a lady her age. The last one is . . . Oh, crap . . . this is Benjamin Franks. He looks to be about ten. And he's been here wayyyy too long. Don't look, Maggie."

Dennis was busy dialing 911. He explained the situation and said, "We'll be waiting outside. Please be careful, Agnes is right up against the door. There's no way we can get that gurney back up the ramp. And when you do get her you might want to . . . to . . . adjust her pearls. It's a lady thing. Women and their pearls."

"We need a cover story for all of this," Ted said, waving his arms about.

"We were here to meet with the Obermans to do a story on how they came up with the name for the mortuary. Human interest. That kind of thing. The door was open so we walked in and felt something was wrong. Soon as we discovered what we . . . discovered . . . we called nine-one-one. We do *not* mention the men at the door. Is that clear?" Maggie said in her take-charge voice that no one in their right mind would ever argue with.

"I guess that will work," Espinosa said as he packed his camera in his backpack.

"What do you think would have happened to those . . . the deceased if we hadn't come here?" asked Dennis. "What do you think those men would have done with . . ."

"Don't go there, kid," said Ted. "It didn't happen. That's the good thing. This is in other hands now."

"Amen," Maggie said solemnly.

Chapter Nine

The *Post* reporters dutifully answered all the questions the local Virginia authorities asked them, stressing the fact that they hadn't touched anything inside the building other than bumping into the coffin that led to the accident with Agnes Twitt, who slept peacefully her forever sleep by the front door. It took one of the officers twenty minutes before he lowered the top of the coffin. No one seemed to care about the pearls that were askew around Agnes's neck but Dennis, who walked around asking someone to please take care of the matter. No one paid the slightest attention to his pleas.

Ninety minutes later, Maggie put her foot down. Hard. "We told you everything we know. There is nothing more we can do here. We need to leave. You can get in touch with us at the paper or call us personally at the BOLO Building. The number is on each card we turned over to you. We all gave you our personal cell-phone numbers as well."

A young officer who looked like he wasn't old enough to shave nodded and thanked them for their help, saying they would be in touch but reminding them they all needed to go by the station to sign the statements they'd just given. The gang agreed and climbed into the van. Dennis pressed hard on the gas as they flew out of the parking lot. No one paid attention to the scenery or the Best Western as Dennis whizzed down the road.

"Someone should say something," Maggie groused. "I've been doing all the talking, it seems."

"That's because you never shut up and forever tell us you are the boss, so we are just doing what you want us to do. Make up your damn mind already," Ted growled.

"What do you think they are going to do with the . . . the . . . deceased?" Maggie asked.

Espinosa raised his hand. "I know the answer to that because I asked. Last Stop before Heaven is where the local authorities send all their Jane and John Does, and the county pays for burial. In other words, the indigent. Supposedly. Which does not compute to me because of that Springfield casket that goes for 25K. LSBH is one in a chain of close to three hundred throughout the country. The coroner himself told me that. He also said this was so far out in the country that most people opt to use funeral homes in town closer to where they live. The indigent get buried in pine boxes or cremated. There were all those . . . jars lined up in that one room, so I guess what he said is true, as he should know. He is the coroner, after all."

"What's going to happen to Agnes and the other four?" Maggie fretted.

"They're calling the Dylan Funeral Home in Alexandria to come for the deceased. There's a ton of paperwork someone is going to have to go through to . . . you know, notify next of kin if there are any and to find a new home for all those jars. This is not sitting well with me, guys," Espinosa said. "In point of fact, it's making me sick to my stomach."

"You need to get over yourself, Joe. We're reporters; we're supposed to be able to handle anything we report on," Ted said, but there was no conviction in his voice.

"We're here!" Dennis shouted, as the gates to the alley behind the BOLO Building opened up. The moment the iron gates clanged shut, he let loose with a loud roar. "*Safe*!!"

Everyone started talking at once. "Why are we here? I Thought we were going to the farm! No one is here! The lot is empty!"

Dennis looked around, befuddled. "You told the officers we were coming here, and this is where we could be reached. None of you said anything on the drive here," he said as they were exiting the van.

"Easy, kid! We're all in a daze here in case you haven't noticed. Let's just get back in the van and head out to the farm. It's not your fault. I'll drive this time," Ted said.

Dennis was the last to climb aboard. He felt foolish until Maggie wrapped her arms around his shoulders. "If it's any consolation, Dennis, I didn't even know we'd arrived until you yelled, 'Safe'! We're all having a bad day here, so don't take it personally."

Espinosa clapped him on the back to show that he agreed.

Dennis felt better immediately, so he leaned back and closed his eyes, pretending sleep, while his mind raced around thinking about what the four of them had just been through.

Forty-five minutes later, Ted steered the van through the gates of Pinewood. The sound of all the dogs barking was like music to his ears. The kitchen door opened as Jack, Harry, and Abner stepped out onto the small porch, the dogs clustered at their legs.

"Hurry, get in here before you drown," Charles called out. "Fergus just washed and dried all the towels from earlier."

"You are not going to believe—"

"Save it, dear, for when we can all pay attention down below," Charles said as he handed out towels. Only Jack noticed Cyrus slinking off to his spot under the table. The big shepherd hated folding towels.

"You guys look . . . oh, I don't know, like you just saw a ghost, green around the gills, if you like that cliché," Abner said flippantly. "Coffee is fresh. Sandwiches are wrapped in the fridge."

"Food! Food! Is that what you said? Don't ever say that word out loud in front of me ever again. Do you hear me? I'll probably never ever eat again for the rest of my life," Maggie wailed dramatically.

"We aren't hungry," Dennis said.

"No, we aren't hungry," Ted and Espinosa said in unison.

"Everyone dry?" Not bothering to wait for a response from the foursome, Charles headed for the secret staircase to the war room, where they could get to work.

Cyrus was first in the parade, Lady staying behind with her pups to do her job, which was to guard the premises and make sure no one approached the door that she guarded by lying down on the mat in front of it. Her pups took up their positions and went to sleep.

Outside, the rain continued to pour down like a tsunami.

Down below in the old dungeons that now housed the war room of Pinewood, the gang saluted Lady Justice before they took their seats at the huge round table, where they immediately started to babble and talk over one another for a good fifteen minutes. Somehow, it all made sense to the gang when they finally wound down, and Jack said, "So this is where we are right now. I think this is also the moment when Charles will give us his favorite Leo Tolstoy quote: 'The two most powerful warriors are patience and time.'"

"Thank you for that, Jack," Charles said tongue in cheek. "It truly does apply here. There is no immediate rush on anything at the moment. The children are safe. I think we can all agree that is paramount. Their mother is on the way. So we have time on that. Patience is something none of us have, and that's okay to a point. We now need to focus on the Karas brothers. Abner has more to say on that subject, which he will share with the rest of us shortly.

"Maggie's report on the Last Stop before Heaven establishment right now is what we need to discuss." Like Myra and Annie, Charles never referred to the photo journalist by his last name and always called him Joseph. "Joseph is going to show us all the pictures he took on the big screen. We all need to look at them carefully; then we'll discuss everyone's opinion. Next up will be Abner, who has been in constant contact with his . . . ah . . . colleague, Philonias Needlemeyer. From there, we will go wherever we need to go. You have the floor, Joseph."

"I'll put the pictures up, and Ted can narrate."

"I haven't been in all that many funeral homes, but this one appears to be the same as the ones I've seen. By that I mean the areas that the public see. Lots of velvet draping behind where the caskets are set up for viewing. They, the caskets, sit on gurneys. With wheels that lock. The lids, covers, the tops, whatever they're called, are in two pieces. Only half is open to view . . . uh . . . the upper extremities.

"The place smelled. Like incense and dead flowers, and there were plenty of those around. If I had to take a guess, I don't think the owners have been gone long, a few days at the most. Dennis said this license Joe is showing you now is bogus because there is no raised seal, so who knows if Eli and Ethel Oberman are the true owners or not. Or if the persons who were running the funeral home were really named Eli and Ethel Oberman.

"There are ramps everywhere and no steps. I don't know if that's a handicap law or not. The few funeral homes I've been in had no ramps. I don't know if that's important or not. If it weren't for the ramp, Agnes Twitt wouldn't be where she is by the front door in the picture you're now seeing," Ted said, as a picture of the deceased appeared on the screen. "What happened was, we couldn't get to the handles quick enough and the casket got away from us and she . . . well, what she did was kind of . . . bounce in the air and fall back and that's why she . . . she looks like what you're seeing."

A new picture appeared on the screen, the room where all the caskets were lined up. "This is where we think the kids were kept. Or at least they slept in . . . in them. The covers or whatever you call them were mussed up. Carrie was right when she said they slept in boxes. To a kid, a casket would seem like a box."

More pictures appeared. "File room. We didn't touch those at all. We did look inside each cabinet. All of them were full. Either a lot of dead people went through there, or those were the files for the kids who passed through. No way to know. We were just getting into it when the doorbell rang, and all those men appeared with their story of their grandfather dying. That's when Agnes Twitt rolled down the ramp and slammed into the door. Trust me when I tell you there was no dead grandfather. The guys looked like thugs who had come there to do some serious work, like cleaning out the place. And we didn't get a chance to explore the back, where they . . . where the crematorium is."

"Ted, you forgot the room with the jars," Dennis said.

"No, I didn't forget. Joe didn't put it up on the screen. Let's see it!" Ted said.

Espinosa scrolled through his camera till he found what he was looking for, and in seconds, the room appeared on the big screen. What looked to be well over a thousand jars, some large, some small, in different colors with labeled names on the tops that were sealed shut made everyone in the room blink.

"I'm not sure about this, but I think I read somewhere that you have to pay to have a funeral home store . . . display, don't know the correct term for a person's remains. Most people take their loved one's ashes home with them. I have a friend I went to school with who keeps his parents' ashes on the top shelf of his bedroom. I don't think I could do that," Ted said in a strangled-sounding voice.

"So, that's it?" Charles asked.

"Pretty much. I took some pictures of the empty parking lot, the landscaping, the front of the building, the sign, but that's it, yes," Espinosa responded.

"Anyone have any questions?" Charles asked. There were no questions. "Then I guess it's up to Abner to tell us what he has if anything. You have the floor, Abner."

"Look, I'm not a miracle worker here. I can only go by what's out there to find. First, and to me the most important, is the BOLO out on Allison Bannon. Every law-enforcement agency in this crazy alphabet city is on the hunt for her. I assume you haven't heard anything more, Harry?"

"She said she would call. That lady knows what she's doing. Somehow or other, she will find a way to get here because she knows we have her kids, and that's the only thing on her mind right now. We just have to wait for her to call."

"I'm on top of the different agencies, and so are my . . . colleagues. I'll hear the minute there is a sighting of any kind, real or not. Trust me on that. I'm also working on the husband angle. It would appear, and Phil agrees, that he is a traitor and on someone else's payroll besides the CIA's. For Allison to run like that without her husband pretty much buttons that up where I'm concerned.

"I was on the Net with Phil most of the night. I'm going to call him in a bit and put him on speaker, so you can all hear what he has to say. He said there is no history, no legend created for the Karas brothers. It's just not there. What he was able to pick up was the day the brothers made their entrance into the world in Paris, France at the age of twenty-two. He said it was as if they had been born that very day. Now, he did hack into the passport records. This you might find interesting. The brothers are forty-eight, according to their passports and international driving licenses. So, twenty-six years ago, they stayed in France for close to six years. They lived high in a villa with a houseful of servants. They rarely ventured out, and when they did, it was with a retinue of many. Then, when the six years were up, they stormed the international scene. They were handsome, charming, charismatic, spoke many languages, and had money to burn. They did not entangle themselves with women. Occasionally, they were seen and photographed with beautiful women, but there were no relationships anyone talked about. This is when they started to travel extensively, never staying in one place more than a few days at a time.

"Phil backtracked the slave-trafficking stats, and that's when it all started to heat up. Every agency under the sun was on it, but no one has been able to trace the source. But, with the aid of all our colleagues, Phil and I have come to the conclusion that wherever they traveled, either before, during, or after, a group of children went missing in the vicinity. That they are responsible is just a theory, nothing more. But I strongly agree with it. Back then, the agencies went public, asking for the citizens' help. When that didn't work, they shut down and kept it all close to the vest."

Jack leaned forward. "I do not understand how so many children could have gone missing without the world's going crazy. Where are the parents? I'd leave no stone unturned if I had a kid and he or she got snatched. I'd be screaming my head off to the authorities, and now, with social media, I just don't see why there is not more of an uproar.

Someone needs to explain that to me. The only thing I ever see on TV is that guy John Walsh," Jack said, anger ringing in his voice.

"I think we all feel like that. Where do the Karas brothers, if it turns out they are responsible, get the children they're selling? Are they orphans, foster kids, kids off the street? Tell me where?" Ted asked in frustration.

"All of the above. The hue and cry in the Asian and European countries is not what it is here. A lot of the kids are the throwaways. The ones no one wants, which is sad to say. Then there is the Net, where all kinds of crap is posted that kids see and believe. Young women offered glamorous jobs overseas, a life of richness and fame. They fall for it. What we found out also are blond young women are at the top of the list. Little blond girls go for so much money it's sinful.

"Phil read me a statistic that made me run for the bathroom. He said a ten-year-old blonde with good teeth, and he stressed good teeth, goes for several million dollars. The buyer or buyers, as in plural, use her till she's fourteen or fifteen, depending on her breast size, then put her out on the sex circuit. By that time, the years of drugs and decadence generally lead to death by age seventeen. The same thing for the older ones. The fresh ones are used up by twenty-three or -four. Then they go on the circuit, too. It's a filthy, rotten business."

"But how . . ." Dennis tried to speak.

"It's all done on the dark side of the Web, the underbelly. Dennis, you have no idea what goes on there. I can truthfully say I wish I didn't know," Abner said.

"But everything points to the Karas brothers, right?" Charles asked.

"Yes. Points to. No proof. Phil's wife and former hacker, PIP, which stands for Pretty in Pink, has a theory that Phil and I both more or less agree with. It's just a theory, understand that."

"Well, what is it?" Jack demanded.

"We think the Karas brothers were given their names by the masterminds behind all of the child trafficking when they plucked them out of nowhere. Then they took them to France, where, as I told you, they stayed for six years. PIP thinks they were schooled in every phase of life to turn them into what they are today, the charming international playboys with money to burn. She also thinks, and this is where we all three agree, that the brothers were hypnotized, or if you like the term *programmed* better, go with it, and they have no memory of their life before they were taken to France. I don't know too much about hypnotism or being programmed, but from what I've read, the process has to be reinforced from time to time or their real memories would come back. I know it sounds crazy and way out there, but still, it does make sense since we have nothing better to go by."

"That is so . . . preposterous!" Maggie stuttered as she grappled with what she'd just heard.

"No it isn't. It makes perfect sense," Jack said. "More sense than anything we can come up with. Think about it. They've been literally programmed. That has to be another reason why they travel with the entourage they do, so no one can get close to them. I guess what we're saying is that they oversee the operation, but their hands are clean. So we now also have to find the masterminds behind all of this, not just the Karas brothers."

"Correct. And for doing what they do, they get to lead the life they lead. And before you can ask, no, they do not have a conscience. That was wiped out. The answer to the other question you haven't asked yet is yes, they probably had as extensive plastic surgery as you can get these days, not back then, to fool all the facial-recognition programs. As I said, they were born the day they were picked up from wherever they lived. Somewhere in Europe would be my guess," Abner said.

"How do we fight this? What can we do? Where do we start?" Harry finally said.

No one had an answer.

"I guess we have to wait for Allison Bannon to get in touch. She and her team have been on this case for years. I hate saying it, but it looks like she's our only lead right now," Harry said.

"There is one other thing. Phil, PIP, and I all agree that the Karas brothers are on the move. As of this morning, they were registered at the Ritz-Carlton hotel in Buckhead in Atlanta. They rented three entire floors for three weeks. They had a full week to go on their reservation when they packed up and left. Several hours ago, to be precise. They did pay for the whole week for all three floors. We have Phil to thank for this information, wizard that he is. Like I said, they're on the move. Phil is waiting for some satellite to go overhead to pick them up. Seems he has a contact at NASA that . . . ah . . . helps him out from time to time."

"Oh jeez, are you saying you guys are messing with the . . . oh jeez," Dennis twitted. "That's really, like, you know, breaking some serious laws. NASA?"

Harry turned and, with one look at the young reporter, reduced him to pure misery. "No one is forcing you to do anything you don't want to do, kid. You can leave now if you want to, no hard feelings. Where is all this coming from all of a sudden?"

Dennis squared his shoulders and eyeballed Harry. "I panicked for a moment, okay? My bad. It won't happen again. If we need the satellite, then we need it. I'm good, Harry."

Harry clapped Dennis on the shoulder and grinned. Harry never grinned. Dennis lit up like a Christmas tree.

"Listen, people, I need to say something," Maggie said. "I'm going to backpedal here on a suggestion I made about arranging a contest for the kids or whatever we were going to call it in the hopes that would bring the Karas brothers to us since we can't seem to get to them. It's too risky. Especially for the children."

"Psychologist Leo Buscaglia said the person who risks nothing does nothing," Charles announced in a tone of voice that reminded many of Sundays spent in church.

"Yeah, well, tell Leo I'm not buying into that little ditty," Maggie said, her voice sounding sour. "I found, I think, a better way. And . . . I even sent Annie a text, and she okayed it. So there!"

"Well, in that case . . ." Charles started to say, until Maggie held up her hand for silence on his part.

"We—I guess that comes down to me—I am going to write an open invitation for the morning issue of the *Post* tomorrow. Location to be determined. Which means I have to get on it ASAP. A black tie dinner event to raise money for missing and exploited children. Annie promised ten million dollars to kick it off. And she promised to match, dollar for dollar, what we raise. Here is my plan. I am going to publish a list of every famous person I can come up with, right down to the president and vice president. I'm going to say the list of people is the tentative invitation list. Not that we're actually going to send out the invitations. But, as Annie pointed out, if it looks like it will fly, then we should actually do it. Movie stars, politicians, socialites. Everyone will be buzzing and talking and asking if they got their invitation, and, of course, the answer will be no, which will generate all kinds of interest. We'll use social media every way we can. Abner can take care of that. Of course, the Karas brothers will be on the list. How could they pass up something like that? Countess Anna de Silva, who I am sure has a net worth much much greater than they do. We always worry at the paper about being sued. Annie said if we do it this way, there is no problem. I suspect she knows what she's talking about and is right. I'm also sure she has her lawyers on it as we speak. She'll let me know if I'm going off the rails. So, until something else happens here, can you all help me come up with the list of the most important people in the country? Or the world. Start on your lists, people. Remember now, we're just saying they might be on the list to be invited. There's a big difference between being on a possible list and actually being invited."

"Pure genius," Jack said, reaching for a yellow pad. "I assume we want a mix of old and new for all ages."

"Hmmmm, yes," Maggie said as she started tapping out the article she planned to write for the morning edition.

"Above the fold?" Ted queried.

"Absolutely! Since Annie owns the paper, where else would you expect to see something about her throwing a party for charity?"

Dennis jumped up and down, waving his arms. "I have a great headline if you don't already have one."

"I don't, not yet. Share."

"ARE YOU ON THE LIST?"

Maggie's eyes popped wide. "Damn, Dennis, you're good! We'll run with that. Thanks. Now get to work on the 'supposed' list."

Ted started to laugh and couldn't stop.

"What's so funny?" Harry demanded.

"By noon tomorrow, the paper's phone system will have crashed. I guess it isn't all that funny. For some reason, I suddenly got this mental picture of everyone in Washington dialing into the *Post* to ask if they're on the list. You know, all those people who love to be seen and love to get mentioned on Page Six."

"Do you want me to run with the same banner on the Net?" Abner asked.

"Yep," Maggie retorted. "Everywhere you can think of. Make sure you post some pictures of Annie in full regalia, wearing her tiara. How long is that going to take? Are you planning on doing it as a tease or a full-out statement?"

"Both," Abner responded, his fingers flying over the keys. "What's your feeling on my getting in touch with Phil and my . . . colleagues for some added help? I was also thinking of having Phil go to the dark side and start a campaign. If he does that, it will be a wildfire."

Before Maggie could respond, Jack said, "Just do it!"

"Well then, okayyyyyy!" Abner said, getting into the spirit of things. "Oh, by the way, do you want us to crash the Internet with the news?"

The war room went totally silent as everyone stopped what they were doing to stare at Abner.

"Can you do *that*?" Dennis asked, his eyes almost bugging out of his head.

Abner stared at the young reporter. "Seriously, Dennis, did you just say what I think you said?" At the look of chagrin on Dennis's face, Abner laughed. "So, should I take that as a yes or a no?"

"Do it!" Jack barked again. "That should make the Karas brothers or their people sit up and take notice. Do it in . . . what? Two hours from now. Does that work for everyone? Or should we wait until the *Post* comes out in the morning? I opt for morning if my vote counts."

Everyone agreed that it worked for them.

"How long do you want it to stay down?" Abner grinned.

"Long enough so that it's all people are talking about. I

say talking because that's the only way people will have to communicate. How about six hours?" Jack asked.

"Your wish is my command. Phil is going to go over the moon. So will my fellow colleagues. We talk all the time about doing it just to see what would happen. Guess we'll finally get an answer."

Charles cleared his throat. "There is a risk according to—"

"Please, Charles, forget Leo Buscaglia and his ditties. We're doing it. Period," Fergus said, opting to contribute for the first time.

Dennis was about to make a comment about all of them going to some federal pen and they wouldn't have to worry about communicating with anyone but thought better of it when he caught Harry looking at him. He offered up a sickly smile and went back to his list to add Taylor Swift and Beyoncé, whom he loved and adored.

"Showtime!" Abner said, raising his hands and flexing his fingers.

Dennis felt his insides gather into a tight knot. He knew he wouldn't do well in prison. Then his spine stiffened, and he squared his shoulders. He really needed to stop being such a *wuss*. He really did.

Chapter Ten

Allison Bannon rolled over in the comfortable bed, instantly awake and knowing exactly where she was. She even knew the time by some quirk of fate. She always knew the time, Give or take a few minutes, no matter where she was or what she was doing.

What she also knew was she didn't have to get out of bed this exact second. In fact, she could roll over and go back to sleep if she wanted to. But she wouldn't do that. She had things to do, plans to make. Now that she knew her children were in safe hands, there was no reason to rush to find them. With every law-enforcement agency hot on her trail, she needed to be extra careful. Extra, *extra* careful.

Still, she stretched luxuriously, enjoying the feel of the soft sheets, the light blanket, and the down pillows. Luxury. At least it was luxury to her. She thought about the hard, lumpy mattress she had slept on just days ago before she cut and ran. She let her mind roam to all the foul, ugly places she'd slept in over the years, her husband, whom she had once loved, at her side. Not anymore.

She was alone now. She couldn't remember the last time she'd worked alone. There had always been Steven and the team. The team. The team who had her back the way she had their back. Like brothers and sisters. They had all knowingly and willingly trusted their very lives to one another. And it worked. It worked because she had hand-picked and trained her team. Steven just happened to be her first partner and her husband.

If she'd made any mistakes along the way, Steven was the mistake. But if she admitted to that, she wouldn't have her children, the children she loved more than life itself.

Now the only one she could count on was herself. She had no backup. Well, that wasn't entirely true, she told herself. She had Harry Wong and his friends. And she had Lizzie Fox.

Right now, though, she needed to think about what Steven was telling their section chief and handler, Luka, and the other nameless, faceless people they worked for. Steven was her husband, he knew her better than anyone. He would tell them everything he knew to make sure he came out smelling like the proverbial rose. More importantly, he would be trying to cut a deal that would benefit him. But Luka was no fool. He'd see through Steven in a second. That meant she had to transform herself into the opposite of what Luka and the others would expect.

She was Doris Brown now, with an excellent set of forged identity papers. She even had a car registered to Doris Brown, and all her creds were backdated. She felt reasonably secure in that regard thanks to Lizzie Fox.

Allison swung her legs over the side of the bed and sat there for a few moments, wondering if she should make the bed or not. Would she ever come back here, or was this her port in the storm that she'd never see again? She decided to make the bed.

In the bathroom, which was pretty and charming, she stared at herself in the mirror. She was no beauty. Once, maybe. The years had taken a toll on her. No time for facials, fancy creams, plucked eyebrows. Her hair was a disaster, mostly cut and trimmed by herself. Now it was long, in a ponytail. She'd correct all that momentarily with a new haircut and some hair dye. She'd go pixie short, and Doris Brown would become a strawberry blonde just like the picture on her passport and driver's license.

Under the sink was a full makeup kit complete with latex she would apply to smooth out her face. She could widen her nostrils, square off her chin, redefine her eyebrows, and plump up her cheeks. She could add ten pounds to her 110-pound frame simply by adding some extra padding around her middle. Glasses with plain glass in them would complete Doris Brown's identity. Tea Pope, aka a dozen different aliases, would cease to exist.

Shower or not to shower? She'd taken three yesterday when she'd arrived. When she'd finally climbed into bed, she still felt dirty. Definitely take a shower. She soaped up and stood under the hot water until it ran cold.

Allison spent the next few minutes trying to decide whether she should work on her hair first or have some coffee. Good coffee, not the swill she was used to drinking on the run. Years of drinking sludge that passed for coffee was something she didn't want to think about anymore. There was so much she didn't want to think about but knew she had to. But not just yet. First, she needed to get rid of the squirrelly stuff whirling around in her head. That meant the agency, her husband, and her team.

Steven first. Steven was on her shoulders, no one else. Not her team, although now when she thought back to the last three encounters, when they all thought they had the Karas brothers' people cornered, it had all culminated in a dead end. Zack Henry had almost come to blows with Steven the second time it happened, but she'd broken it up because she hadn't wanted to hear one of her team members saying her husband had sold them out. Even though, to be honest about it, she had thought the same thing herself, she refused to consciously believe that her husband would sell out the team.

Allison stared off into space. It was the first time she noticed the wallpaper in the kitchen. Big yellow sunflowers. So pretty. If Steven sold them out, he had to have inside information. The question was, how and where did he get that information? How did he make contact? He was never out of her sight or away from her side. Did he do it for money or did he do it to plow her under? Probably both. She wished she could turn the clock back and not have intervened when Zack and Steven almost came to blows. He was her husband. That was the bottom line. She'd been a stupid fool. That was on her, too.

As she sipped her coffee, she realized that she needed to be completely honest with herself now. The marriage was over after Andy was born. She knew that the minute Steven stared down at his infant son. She'd seen nothing in his eyes or his expression. He hadn't wanted to hold the infant, either. Five years of staying married after his birth. For what? And while the marriage was sexless, neither one had made a move to dissolve it. Why? Because the team would get split up. That was her side of it. Steven's side, if he had a side, was . . . she had to admit she didn't know what his motivation was.

What she did know was Steven hated being her second in command. He wanted his own team, but Luka had told her in private that that would never happen because Steven was a hothead and resented authority. And now Steven was spilling his guts to Luka. Half would be lies, she knew that. Hopefully, Luka would call in the rest of the team and listen to what they had to say. Luka was no fool. Simon Spinelli, aka Steven Bannon, was a traitor. That was the bottom line. Her husband, her children's father, was a traitor. How was she ever going to live with that? How?

Allison got up to refill her coffee cup. She loved that whoever it was who cleaned the cottage had provided real cream and real sugar for her coffee. She knew she'd drink the entire pot and probably make another one before she took on the day.

Allison stared at the laptop in the middle of the table, where she'd left it last night, then over at the small television on the kitchen counter. The laptop was new. She'd trashed the old one on her way here, tossing it into a Dumpster at a Burger King but not before she'd dismantled it and crushed the guts to shreds. No point in giving the hunters an edge. She'd programmed the new one last night, along with her latest stash of burner phones, paying cash at a Target store. The Doris Brown ATM card had worked perfectly. She had a bundle of money now. She was good to go electronically.

The laptop could wait. Allison decided she'd delayed the inevitable long enough and needed to know what was going on newswise before she left here. She turned on the small TV and gasped as she saw a picture of herself that was less than flattering. She blinked, then blinked again as she struggled with what she was hearing. She bit down on her lower lip so she wouldn't cry. She was none of those things the news anchor was saying. And then, thankfully, her picture was gone, and Luka appeared, all solemn and stiff and begging her to call him, to give herself up. Like that was really going to happen. She waited another minute to see if there would be any mention of Steven or her team. There wasn't. She pressed the MUTE button on the remote and settled back in her chair, the chilling words of a nationwide manhunt ricocheting around and around inside her head.

Allison wondered if Lizzie Fox and Harry Wong would rescind their offer of help once they heard the news. She eyed the pile of burner phones. Should she call or not? No. Better to stick with her original plan. She continued to stare at the silent TV, reading the commentator's lips. And then a regal picture of an older woman dressed by some fabulous person and wearing a tiara appeared on the screen with a caption running underneath. Allison turned up the sound as she read. *War!* Countess Anna de Silva, one of the richest women in the entire world, was declaring war on the people who kidnapped and exploited children by throwing a black tie event that she would kick off with $10 million.

"Well, well, well, how do you like them apples?" Allison muttered under her breath. Her gut told her this was no ordinary, run-of-the-mill party. No, no, this was part of . . . of . . . *something*. Something that had to do with her, Allison Bannon. And with Lizzie and Harry Wong. Lizzie had alluded to the people Harry was hanging with these days. The good thing here was, her gut was *never* wrong. Never.

Suddenly, Allison felt like a lightning bolt had ripped through her entire body. She could donate, anonymously all that money she'd found in the woods years ago. Instead of giving it over to some governmental agency, she could donate it. She took a second to wonder if the countess would really match it dollar for dollar.

Allison got up, disconnected the coffeemaker, then rinsed her cup. Time to get this show on the road. She headed for the bathroom, where she went to work on her hair. Slice, chop, shear, chop some more. Done. The last time her hair had been this length was when she was one year old. She hardly recognized herself. She gathered up all the hair and flushed it three times. She cleaned up the rest of the long strands with wet tissue and flushed them. She mixed the hair dye, and within minutes, her head was covered in a thick cream. She sat down on the edge of the tub and let her thoughts go to her children and how wonderful it was going to be to see them. She hoped her new appearance wouldn't scare them.

When the thirty minutes required for the dye to set were up, instead of rinsing off the color in the sink, she hopped in the shower again. Mrs. Clean herself. She giggled. As she washed the dye out of her hair, she thought about the money she was going to donate. All clean-laundered money. She almost burst out laughing as she imagined the look on the Karas brothers' faces when they heard how much money the countess raised to fight for the kids. Bastards. "If it's the last thing I do, and if I die doing it, I'm going to find you and kill you with my bare hands," she muttered before she stepped out of the shower. "Bastards!"

Allison worked industriously for the next ninety minutes on changing her appearance. When she was finished, she stared at her reflection in the mirror. She leaned closer to see if there were any imperfections. She couldn't see any.

"Who are you?" she whispered.

"Wife. Not anymore."

"Mother. Always and forever."

"Superagent? The best of the best."

"And what else are you?"

"I'm an *assassin* doing my government's bidding." Tears burned her eyes at the out-loud declaration.

"*Was* an assassin is the operative word from here on in," she told her reflection in the mirror.

Enough of that kind of thinking. Time to get a move on.

Allison pulled on a knee-length summery flowered dress with three-quarter sleeves. She stopped just short of looking dowdy. The padded corselet around her stomach gave her small frame a pear shape that made her look ten pounds heavier. The padded bra pushed her breasts up and out. She eyed herself in the wide mirror from all angles to make sure she hadn't missed anything.

"Well, helloooooo there, Doris Brown," she said, giggling.

Shoes. The dress called for sandals but this new Doris Brown opted for a pair of white Keds in case she had to run. No way could she outrun someone pursuing her if she was wearing leather sandals.

Every year at the fitness trials at the farm, she'd always come in first, outrunning the star athletes. Like Luka said, she was the best of the best.

Allison looked down at the bottle of cherry-red nail polish in the nail kit sitting on the vanity. The last time she'd worn nail polish, she had been fourteen years old. She went to work filing and buffing her nails, then polishing them. She whipped her hands through the air to dry the polish and applied a clear coat to protect the polish. She was slowly getting the hang of all this. Oh so slowly. She kept waving her hands in the air until she was satisfied her nails were dry. She wondered what it would be like to actually get a manicure and a pedicure, to be pampered. Maybe someday she'd find out.

She looked down at her Doris Brown watch, big face, bright red wristband that matched the dress she was wearing. She'd spent two hours decorating herself. Time for a last cup of coffee. And then she'd leave. She wondered if there would be anything new on the news after the two hours she'd spent in the bathroom.

Allison plugged in the coffeemaker again, then started to make herself some coffee. She turned up the volume on the local TV channel to hear a frenzied anchor screeching that the Internet had crashed. "*Crashed!!*" he thundered to his unseen audience. Allison whipped around to pick up her laptop, turned it on, started her browser, and tried some Web sites. Nothing. Dead as yesterday's newspaper.

Allison laughed. She had always been good at puzzles, analyzing things. It took her only a few seconds to put together in her mind the news she'd heard earlier about the war that was on for missing and exploited children with some beautiful wealthy countess. And now this! She was still laughing as she poured coffee while listening to all the talking heads screaming over one another on the TV set.

Allison sat down, coffee cup in hand as she stared at the frantic people on the TV set. They were acting like it were the end of the world. One of the commentators on the screen was saying, "Good Lord, people will have to actually talk to one another. Service providers cannot explain what's going on; nor can they say when and if they can get the Internet back up and running. Furthermore, for some reason, the major cell-phone towers are also having trouble."

Allison eyed the pile of burner phones on the table that were probably inoperable for now. *God does work in mysterious ways*, she thought. She'd be off the tube; no one would be able to get in touch with anyone else. She needed to move now and head to Washington in the hopes of hooking up with Harry Wong. If she couldn't make verbal or text contact, she knew where his dojo was. She'd simply go there and hope for the best.

Allison finished her coffee, disconnected the coffeemaker for the second time that morning, rinsed her cup, and put the cup back into the cabinet.

Doris Brown was not the type of woman who would travel with a backpack, so she packed the laptop and the burner phones in a wide plastic produce carryall she found under the sink. In the bedroom, she found a duffel bag she filled with two other flowery dresses, a pair of jeans, three T-shirts, and several sets of underwear.

Allison made sure the back door was locked, and nothing was out of place. She was satisfied that the whole house looked like no one had been there recently.

Ten minutes later, Doris Brown programmed the GPS and was on the road and headed for Washington, D.C.

Allison turned on the radio and listened to the world going crazy. Yes sir, God did work in mysterious ways. And the best part was only twenty minutes had gone by since the crash of the Internet. Hopefully, it would stay down till she reached her destination, giving her the anonymity she needed for now.

Everyone in the war room gasped when each and every computer and laptop stopped being able to access the World Wide Web. Lady Justice disappeared in the blink of an eye.

"Holy crap! You honest to God shut down the Internet!" Dennis said in awe.

Abner leaned back in his chair and propped his size 13s on the desk. "I had some help," he drawled. "But, yeah it's shut down. We should go topside to see what's going on. We won't have cable, but the local stations will be broadcasting. I'm not sure which cell-phone towers are down. I need to talk to Phil. No reception down here. And, there's nothing we can do down here anyway."

The mad scramble for the stairs irked Cyrus, who was always first. He let it be known in no uncertain terms, and everyone stopped in their tracks to allow the magnificent shepherd to do his thing, which was tantamount to taking a bullet for whoever was behind him. In theory. Cyrus barked and took his sweet time sauntering to the staircase. He knew when things were at emergency level, and this was not an emergency. When he reached the moss-covered steps, he bounded up them like a gazelle, the others right behind.

Charles immediately turned on the twenty-one-inch television sitting on the far counter. He reared back for a better look at what he was seeing, a frantic anchor and his colleagues trying to explain something to the viewing public that even he didn't understand himself.

"All we can do at this point is speculate. Our communication system crashed along with the Internet. I think it's safe to say people were calling in wanting answers." He stepped back to show a row of agitated people, talking heads, who were waiting to voice the same information only in a different tone of voice.

Jack looked over at Abner, who was staring at the TV, a satisfied grin on his face.

"You do good work, bro!"

"C'mon, guys, and you too, Maggie. I'm good, but I'm not *that* good. The honors go to Phil and his star pupils. PIP played a part in this, too."

Dennis inched forward. "So, tell me, when it's time to kick it back up, what's involved?"

"Dennis! Dennis! Dennis! If I told you that, then I'd have to seriously compromise you. That means kill you. You still want to know?"

"Absolutely not. No sir, I do not want or need to know. I'm good, Abner. I mean I'm really good." Dennis tried to make himself invisible. All eyes went back to the idiotic talking heads repeating the same thing over and over.

"People, check your cell phones to see if they're working."

"Dead," Maggie said. Ted, Espinosa, and Dennis seconded Maggie.

Charles and Fergus shook their heads. "We're down, too," Fergus said.

"I have one bar," Jack said.

Harry stared down at his phone, a look of surprise on his face. "I have four bars. For how long, I don't know."

"What about you, Abner?" Jack asked.

"I'm good. It's a good thing, too, because I have to be able to get in touch with Phil."

Jack mumbled under his breath about all things electronic and satellites and all the other stuff he would never understand in a million years, yet Abner knew it all and even understood it. As did his colleagues.

"Do you think you should check in with your pals?" Jack asked, addressing his question to Abner.

"Nah. I don't want to waste my bars. He'll get in touch if need be. Is it just me, or aren't you guys hungry? It's past lunchtime," Abner said, looking directly at Charles.

"How can you even think about food at a time like this?" Maggie barked.

"I can think about it because my stomach is letting me know it's time to fill it. You don't have to eat, but I do," Abner barked in return. Maggie clamped her lips shut and stared at the TV, wanting to put her fist through it.

"What's the game plan? Are we just going to sit here and look at one another, or maybe eat, then take a nap? What?" Ted demanded.

"We could read or talk to each other," Dennis said. With no response, Dennis went back to staring at the TV along with Maggie.

Fergus started to bang pots and pans as Charles scoured the refrigerator for a simple lunch. "Omelets!" he proclaimed. "And tapioca pudding!"

Lunch over, Jack proclaimed the Internet had been down one hour and twenty-five minutes. "And we don't know anything. The local news is just that, local. We know as much as they know. I think you should call your buddy to see what's going on, and don't tell me he won't know. If he can crash the Internet, then he knows what the hell is going on. Government is shut down. Not that people care about the government, but they do care about not being able to get on Facebook. Which I agree is a sad state of affairs. Well, Abner, are you going to do it?" Jack demanded.

Abner was about to respond when his cell phone pinged. He almost jumped out of his skin. "It's the CIA. I recognize the number. I bet it's my old boss. Should I answer it?"

"Of course," Charles said. "Information is power, remember that."

Abner said hello and waited to see who was on the other end of the phone. Ah, the man he had worked for whose real name he didn't know or want to know. The voice got right to the point. "I need you to come out here right now. The Internet went down. No one here has a clue as to what they should do. I was told to call you."

"I don't work for you anymore. I quit, remember? What makes you think I can fix whatever it is you want fixed?"

"Because . . . our mutual friend, the one who recommended you, said you were the best of the best."

"Then you should be calling him and not me. I can't help you; this is above my pay grade."

"I tried and couldn't reach him. Listen to me, Tookus. We're talking national security here. Your country needs you. I've been authorized to tell you they'll pay you whatever you want. Name your price."

"This isn't about money, sir. I'd do it for nothing if I could. I can't even begin to know how to fix something like this."

The voice grew desperate. "A million! Five! Ten! Get your ass out here right now before I send someone to fetch you. You won't like that."

Abner laughed. "You don't know where I am. And, you don't scare me. But let's suppose I do . . . ah . . . know someone who just might, I say *just might*, know how to get you up and running, what would you say? Same deal? Anything he or she wants?"

"Yes, yes, for God's sake. Whatever it takes."

"I'll check with the person and get back to you."

Abner looked at the gang, and said, "Well! That just kind of fell into our laps. What do you want me to do?"

"Call Phil. Then call that person back and tell him Phil has a price. You want all they have on the Karas brothers, every scrap of information. When we have it in hand, he'll get the Internet back for them, along with millions of other people."

"Oh, man, Jack, you drive a hard bargain. Okay, let me call Phil to see what he has to say."

Abner pressed the number three on his phone. Philonias Needlemeyer picked up immediately. "Get what you can out of him. Tell him if he holds anything back or isn't shooting straight, you will bring the wrath of God down on him."

"Dammit, Phil, you need to stop listening in on my conversations," Abner said with no real anger in his retort. "I'm not calling you back because you can listen in on your own."

"Ten four and out," Phil said playfully before he broke the connection.

Abner looked at the gang enjoying the expressions on their faces. "Okay, here we go," he said, entering the number that had just called him. It was picked up midway through the first ring.

"Well?"

"Well?" Abner said, parroting the man on the other end of the line. "I spoke to the only person in this whole entire world who can possibly help you. I say possibly. He wants to know what's in it for him. I told him what you offered me. Unfortunately, he is not interested in money; he has plenty of his own. He's willing to help, but for a price. A price you might not be willing to pay. No resets. One chance, and that's all you get, so you might want to gather your people from the top of the food chain who have the authority to grant a one-of-a-kind wish. I'll give you ten minutes, then I'll call you back. Are we clear here?"

"Is it guaranteed?"

"Of course it's guaranteed. The minute my colleague is

satisfied that you delivered on your end, you and everyone else in the world will be up and running within ten minutes, twenty minutes tops. Or maybe six hours. That's his timetable, and it's a take-it-or-leave-it offer. Screw this up, and your whole agency is in the toilet. Those are my ... ah ... source's words, not mine. I'm ending this call now." Abner leaned back in his chair and closed his eyes, a dreamy look on his face. "I hated that son of a bitch when I worked there."

"I think we all figured that out already," Harry said.

The minutes crawled by. When the ten minutes were up, Maggie raised her hand.

"Let's let him sweat another five minutes," Abner said.

Maggie thought the next five minutes were the slowest of her life. She literally screamed out loud when she said, "Time's up!"

Abner bolted upright and pressed in the digits that would connect him with the man he'd spoken to earlier. He didn't bother with the niceties. "What's it gonna be, boys?"

"There are two ladies here," came the inane response.

"And two ladies," Abner drawled. "I repeat, what's it gonna be?"

A voice that sounded old and reedy spoke. "We want a guarantee, young man."

"I gave it to you earlier. Ten minutes, twenty, six hours tops. Turn up your hearing aid, mister."

Another strange voice spoke. This one had authority resonating all over the room. "What is it your source wants in return?"

"Not much. The total file you all have on the Karas brothers. If there's even one page missing, one omission, down you go, never to return. Ah, your silence tells me this was the last thing you expected. I'm going to hang up, give you five minutes, and if you don't get back to me, I'm going to turn off my phone." Not bothering to wait for a reply, Abner ended the connection.

"And how are we supposed to take possession of the Karas file, Abner?" Jack asked.

"What! You expect me to do everything! Figure something out. I did my part."

Cyrus barked, then barked again to show he didn't appreciate Abner's tone, to which Abner made a barking sound in return, which meant cool your jets, dog.

The team looked at one another in a daze.

"I know! I know! We send Dennis, who will pretend to be a messenger. The *Post* uses a courier service in town. I know the manager, who will back up any story we give him to tell. He can be trusted. Dennis!"

Dennis was scared out of his wits. He didn't trust himself to speak, so he simply nodded.

"A piece of cake, kid. Really, a piece of cake," Ted said.

"Oh dear, we're three minutes past the five-minute deadline," Maggie said.

Abner reached for the phone. "You sure you want me to make this call, because I can tell you exactly what they're going to say. They have no file on anyone named Karas. So, what do you want me to do?"

"If that's how it turns out, simply hang up," Charles said. "If they are as desperate as we know they are, they'll call back. Make the call, young man."

Since Abner always, well almost always, followed instructions, he placed the call. A third, never-before-heard voice said, "This agency does not—"

"I don't want to hear your bullshit, General. I'm assuming you are a general who basks in his authority, but you have no authority over me or my source." He ended the call and once again leaned back in his chair.

"We should start a pool. How long do you think it will

take for them to call back?" Maggie asked. The entries
were from eight minutes to an hour.

They all stared down at Abner's phone, sitting on the
kitchen table, waiting for it to ring.

"Doncha get it, guys. This is all a game to them. Trust
me, they're scrambling. Right now, it's who blinks first. A
no-brainer. We should go in the dining room, where the
table is bigger, and play cards or something."

Maggie threw a dish towel at him and missed.

"What now?" Ted asked.

"We wait."

Chapter Eleven

Allison Bannon, now Doris Brown, settled herself behind the wheel of the SUV. She checked the rearview mirror and the side mirrors, which had all gone back to where the previous owner had set them when she shut off the engine. For some reason, the same thing had happened when she drove the SUV for the first time. She adjusted the steering wheel to match with her small frame, pushed the seat forward, then flexed her hands on the wheel. The nearly five hundred–mile trip she was certain would be made in relative comfort, with a few stops along the way for coffee and bathroom breaks. On the passenger seat was a map that she had to follow since the GPS wasn't working. Following a route on a map was no big deal, but a GPS was the way to go. Since that wasn't an option, she'd marked her route, estimating she would arrive in the District of Columbia after dark. A good thing. She had one stop to make once she drove out of the cozy little neighborhood—the nearest convenience store, where she could pick up a portable, battery-operated radio since the one that was installed in the SUV was stone-cold dead.

Allison wondered if once she left the area and hit the open highway any of the burner phones would come to life. Highly doubtful was her opinion. Maybe once she arrived in Washington, the cell towers might be up and working. Everything right now was a crapshoot. Everything.

With nothing to occupy her mind except the open road in front of her, Allison let her mind wander back three years to the day Luka had called her team into his sterile offices and stared them down. He'd started off with a compliment mostly directed at her, and said, "This mission I'm sending you on is so top secret that until this moment only one other person knew about it. And now you five will also know. That makes seven in total. The only other person beside myself is the director. If there are any mistakes, any screwups, they're on your heads."

Allison liked Luka. More than that, she respected him. He eyeballed her as he outlined why he'd called her team into his offices, which no one was ever invited into. All meetings were in bug-swept, soundproof, bulletproof rooms. Why this meeting was being held in this spartan office was a mystery to her. Knowing Luka, she realized that by the time they walked out the door, she'd have her answer. Then again, knowing Luka, maybe not.

Luka got right to the point the moment everyone was seated. "I am assuming that there is no one in this room who doesn't know or has never heard of the international playboys Ryland and Roland Karas? Am I correct?" Luka, a bear of a man weighing 250 with a beard almost down to his neck and a ponytail tied in back, nodded in pleasure when they all agreed that he was correct.

"Good! So you all know who I'm talking about. Take a look at the screen because this is what the brothers look like as of two days ago. Burn that image into your brains." He clicked a remote in his hand. "Now look at these pictures. These are their closest protectors. That would mean to you retired Seals, Deltas, Mossad . . . the best of the best recruited at a great cost to them. If you like the word *mercenary*, substitute it if you choose.

"The brothers are never alone. Never. It wouldn't be a lie to say they have an army within a few feet of them. Ordinary people you'd never take for who they really are. We have it on excellent intel that the Karas brothers are behind the child-trafficking ring that's escalated abductions to epic proportions during the past year. Every alphabet agency in Washington has tried to get the proof we need to reel them in. They are so well connected, there is no accountability. It's only been whispered about on the dark side of the Net. We literally cannot touch them. We have had three different people we promised the world to if they would tell us what they know from the dark side. They did help us, and now they're all dead. This is the part that really hurts. They were under our protection. We promised them a life, a good life, if they'd help us, and still the brothers or their people got to them, which doesn't say much for us or our agency or the FBI, NSA, and Homeland Security. We worked together on a joint mission, and we blew it. We goddamn blew it," he snarled.

"And after all that, you think . . . what . . . the five of us can do what you and the others couldn't do?" Allison asked incredulously.

"Yes, that's exactly what I think. Back then, when the idea of this joint task force was being discussed, I had serious doubts. Not only did I have them, but I voiced them. All to no avail. Too many people, too many agencies, too many chances for mistakes and leaks. That's what happened. Somewhere along the way, someone said the wrong thing, did the wrong thing by mistake, or else someone took a bribe and is now on some island surrounded by beautiful women and living the life of a king.

"I'm not *asking* you and your team to take this mission on. I'm *telling* you it's yours. See those boxes in the corner? Those are the files on the Karas brothers from the time they hit the international scene twenty-some years ago. Remember, they are the darlings of the jet set. They donate millions and millions to worthy causes. They champion everything that even smells like a good cause. No one wants that well to dry up. Even our own president thinks the sun rises and sets on the brothers. Did you know they've been to the White House for two dinners? It's been rumored that the Queen might knight them for all their philanthropic generosity. Are you all getting the picture here?"

"Where are they now?" Allison asked.

"An hour ago, they were taking a gondola ride in Venice. We know that thanks to our satellites. I'm going to leave you and your team here in my office to read up on the brothers. I'll send in some lunch and coffee in a bit. By the close of business today, I want to hear a plan from all of you. Whatever you want or need, it's yours. Allison is your team leader. You do what she says when she says it. Her orders are absolute, and she answers only to me. Now, get to work!"

Allison was shaken from her thoughts when she saw a roadblock a half mile up the road. Her stomach crunched into a knot. She slowed down, glad she'd shoved her bag of burner phones under the car seat. The little portable radio on top of the map, along with the small purse she figured someone like Doris Brown would carry, were spread out on the passenger seat. Nothing wrong with that or out of the ordinary. Nothing to arouse suspicion.

Allison popped a piece of gum in her mouth and started to chew. She didn't know why, but she thought Doris Brown would be a gum chewer. She crept along, her stomach churning as she listened to the person on the radio spout the same thing he'd been saying for the past hour. Nothing new.

And then it was her turn. She lowered the window and waited.

"Ma'am, can we see some identification?"

"Sure. Can I ask why? Did something happen? As you can see, I'm traveling alone. I wish I had a dog," she said wistfully. She handed over her credentials.

"Why are you going to Washington, D.C., ma'am?"

"Two reasons really. One, I've never been there, and I've always wanted to see the cherry blossoms, and the other reason is I'm thinking of moving to Virginia to take a job in a library there. I have an interview tomorrow. Is there a convict on the loose or something?" she asked in a jittery voice.

The officer handed back her credentials and waved her on without responding to her question, which was more than okay with Allison. She moved the SUV slowly, watching out of the corner of her eye to see if anyone was paying attention to her. No one was. She swept past the police cruisers and accelerated. "Good job, Doris Brown," she muttered under her breath. "Let's just hope the rest of the trip goes as smoothly."

The SUV ate up mile after mile as Allison cruised down the road. Two hours passed before she saw a huge sign that said gas, lodging, and food were five miles ahead. Maybe she could gather some information in the restaurant. Travelers did love to talk.

Allison gassed up and paid in cash at the lodge, then went inside and sat down at the counter next to an elderly couple who said they were headed to Florida after a stop in Virginia to see their grandson. They were pleasant and talkative, bemoaning the loss of Facebook. "That's how we stay in touch with our kids and grandkids. We're on it every day," the woman, who said her name was Esther, said. "This is Stan, my husband."

"Doris Brown," Allison said by way of introduction. "So is there anything new? Does anyone know what happened?" Allison asked as she scanned the menu in front of her.

Stan looked across at her, and said, "Everything just

stopped working. Even our cell phones. Every so often, one bar shows up, and by the time you hit the number you want to call, it's dead again. It's the Russians, sure as hell," he said, authority ringing in his voice.

Allison ordered two eggs over easy, extra-crisp bacon, and home fries. No matter the time of day, she could eat breakfast and preferred it to any other meal of the day. The coffee was good, strong, just the way she liked it. She'd get two more to go when she left.

"And did you hear about what's going on in Washington, D.C., with that countess going to war?" Stan asked.

Not wanting to listen to a recap of the morning headlines, Allison nodded. "It's a good thing. Child trafficking is a terrible thing. I hope it works."

Stan got up, offered his arm to Esther to let her hop off her stool, and they headed to the cashier to pay their bill. Allison welcomed the silence. Now she could listen to what the local commentator was saying, which, as per usual, was nothing new. Still, she listened as her food arrived, and she started to eat. Her ears perked up when she heard a truck driver speaking with the waitress. "Three roadblocks! Do you believe that? Puts me forty-five minutes behind schedule."

"Why?" the waitress asked as she poured coffee for the truck driver.

"Some agent from the CIA cut and ran with government secrets locked in her head, and they want her dead or alive," the truck driver said dramatically. "No offense to you, little lady, but that's what happens when you have a woman doing a man's job. Secret agents are supposed to be men like Jason Bourne or James Bond. I wonder if she's as smart as he is."

The waitress looked at the driver for a second, then filled his coffee cup so full it splashed out and over the counter to run down his leg. He yelped and cursed. The waitress winked at Allison as the man made a hasty exit for the men's room.

"He deserved it." Allison giggled.

"I hope they don't catch her. I bet some man did something to her, and she's going to get the blame for it because she's a woman, and that's why she's on the run, to exonerate herself. Maybe when those vigilante women hear about her case, they'll help her out. Now, wouldn't that be something?"

Allison's head bobbed up and down, as she agreed that it would indeed be something. "You know, that's exactly what I was thinking," Allison said as she crunched down on her stick of bacon. She did love bacon. Actually she loved food. Period.

"Anything else, hon, before I ring you up?"

"Two coffees to go and a slice of that cherry pie."

"You got it. Where you headed?"

"Virginia. For a job interview, with a stop in D.C. to see the cherry blossoms, if there are any left."

"Well, drive safely." The waitress walked away to fill two Styrofoam cups for Allison's coffee. Allison watched as she wrapped the slice of pie carefully and then tucked a plastic fork in the bag. For no other reason than she liked the waitress, Allison left her a fifty-dollar bill as a tip. She grinned at the waitress, who was bug eyed; grabbed her food; and left.

Tooling down the road, she wondered if she'd made a mistake in leaving the fifty-dollar tip. The waitress would remember her now. She was probably right now chatting up her coworkers and showing off the fifty-dollar bill. A person going on a job interview would *not* leave that kind of tip. *Allison Bannon, I hope you didn't just make a mistake.* Well, if she had, it was too late to rectify it.

Three hundred and eighty miles to go.

* * *

Ted looked at Maggie, and said, "Do you think we should head back to the District? That guy on the TV who is losing his voice for saying the same thing over and over again just said people are calling in saying their phone systems crashed. The *Post* was on his last go-round."

"No. There's nothing we can do there. I want to be here to hear what the CIA says to Abner on the return call. That's where the real story is."

Abner looked down at his phone when it pinged. "Here we go!"

"Abner Tookus here," he drawled.

Abner's old boss, the man whose name he didn't know or want to know, said, "I'm asking you to be reasonable here, Mr. Tookus. I'm talking to you in the interests of national security. We can't trust just anybody willy-nilly. We're the CIA!"

"How funny is that? You trusted me when I worked for you. I have all your secrets stored in my head and ... other places. So, like I said before, cut the bullshit and let's get down to business. You give me that line of 'We don't know what you're talking about—we never heard of the Paris brothers,' and I'm hanging up, so don't play dumb here. And don't threaten me, either. When I walked out of your doors, I told you what I would do if you retaliated against me. I stress *I*. So what do you have for me? I have no clue what my source will do, so bear that in mind."

The second voice spoke. The director of the CIA, Tookus surmised. "We can't give you something we don't have, young man. And your source, whoever that may be, is barking up the wrong tree."

Abner looked at the gang and shrugged, his eyes asking the question he was ready to ask. The gang nodded.

"So then you guys are saying you didn't assign Allison Bannon and her team, which includes her husband, who just happens to be a traitor, to track down the Karas brothers. By the way, it is Karas with a *K*, not Paris as in France.

"And I guess you're also saying the Bannon children weren't kidnapped, either. Is that what you're telling me? You've been tracking the brothers for over three years with no luck. That means you must have an extensive file, and my source wants it.

"Just so we're clear on this, Mr. Director. The entire Internet is down across the country. Me coming out to Langley would serve no purpose. I can't fix your Internet. No one can. You have a roomful of brainiacs who probably told you the same thing, but for some reason, you don't believe your own people. You only have one option as far as I can tell. My source is waiting. I should tell you he has a short fuse and zero patience.

"Now if you guys were really serious about reeling in the Karas brothers, you would be falling all over yourselves to cooperate. But here is what I see your immediate problem is. You're only allowed to operate on foreign soil, and Allison Bannon is here in the good old U.S. of A., meaning you all are doing something illegal. I'm thinking I should be talking to the FBI instead of you lunkheads. I bet they'll be more than happy to help my . . . source."

"Now see here, Tookus—"

"Stuff it, Mr. Director. Give me a time and a place for the handover. You get back the Internet. Win-win. If you choose not to play ball—and you have sixty seconds to make up your mind—this line goes down, and I'm on the way to the FBI."

"All right, all right, you son of a bitch. Be warned, you're going on the list."

"To that countess's shindig! Man, I so want to go to that! Are you saying you can arrange it? Wow! Double wow!" Abner laughed. He stopped laughing and said, "Where?"

"How do we know your source will come through?"

"Because I said so. I have an idea. Bundle up all those files and have them delivered to the Starbucks on Constitution Avenue. One driver. That's it. Bring them in the back of a pickup truck with a tarp over them. A messenger who is totally innocent and knows nothing about what is going on will be waiting for you to transfer them to another vehicle. He drives away. Your people drive away. We'll be watching, so don't try any tricks. Do we have a deal?"

"We need time," the director said.

"You don't have time. You have ninety minutes. You'd better get cracking if you want to meet the deadline." Abner broke the connection and looked around. Dennis looked like he was going to explode.

"Come along, young man. I'm going to show you where the farm truck is. It has a few kinks you need to be aware of. Do not speed on your way. You do know where the Starbucks is, don't you?"

"Yes. I. Do."

"After the transfer, you head straight for the BOLO Building. Cyrus is going to go with you if Jack okays it." Jack nodded. Cyrus was already at the door, his tail swishing so fast it felt like a breeze was whipping through the old kitchen.

When the kitchen door closed behind Charles and Dennis, Abner frowned. "I don't trust those guys at the CIA."

"What? You worked for them for three years!" Ted said.

"Yeah, and that's why I don't trust them. I know what they do, what they're capable of. They'll come through. It's what they'll do afterward that concerns me. But once the handover happens, we need to create a diversion of some kind so the kid can make a clean getaway."

"We just call in to the locals and say there is a sighting of Allison Bannon, their rogue agent, in the area of Starbucks. All hell will break loose, and the kid takes it on the lam, with us watching for tails," Jack said breezily.

"We need to leave right now," Charles said when he entered the kitchen. "Like right now. We need to get there ahead of young Dennis. That old truck won't go over forty-five miles an hour, so it's safe to say we'll beat him into town."

Five minutes later, a parade of cars roared through the open gates and out to the highway.

Chapter Twelve

Dennis parked the old farm truck in the Starbucks parking lot and turned off the engine. He opened the door and swung his legs out just as Cyrus let himself out and walked over to take up his position near Dennis. Dennis stroked the animal's head as he talked to the dog, who appeared to be listening intently. "I know this hunk of junk looks terrible, but it has a new engine. Charles told me the truck was willed to him by an old war buddy who emigrated to Minnesota when their cover was blown while serving under Her Majesty. Charles flew to Minnesota for the funeral and was presented with the truck by his colleague's children afterward. He treasures it. He also put in seat belts. It has new tires. It's just the shell that is an eyesore. One eyesore people will remember, like the dudes we're meeting up with. You following all this, Cyrus?" Dennis asked nervously.

Cyrus yipped to signal his answer in the affirmative.

"Charles doesn't think they'll follow us back to the farm. Why would they—all they have to do is run the license plate, which is still registered in Minnesota. Charles is really smart to have thought that far ahead back then. Every year, he has faithfully renewed it. Ah, I hear Harry and your master. You know the rule. You stay here and don't give up anything like running to greet Jack. Yeah, yeah, I know he talked to you before he left, but you're a *dog*, Cyrus!" Cyrus bared his teeth in a vicious snarl. "Stop trying to scare me. I got your *schtick* a long time ago. And you obey orders. Okay, there they go. Look sharp, Cyrus! I know you live to bite someone's ass, and it might happen, so stay alert." Cyrus quivered from head to toe in wild anticipation of the possibility signaled by the reporter's words actually happening.

Inside Starbucks, Jack looked out the window to see a black panel van pull up two parking spaces away from the farm pickup truck. "It's going to go down now. Ahhh, four guys. Back is opening up. Bankers boxes. We need to go outside now, so Dennis doesn't do anything stupid. Even with Cyrus there."

Harry was already halfway out the door before Jack stopped talking. They casually sauntered toward where Harry had parked his Ducati. As they strolled past Dennis, they could hear one of the buttoned-up suits say to Dennis, "Well, aren't you going to help?"

"You talking to me? If so, no. I just pick up and deliver. Says so in my contract."

One of the bankers boxes hit the bed of the truck, and the lid flew off. Dennis stretched his neck, and said, "Not nice. I'm not responsible for the contents if anything blows away. One way or another, you guys will pay for any loss or damage. Do that again, and this dog will chew your ass off. Nice and easy, boys." Dennis felt like a badass and hoped it showed.

Cyrus advanced to within striking distance and froze before he let loose with a bloodcurdling growl, then showed the pearly whites that Jack faithfully brushed twice a day. The four men paused as they stared at the dog, then at Dennis, who was staring at Jack as both men fought to control their laughter.

"Easy, Cyrus," Dennis crooned under his breath as the balance of the cartons were carefully slid into the truck bed. The sound of the tailgate slamming shut ten minutes later clued Dennis to the fact the transfer was complete.

"Okay, buddy, sign here that you got all sixteen boxes and the one labeled 'United States'!" one of the men shouted.

"What! What! You didn't hear me? I said I just pick up and deliver. You want me to sign something, bring it here, and I'll sign it; otherwise, I'm outta here. I'm on a deadline. I get paid by the trip, and any failure to meet the deadline comes out of my pay." Dennis swung his legs back inside the truck and turned on the engine, but he didn't close the rusty door.

The four men eyed one another uneasily as Cyrus moved to go around to the passenger side of the truck. "Get that mutt outta here!" one of the men shouted.

Cyrus stopped when he heard the word *mutt* and lunged at the man holding a slip of paper.

Dennis gasped as guns appeared out of nowhere in the hands of the other three men. Out of the corner of his eye, he saw Harry and Jack seem to fly through the air, their arms and legs going every which way. And then it went deathly quiet, with the only sound coming from the man whose buttocks Cyrus had in his jaw. The other three men looked to be sleeping peacefully on the ground. Dennis decided right then and there that he had just learned more curse words in one minute than he had his entire life.

"Good job, Cyrus!" Jack said. "You can let him go now. You had your fun, so it's back to work." Cyrus yipped happily as he hopped into the old farm truck and buckled up.

"You did good, kid," Harry said, slapping Dennis on the back. "Head for home. We'll stick around a while to make sure these guys get off okay. Keep an eye on the rearview mirror, but I don't think there will be anyone following you. They'll think they're ahead of the game with the license-plate number."

The only agent still standing, and Jack and Harry simply assumed they were agents, rubbed his buttocks and turned white when he saw blood puddling around his shoe. "You're under arrest!"

Jack and Harry laughed. Harry reached out, tweaked the agent under his ear, and watched as he joined his fellow agents on the concrete parking lot.

"Some people are just plain silly, don't you agree, Harry?" Jack bent down, picked up the slip of paper, and signed it Donald J. Trump. He guffawed as he tried to outrun Harry to the Ducati. Harry beat him by a nanosecond.

Ten minutes later, Harry whizzed by the rusty farm truck. Dennis tapped the horn, a froggy, wheezing sound. He waved. Cyrus slept peacefully on the passenger seat. He'd had enough action for one day.

As Dennis headed back to Pinewood, the Karas brothers were stalled in traffic on their way into the District of Columbia. Roland, the younger brother by two minutes, was irritated, and he let it show. "This is a mistake, Ryland. You should have said something, explained in more detail. Why didn't you?"

"We were told never to question our benefactor. I simply did as I was told. And then the Internet and the phones went down. Not that I would have called him back because I would never do that. Nor would you if you stop and think about it. It's easy to say something after the fact."

"And you're right. It's a mistake, Ry. You know it, and I know it. No matter what fiction says, you do not, I repeat, you do not return to the scene of the crime. What is he thinking?"

"I have no idea, and I do not want to know. He said

drive to Washington, do not fly. Check in at the Sofitel. All the arrangements have been made. That's it. So, that's what we're going to do if we ever get there."

Roland handed over the newspaper he'd read from cover to cover to his brother. "You should read the article on the front page, the one above the fold, then the article on the CIA agent who has gone rogue. Seriously, Ryland, read both articles."

With nothing else to do but twiddle his thumbs, Ryland scanned the printed matter on top of the fold. "Well, this explains why we're going to Washington. Our benefactor assumes we will be on the list, and he wants us available to attend this black tie event."

Roland made a rude sound deep in his throat that caused his brother to look at him in alarm. "What?"

"I don't think we're going to be on that list. The countess has hosted many a soiree to raise money here and abroad, and we have never been invited before this. What makes our benefactor think this time will be different? It's too close. . . . Something isn't right. Think, Ryland, for God's sake, think for once instead of blindly obeying our benefactor."

"You think we're being set up for . . . for . . ."

"Yes. Yes, that's exactly what I think. We made mistakes. That rogue agent is on the hunt for us. She wants her children. It's all tied in together. Don't you get it?"

"And you are visualizing a very nasty outcome to this visit, is that what you are saying? Or should I say predicting?"

"Exactly. I'm glad you are finally seeing it."

"Roland, what would you have us do? There's nothing for us outside of this car. Our benefactor owns us, body and soul. There's nothing we can do but follow his orders. Unless you have a death wish, which I do not share."

"Think about this, brother. Assume we get caught. Can you even begin to imagine what life will be like for us here in an American prison, considering the business we're in? I do so wish you would read more. You would not do well, nor would I, as prison bitches."

"It will never come to that, Roland. Our benefactor will take care of us."

"No, Ryland, he won't. He will only protect himself and those closest to him. He'll toss us to the wolves. Or he'll kill us first."

Ryland closed his eyes and thought about what his brother had just said. Roland was no fool, and he did read. Roland was worldlier, and he understood society much more than Ryland himself did. He should pay attention to what he was hearing. Even agreeing with him would do no good if he was right.

Roland stared at his brother until his eyes snapped open. "What would you have us do? Do you have a plan? What, brother?"

"Sadly, no. But if we work together, surely we can come up with something."

Ryland surprised his brother with his next question. "What has you the most worried, the countess's party list or the rogue agent?"

Roland didn't hesitate before replying. "Both, because I think they are tied together."

"The agent concerns me the most," Ryland confided.

"And it should because that's on you. You gave the order to snatch her kids. I said no, and you overruled me."

"As you pointed out, I made a mistake. We have to find a way to correct that mistake."

"You really need to start listening to me, Ry. It's too late. We *can't* correct it."

"I refuse to believe that," Ryland said, leaning back into the softness of the leather seat. He put in his earbuds and closed his eyes.

With nothing else to do while sitting in stalled traffic,

Roland reached for the paper and started to read it a second time, hoping he had missed something that would give him pleasure the second time around.

Harry Wong knew the moment he stepped into his dojo that someone was inside. He took a deep breath, held it, and let it out slowly. He did it again and again until he had his heart rate where he wanted it.

He walked about, turning on lights. His senses were functioning at an all-time high. He was aware of everything at a glance. Choa, his lead instructor, had once again forgotten to put the cap on the eucalyptus liniment. He put the top on and twisted it. He was aware of the smell of sweat, disinfectant, and eucalyptus. Sometimes, the smell bothered him; other times, he didn't even notice it. The dojo was clean, and that was all that mattered to him.

There was no one in any of the workout rooms. That had to mean whoever was in the dojo was upstairs in his apartment. It wasn't his wife, Yoko—she was somewhere with the sisters—and it wasn't his daughter, Lily—she was at school.

Harry didn't hesitate or break step. He did what he always did: he headed for the stairs that would take him to the second floor, where he lived with his family. He turned on the light at the bottom of the staircase that lit up the entire stairway and the small foyer at the top. Then he ascended the stairs. To his left was the kitchen, to his right, the living room. Then another small hallway where two bedrooms were side to side with the bathroom on the left.

He didn't miss a step when he turned on another light, and his kitchen appeared. A woman was sitting at the kitchen table, her hands folded. "I didn't touch anything, Harry. I've just been sitting here waiting. This is your home, but I was afraid to stay outside, too many eyes out there. I swear, Harry, I didn't even look around."

"It's okay. How are you, Tea Pope?"

Allison Bannon didn't move. "Oh, God, Harry, do you know how good it is to hear my real name said out loud?" A sob caught in her throat. "They erased me, Harry. But that's not why I'm here. How are my children? Are they okay? Lizzie . . ."

"I know. The kids are fine, or as fine as they can be. We've been taking care of them. They're healthy. Resilient. They miss you, of course. They talk about you all the time, especially Andy. He said you are going to be proud of him because he doesn't eat with his fingers anymore. He's pretty good with a spoon."

Allison's shoulders started to shake. "Oh, God, Harry! I need to see them. Can you take me to where they are? Like right now?"

"They're asleep. They had just gone to bed when I left to come home. We'll go first thing in the morning. You look different."

"Not different enough to fool you, though, right?"

"It's the eyes. The eyes are always a dead giveaway. How did you get here?"

"Lizzie helped me. My new name is Doris Brown—all the creds say so. She got me an SUV. I have a bank account and an ATM card. I'm good for the moment. I parked a block away and walked the rest of the way."

"What happened, Tea? Who the hell are you working for?"

"I, along with my team, are on loan to Homeland Security. Three years now. I'm on the CIA payroll, but as you know, they are forbidden to operate domestically."

"Where's Steven?"

"Hopefully in custody, singing his heart out. He was a mole. He'll try to cut a deal, and who knows what will happen. He sold us out. I didn't see it coming, Harry. That means I'm slipping. The marriage was over years ago, after Andy's birth, if you want me to be specific. He wanted his own team, resented being my number two. While the rest of the team worked with him, they wouldn't take orders from him. I talked to my handler, but he said he wasn't going to make any changes until this mission had been completed. Guess that didn't sit well with Steven.

"We had the guys we wanted nailed down. Easy peasy. When we got there, they were gone, the place sterilized. I knew in my gut it was Steven who sold us out, but when I saw the smug look on his face, I knew for certain. So did the team. He wanted me to look bad, to show I was chasing phantoms.

"I went nuts when I found out my kids had been kidnapped. I raised all kinds of hell. Luka told me everything was being done by the agency and every other agency, specifically the FBI, to find them. I believed him. I still believe that. They've taken good care of my kids over the years. Steven didn't seem to care. Harry, he didn't care.

"I made the decision that it was time to get out. So, I cut and ran. My kids are more important to me than the CIA. I don't care how much money they spent training me, I don't care that I'm number one. I gave them fifteen years. Fifteen years I can never get back. I allowed them to turn me into what I am today. Harry, look at me," Allison said, tears pooling in her eyes. "I'm an assassin. I have a license to kill bad people. I have the blessing of the president and the director of the FBI. I'm in demand by every damn agency in Washington. Do you believe that?" She sobbed.

"They won't let me out. I know too much. They'll kill me, Harry. They will. They won't want to, and they might try to find another way, but in the end, the next BOLO that goes out will be STK. Shoot to kill. I'm good, but I can't run for the rest of my life, even I know that. And what's going to happen to my kids? Steven is going to go to prison. Neither of us has any family. I need help, Harry. Lizzie said you and your friends would help me. Can you?"

"Of course."

"Today, the Internet went down. I never thought that was possible. It's like the world came to a stop. Most of the cell-phone towers didn't work, either. Somebody up there must be watching over me. I was able to make it here from Tennessee with no problems. There were some road-blocks, but I aced them. Communication, orders, directives . . . they all came to a standstill. It worked for me. Did the Internet come back up?"

Harry laughed. "It did."

Allison stared at Harry, her eyes wide in shock. "You shut it down, you crashed it!"

"Ah . . . it was a collaborative effort, but yes, we shut it down. We brought the CIA to their knees. They gave us what we wanted, which was basically everything they had on your current mission. They buckled."

"Lizzie said you run with some . . . some powerful people. Want to share more?"

"No."

"You sure my kids are okay? Seriously, Harry, don't pacify me. I need to know. I'm a mother."

"Your kids are fine. I swear on my own daughter. They're very intelligent. They escaped. Carrie took care of Emily and Andy. They were held in a funeral home. They slept in coffins. They think they just slept in boxes. Sooner or later, as they get older, they're going to remember, and they might need some counseling. I'm a grown man, and it creeps me out no end. They're troopers, Tea, chips off the old block. You need to trust me . . . us."

"While I was sitting here, I started to think about the past, what if anything will be my future. I think, at least right now, that I, too, might have to talk with a shrink at some point if they don't get to me first. How do I live with it, Harry?"

Harry propped his elbows up on the table and stared

across at the woman who was staring at him and hoping that he had an answer to her question. "You saved a lot of lives. You and your team have made the world a better, safer place. You learn to live with it. The end justifies the means, that kind of thing. Console yourself with what happened after you made your hit. No one is ever going to know except the people who need to know. I know you got commendations, medals for your service. I also know the president himself thanked you and shook your hand. If it weren't you, there would have been someone else taking the shot. Think what would have happened if that person missed and the end result was catastrophic. You did it because you're the best. You made all the difference. The difference is what counts. Think about that! Jack laughs at me when I say everything ends just the way it was meant to end. He said that's Chinese philosophy. I prefer my thinking. You did a job you were trained to do. You can't blame yourself that you're the best of the best. You proved it here in the dojo. We good here? Want some tea, some food?"

"Who is Jack? Forget that crappy tea you drink. I don't think my stomach can handle your seeds and sprouts. Now if you offer me hot, strong coffee and a ham sandwich or a cheese one, then I'm your girl."

Harry grinned. "I have coffee. And there is ham and cheese in the fridge. My daughter comes home from school on weekends, and she likes ham and cheese. She detests Chinese and Japanese food. Go figure. Jack is . . . Jack is . . . my friend. He's like a brother."

"A close friend then. I understand. I don't have any friends. No relatives, either. For a while, Steven was my friend. That's back when the marriage worked." Allison wound down and watched Harry as he put water on to boil for his tea, and then he made coffee before he made her a thick sandwich that looked delicious.

"So, Harry," Allison said between mouthfuls of food, "who are these . . . ah . . . special people you are aligned with? Lizzie spoke glowingly of you, but she wouldn't divulge anything other than that I should trust you. I trust you, Harry."

"Tomorrow morning, when we head out to Pinewood, will be time enough. You need to eat and go to bed. We'll head out early to beat the rush-hour traffic. You will need to park your vehicle in the alley outside the dojo. We'll take my motorcycle."

"You still have the Ducati?" Allison asked in surprise.

Harry was shocked at the question. "You remembered the Ducati."

"Harry, I remember every single minute I spent here at the dojo. I remember all the aches, the pains, the brutality. I remember crying myself to sleep at night because I hurt so bad. I remember the humiliation on the bad days. The guys who talked behind my back, the names they called me. I remember that even though I never said anything to you, you were going to interfere, but I told you no. But what I really remember is the day of the final trials, when you bowed to me. You bowed to *me*. To me that meant I was your equal. That was all I needed to go forward. I felt like you had handed me the Holy Grail. I saw my picture on your wall. You didn't just talk the talk, you walked the walk. I will be forever grateful. Your training saved my life on four separate occasions. To me, that meant I would live to see my kids again. 'Thank you' hardly seems enough."

"It's enough," Harry said gruffly. He had a hard time accepting praise.

"You can sleep in Lily's room. It's late. Morning will be here before you know it."

"If it's all the same to you, Harry, I'll just sit here and wait for morning. You go ahead. You need your sleep."

"We could talk. Tell me about your fifteen years out in

the field. I'm a good listener, and whatever you tell me stays with me."

Allison laughed. "You sure you want to hear all that?"

Harry didn't laugh. "Yes, Tea, I want to hear. And I think you need to get it all out, knowing that whatever you say will stay with me."

"Fine, but first I want to hear about your family. Your wife and daughter. Then we'll get to my stuff. Deal?"

"Deal."

Chapter Thirteen

The early morning cable news was jubilant that the Internet was back up and running. The cell-phone towers were also working, they chortled. Now all the talking heads wanted was someone's head on a platter for causing what one morning anchor referred to as almost the end of the communication world.

The digital clock on the range was one minute away from five o'clock, and Charles and Fergus had already cooked mountains of scrambled eggs and pounds of bacon and sausage for the team.

"So where do we stand?" Abner said, rubbing his red-rimmed eyes.

Avery Snowden looked around the table. "The CIA's files we spent the night going through simply verified pretty much what we already knew. The U.S. file confirmed that the Bannons, their team, were on loan to Homeland Security. We had already assumed that. Team Bannon has been working domestically on the Karas brothers for the past three years for Homeland Security. Off and on. Then, when the brothers packed up and left the U.S. and traveled to wherever they were going, usually abroad, they followed and went back to working for the CIA."

"Do we still think . . . believe that the brothers are untouchable?" Jack asked.

"Pretty much," Snowden said sourly. "I just got a report from a reliable source that there are eight SUVs parked at the Sofitel hotel in D.C. There are forty-eight people, security, protecting the brothers. Same deal they had at the Ritz-Carlton in Atlanta. They've taken over three entire floors."

"I'm not getting this," Ted said. The others agreed. They all looked at Snowden for the answer.

Avery Snowden shrugged. "The only thing I can think of is what Maggie did with the front page of the *Post*. The brothers want to be available. I'm thinking they're thinking they will be on the list. Arriving now is opportune for them. It will be easy for an invitation to be delivered." He flapped his hands to show he was just guessing. "Only a fool returns to the scene of the crime. The brothers are not fools. Someone is jerking their strings."

"How do we get them?" Dennis asked.

"Good question, kid. We need a plan," Jack said. "Where the hell is Harry?"

"He's on his way, along with Allison Bannon," Charles said.

"Forty-eight people is a small army. We're no match for that," Espinosa grumbled.

"Plus what we read in the files, their security is top notch. Retired from their professions. When I say 'retired,' I am not using the term the way Americans think of retirement. These are men who have been kicked out of the agencies they worked for for a variety of reasons. They're mercenaries, soldiers of fortune. Well-paid mercenaries. In other words, they aren't going to kick ass and take names. They're going to shoot to kill. We're no match for that kind of security," Abner said as he got up to carry his plate to the sink.

"Whoa! How can you say we're no match for them?" Jack exclaimed. Cyrus reared up and sprinted over to where Abner was standing. He barked twice. Translation: *Yeah, how can you say that? Did you forget about me?*

Abner reached down to stroke the sweet spot between Cyrus's eyes. He whirled around and barked back. "You're saying you and Harry, just the two of you, can take on forty-eight mercenaries!"

"Well, when you put it like that, no, we obviously can't do that. We'll need some help. Anyway, make that three because Allison Bannon will be on our side. With Cyrus, that adds up to four."

"A diversion of some kind at the hotel. Then we do a snatch and grab," Maggie said, just as Lady and her pups ran to the door.

"Harry's here!" Espinosa said. He turned on the outside light, which bathed the entire courtyard in blinding white light. The sun had yet to creep toward the horizon. He opened the door.

Harry made the introductions. All eyes were on Allison Bannon. She looked like a pixie minus the costume.

Charles held up his hands. "Maggie, take Mrs. Bannon to her children. She's waited long enough to see them." Allison bit down on her lip as her eyes filled with tears. She said nothing, she just waited as Maggie reached for her arm.

"They're still asleep. They usually sleep till around nine, but I'm sure they won't mind waking up early."

"No, no, I won't wake them. I just need to *see* them. Seeing them is all I need right now."

Maggie nodded as she opened the door to Barbara's old room, where the three children slept together in the big bed. "They wanted to sleep together," Maggie whispered.

"Andy likes to cuddle. Carrie is like a little mother to

Emily and Andy," Allison whispered in return as she let her eyes drink in the sight of her children in the dim light provided by the two night-lights. "You have no idea how much I love those kids," she continued to whisper as she backed out of the room.

Cooper's tail thumped on the carpet. Allison reared back. "What was that sound?"

"That's Cooper," Maggie whispered, as the dog's tail thumped twice. "He's protecting your children. He's lying beside the bed. Cooper is . . . it's complicated, Allison."

"I know. Harry said almost exactly the same thing. Maybe someday you'll explain Cooper to me. Or not."

Allison backed out of the doorway before she closed the door quietly behind her.

Maggie smiled. "Oh, I think I have a pretty good idea how much you love your children. Cooper is for another day."

Allison tugged at Maggie's arm. "I heard something in your tone that leads me to believe you care for my children. I saw the way you looked at them while they slept. I . . . during these past fifteen years, I've had to make split-second decisions with no thought to what would happen if I made the wrong one. I trust my gut, my intuition, and I run with it. It's saved my life and my team's lives more times than I want to remember. Having said that, I want to ask you something. But first I want to tell you something."

"Fire away," Maggie said uneasily as she wondered what was coming next.

Allison leaned against the staircase railing that overlooked the first-floor foyer and stared at Maggie in the subdued lighting of the long, narrow hallway. "I made provisions for my children. Me. Not me and my husband. *Me*. I contacted Lizzie Fox, and she took care of everything for me. I've provided for all three of them well into their adulthood. Lizzie is the trustee of the trust that I had set up. I would like you to be part of that. Because . . . be-

cause if I don't . . . if I don't make it, I want to know I left
my kids in good hands. I don't want my husband anywhere near those kids. If there is a God, and if justice pre-
vails, Steven will go to prison for the traitor he is.

"Will you agree, Maggie? I know it's a lot to ask, and
we just met. Will you at least consider it?"

Maggie didn't stop to think, to consider or weigh her response. She simply said, "Yes." Then she hugged the secret
agent and led the way back down to the kitchen, using the
back staircase. "There's nothing stronger than a mother's
love. I've read that, but I've also heard it voiced hundreds
of times over the years. Sadly, I am not a mother. I do have
a cat, though, that I love." She did take a second to wonder where a government agent could come up with enough
money to hire high-dollar attorney Lizzie Fox and provide
for her children into adulthood.

"Works for me," Allison said with a wan smile.

Back in the kitchen, where everyone was gathered, Charles
asked if he could make Allison some breakfast. She shook her
head. "We need to talk."

"Yes, we do," Charles said. He looked around at the
messy kitchen and shrugged. "This can wait. Follow us,
young lady."

If Allison Bannon was surprised at the secret bookcase
and the stone steps that led down to the war room, she gave
no sign. Nor did she show any emotion when she watched
the team salute Lady Justice on the big screen. She sat down
and waited.

"I'm sure Harry has explained everything, am I right?"

"Not *everything*," Harry said carefully.

A wry grin stretched across Allison's face. "He left off
the part about all of you being the male team of the infamous vigilantes. Am I right? And that explaining about
Cooper was complicated."

The collective gasp that echoed in the room brought a

full smile to her face. "I'm a superagent, remember. I recognize this place. Not where we are now but the outside. I worked under the FBI on loan back in the day when the whole world was trying to catch the vigilantes. Even though I was tasked to find them, I was rooting for them to get away. In my heart of hearts. I remember Jack Emery and the reporters. We had them cornered and were getting ready to make our move when the president issued the order to stand down. I didn't know then, but I know now that Lizzie Fox was instrumental in the stand-down. And then they all disappeared. Literally into thin air. The CIA snatched us back from the FBI and sent us to Spain, where it was rumored the vigilantes were holed up on a mountain. Lucky for them, another world crisis that took precedence came up, and again we were told to stand down. I have to say I was relieved. My heart was not in that mission."

The team gaped at Allison, but no one said a word because they were speechless at how close the sisters had been to capture, and they'd had no clue.

"Well, then, let's get down to business," Charles said as he tried to cover up the shock of what he'd just heard from Allison Bannon.

Allison looked over at Avery Snowden and said, "I know of you. You're good."

Surprised, Snowden nodded at her compliment.

Charles cleared his throat. "I think it would help all of us if you go first, Agent Bannon."

"I'm not an agent anymore. I've gone rogue. Allison will be fine."

The team sat transfixed as Allison recited the details of her entire career from the day she was recruited when she finished college to the present, sitting here at the table. Allison looked around at everyone at the table and said, almost playfully, "Your turn. Oh, wait, there is one more thing I need to tell you." She quickly explained about the money she'd *found*. "Lizzie is in charge of that." She almost laughed at the expressions on the team's faces.

Charles took to the floor, explained his background and Fergus's as well. "Mr. Snowden is . . . is a colleague we call on from time to time." He squared his shoulders and started talking. As hard as she tried, Allison found it difficult to conceal her shock at what the people seated at the table did. Lizzie Fox was right. These were the people she needed, people Lizzie said could be trusted. People like her. She would never be able to repay them for keeping her children safe, but by God, she would die trying. She continued to listen, nodding from time to time until Charles finished.

"I'm in," Allison said.

"Now we need a plan," Jack said.

Harry shocked everyone speechless when he said, "I think I might be able to come up with one."

"What? What? You waiting for a bus, Harry? If you have a plan, share it with us. Like now would be good," Jack growled.

"If I heard all this right, we're three plus one killer dog going up against forty-eight mercenaries. The odds of surviving that, much less accomplishing anything valuable, are not favorable." Cyrus bolted upright to stand next to Jack. He loved the term *killer dog* even though he'd never killed anything. Not even squirrels, which he was allowed to chase but not kill. He listened intently to Harry.

"My suggestion is I call the Triad."

Questions flew around the room at the speed of light. "You serious, Harry?" Jack asked, awe in his voice.

"As a heart attack."

"Then you need to share who the Triad is with the people in this room who might think the term has musical implications."

"The Triad consists of three of my best friends, Ky, Ling,

and Momo. They are usually referred to as the Deadly Triad. Ky is in Taiwan; Ling, I believe, is in Hong Kong; and right now I have no idea where Momo is. They might—I say *might*—be willing to come here to help us. That would even the odds quite a bit in *our* favor. Six plus one killer dog."

"How do you figure six plus one killer dog tilts the odds in your favor?" Dennis asked, a worried look on his face.

"Because I said so," Harry said.

And that was the end of that.

"If I have a vote in this, I agree with Harry. I've been, as they say in the business, within spitting distance of those guys. They are their own army, and there is a price on their heads. I guess the question is, how persuasive can you be, Harry? And can we pull it off?" Allison asked.

"The only way we'll know the answer is if I call them. Is everyone in agreement?" Harry looked around the room, waiting for opposition. He wasn't surprised to hear it from Charles, but he was equally stunned at Allison's reaction.

"Don't we need to know more about . . . your friends before we agree?" Charles asked.

"*No!*" The single word shot out of Allison Bannon's mouth like a gunshot.

"Just do it, Harry!" Jack said. Cyrus barked his approval.

Harry shrugged when the room turned silent. He fished around in the many pockets of his cargo pants until he found a funny-looking phone that he used for his business. It took him a minute to locate the number he wanted. All eyes were on him as they watched Harry dial a series of numbers after which he looked up at the different clocks on the wall that told the time all over the world. "There's a thirteen-hour time difference between here and Taiwan. It's not that late in Taiwan, and Ky is a night owl, so he should still be awake."

The wait for Harry's call to be answered seemed to take forever. Harry spoke in English for the benefit of those in the room to show he'd made contact.

"Hello, brother. It's me, Harry. I need to talk to you." He waved his arm so the others would know he had a handle on what he was to do and say. He switched immediately to Chinese and talked a blue streak before he gave up the floor to hear a response. The others waited, hardly daring to breathe. Harry let loose with another long string of rapid-fire Chinese, then waited. And finally, he turned to the team and said, "He wants to know what's in it for him."

"A million dollars each if we're successful," Allison said. "Get his banking information, and I'll pass it on to Lizzie."

More rapid-fire Chinese on both ends of the phone.

Harry turned to the team. "He says it isn't safe for the three of them to fly commercial. He's certain he can talk Ling and Momo into helping, but we need to get them here safely. The million bucks each helped. A lot."

"Tell him to rent a jet and a pilot. Lizzie will take care of the financial end. Or have them just buy a damn plane," Allison said. "Lizzie can take care of that, too. Give him her number."

Harry relayed the information and waited. "He wants to know how long their services will be required."

"Ten days, to be safe," Jack said.

Once again Harry relayed the information. He listened, a frown building between his brows. He turned again to the team and said, "Okay, but here's the tiebreaker. He wants to go to Disney while he's here."

"Done!" Allison all but screamed. "I'll take him myself!"

Harry flicked his phone off and started to laugh. Harry hardly ever laughed, and when he did, no one was sure how to react. "We have a deal! He's going to call Ling and Momo. He'll call me back. He likes the idea of buying a plane and wants assurance it's his when this is all over. I said okay to that.

"He thinks he can get back to me in about three hours," Harry said. "Buying a plane isn't an easy thing, he said. I gave him Lizzie's number, but, Allison, you might want to call her and give her a heads-up so things don't get mired down in bank transactions. Be sure to tell her the plane's registration is to go in the name of Ky Moon. Ky will tell her anything else she needs to know when he calls."

Allison was busy punching in the number on one of her burner phones. The others moved off to give her privacy.

"That all went pretty well, Harry," Jack said, slapping Harry on the back. "How long do you think it will take for a plane sale to go through in Taiwan? You up on stuff like that?"

"Show me the money, and it's instantaneous. If your next question is when can we expect them to set foot on American soil, I'd estimate the day after tomorrow, then again, maybe two. Time for Maggie to run a few more articles in the paper, time for the Karas brothers to sweat a little more, and time for Allison to tell us all the things she left out in her first run-through."

"Then I guess that has to work for us. Now what?" Charles asked.

"Now we have to find a way to get that army and the Karas brothers to a spot where we can take them out. Someplace safe, away from the public. We know for certain there will be firepower on their side. We don't want any innocents hurt," Jack said.

"You can all come back to the table now," Allison said as she slipped the cell phone into her pocket. "Lizzie is on it. She said to say hello to all of you. So, hello from Lizzie Fox."

The team took their seats at the table and looked around

at one another. Ted spoke first. "Think now, and tell us everything you know about the Karas brothers, even if you think it's not important. Little things you picked up during your years of surveillance on the two. You hit the highlights. Now we need the nitty-gritty, the stuff no one else thinks about. The kind of things that make a case in the end."

Allison sighed. "They're weird. That's for starters. They come to a location prior to a handoff. It's like they arrive a week ahead to check things out. They go out and about like they're searching to get the beat and the rhythm of the location. Is it a comfortable fit or is it a trouble spot? That's the best way I can explain it.

"They never lack invitations anywhere they go. They donate handsomely to whatever cause is being presented. They do dinner dates, but as far as I know, those two are eunuchs. There has never, in all the years of my tracking them, been any kind of romantic entanglement. No sleepovers. No second or third dates. Eunuchs.

"There is one thing that had us all hopping about. No matter where they ended up, the first thing they did was to get a manicure, a pedicure, and a facial. Always. They went together. We were never able to figure out if they had made appointments beforehand or if they just picked a place at random. We finally came to the conclusion that the salons were the same as the funeral homes. And still we couldn't nail the bastards."

Fergus was excited. "See, that's what we mean—you never mentioned the salons before. That's important, and it makes sense. Annie told me, and so did Myra, that the turnover at those places is like a revolving door. You never get the same operator twice unless you just happen to get the owner or the person in charge. She even mentioned to me a while back that she thought the owners were smuggling people, young women hardly old enough to work.

And she said the licenses hanging on the wall never matched the people working there."

"Just another avenue in the slave trade. I'm going to call Pearl Barnes to see if she's heard anything. Running her underground railroad, she is certainly in a position to hear and maybe even come across someone lucky enough to have gotten away to find her way to her. It's worth trying," Maggie said.

The others agreed, and Maggie picked up her phone and made the call.

"I'm going back to the farm to see if I can find Annie's invitation box. She had a bunch of invitations made up especially for her. Pricey little devils, too. You can take the invitation and put it in the printer and type in the dates and times on the computer. Looks as real as if a print shop made them by hand, one by one. And they're lined with satin. A hundred bucks a pop!" Fergus said. "When you see me next, I will have the invitations in hand." A moment later, he was gone.

Maggie ended her call. "Pearl said she's heard for years that the nail salons were used for trafficking but she couldn't and wouldn't get involved because the people who ran them were gangsters, and she wanted no part of that. And, she doesn't know anyone who can help us. She practically told me to buzz off. Now, if it was Kathryn who called her, she would have spilled her guts, assuming she had something to spill. She and Kathryn hate each other, as we all know."

"So, that's just another dead end," Charles said. Maggie's head bobbed up and down.

"Anything else, Allison?" Jack asked.

"No, that's it. If I think of anything, you'll be the first to know."

Charles looked at his watch. "The children should be

waking up about now. You might want to find your way upstairs, so you are the first thing they see when they wake up."

Allison's face lit up like a thousand lightbulbs. "Would you be kind enough to allow me to use your kitchen to make my children breakfast?"

"Of course."

Allison sprinted toward the stairs like a gazelle. She was almost to the back staircase when she turned around and came back. "I just remembered something else. It happened in Singapore, maybe five years ago, possibly four. We were tracking the brothers and, as usual, not getting anywhere. They checked into the most expensive hotel in Singapore but I can't remember the name offhand. The army, as we called the Karas brothers' staff, was loading the luggage onto those hotel dollies. There were six of them, that's how much stuff they traveled with. Anyway, they had two dollies already in the elevator and were trying to get a third in when it toppled over. All three were loaded with bankers boxes.

"The hotel staff rushed to help but were waved off. But one precocious young man saw what spilled out and overheard some conversation. The boxes were loaded with books, tapes, and CDs. What the young man heard was the security bitching about how Roland read incessantly and vociferously while Ryland listened to classical music endlessly. The security said there was going to be hell to pay if they didn't get everything put back exactly the way it was because the brothers themselves packed the boxes. He said that's the only thing that mattered to either one of them. Books and music. I don't know if that helps you or not. It didn't do anything for us. Make of it what you will, guys and gal."

"I like her," Charles said. "Imagine that, books and music."

The others agreed. Even Cyrus, who let loose with two prolonged yips.

Jack looked at Harry, and then both men looked at Maggie, whose eyes were shining like stars in a dark night.

"I know where this is going," Jack hissed to Harry.

"Yeah, I do too."

Chapter Fourteen

Allison opened the door to the bedroom where her children were still sleeping soundly. She slid out of her shoes and tiptoed over to the bed, mindful of her children's protector, who was lying at the side of the bed. She waited to see if his tail would thump. It did not.

Allison dropped to her knees and peered at the strange dog in the dim light. "I want to thank you for keeping my children safe. If it's okay with you, I want to climb into that bed with them so I'm the first thing they see and feel when they wake up," she whispered in the dog's ear. Cooper's tail thumped once. *It's okay.*

Her heart beating like a trip-hammer in excitement, Allison wormed her way between Carrie and Emily. Andy squirmed and threw his little arm out. Allison tucked it under her chin, loving the sweet smell of her baby boy. Tears welled in her eyes.

Carrie tried to roll over, mumbling something directed at Andy, then opened her eyes and let out a scream.

"Shhhh, honey, it's me, Mom. Look, Cooper is okay with my being here. He isn't barking. It's okay, Carrie. I just look . . . *different* today. It's me, Mommy, honey."

Allison stretched her free arm out to turn on the lamp on the night table. The room was suddenly bathed in a warm yellow glow. Emily stirred and mumbled something that sounded like, *What is your problem?*

"It's Mommy, dummy. Can't you see her? Wake up! Mommy's home!" Andy was upright on his knees in a heartbeat as he threw his little arms around his mother's neck. He started to kiss her as he cried out his happiness. And then they were all crying, Allison, her daughters, and her son.

"You look different, Mommy," Emily said. "Are you in disguise?"

"Yes, but just for a little while. Then I will go back to looking like you remember me unless you want me to stay looking like this." Allison giggled. "You guys have more hair than I do. How funny is that?"

Still hanging on to Allison for dear life, Andy asked her if she was staying or was she going to leave again. "Where's Daddy?"

Ah, the question she knew was coming and dreaded. "I'm going to stay this time. I quit my job. I decided being a mom is more important than a job. But, I have to finish up what I'm working on before I can officially do that. All these nice people who live here who have been taking care of you are going to help me. And we can't forget Cooper. Then we can leave and be a real family again."

"Where's Daddy?" Andy persisted.

"I'm not sure exactly where he is right now. But he will not be coming with us when we leave here."

"Is that because kids need a mother more than they need a father?" Carrie asked curiously as she hugged her mother so tight Allison squealed in pretended pain.

Allison propped herself up on one elbow, trying not to feel the pain of Andy's strangling weight on her other side. "That's not true in most cases. Ideally, children need both a mother and a father, but sometimes that just doesn't work. This time, for us it doesn't work. I hope you understand."

"Will you stay home with us? Will you always be there?" Emily asked hopefully.

"I promise you all that I will always be there for you. We're going to live in a real house that belongs to us. We're going to plant flowers and a garden with vegetables. I'm going to buy a minivan like all the other mothers have so I can drive you to a real school where you can make friends and go to birthday parties and field trips with your teachers. A real school. We're going to get a dog, a kitten, a bird, and some hamsters and maybe some goldfish. We'll give them all names so they'll be our friends until we make new human ones. We'll go to church on Sunday, and when the town has a parade, we'll go and wave our flags. We're going to put down roots."

"Will leaves and flowers grow out of our heads?" Andy asked in alarm.

Andy's siblings didn't laugh simply because they wondered the same thing.

"No, that won't happen. Putting down roots means we are going to move someplace that we will never have to leave. We'll live there forever."

"Will you bake cookies, help us with our homework?" Emily asked.

"Yes, I will make you the best gingerbread cookies you ever had. And, yes, I will help you with your homework. Yes, I will make sure you learn to play soccer, the piano, and tennis. I will go to all your games and cheer for you. I'm going to be a real mom from this day forward. You will never have to tell fibs to cover for me. You will never have to wonder where I am or when I'm coming home because I will always be there."

"Will you help us decorate a Christmas tree?" Carrie asked.

Allison laughed. "I will do better than that. We'll go to a Christmas tree farm, pick a tree, and watch while the people cut it down for us and put it on top of our car. I think the four of us are strong enough to get the tree in the house and set it all up."

Emily got up on her knees and punched her sister Carrie in the stomach. "See! See!" she screeched. "Dreams come true. Wishes come true. You lied to me, Carrie, you said that would never happen!"

Carrie started to wail. Cooper sprang into action. Somehow, he managed to get up on the bed and between everyone. His tail swished furiously as he yipped four times.

Cool your jets, kids. The wailing and crying stopped.

"I wanted to believe what Emily said, Mommy. I even prayed the way you taught us to pray. I only thought like that on the days I was sad. When I wasn't sad, I didn't think like that."

"It's okay, Carrie. Some days I thought it would never happen, too, but guess what, here I am!" Allison said, throwing her arms out wide. "And I will never leave you again.

"Okay, it's time to get up and dressed. Wash your faces, brush your teeth, and come downstairs when you're ready. I'm going to make breakfast for you."

"Like you used to on Sunday?"

"Yep!"

"Pancakes!" the three children shouted all together. "With lots of bacon and chocolate milk!"

"You got it! Scoot now. I'll be waiting for you downstairs."

When Allison set foot in the kitchen, the only person she saw was Margie Chambers, who introduced herself. "Everything is ready. All you have to do is cook it. The others are downstairs. They said when you're finished to go down. I'll take the kids out to the barn and keep them busy so you can do what you have to do."

"Does that mean you're . . ."

"One of them? In a manner of speaking. I work for Mr. Snowden, but yes, we're all in the same . . . um, business. I'll be in the family room, that's off to the right of the kitchen. I need to catch up on what's going on in the world so far today."

Allison nodded as she started to mix pancake batter. "I don't know how to thank you."

"The kids are great. They're whip smart, even Andy. He gave me a run for my money the first day. You might want to compliment him on how well he's using a spoon and fork. We need some more time on the fork, but he's working at it."

"I'll be sure to do that."

Later, Allison confessed to Maggie that it was the most wonderful hour and a half she'd ever spent with her children, especially the part where Andy couldn't understand why he couldn't scoop up the syrup with a fork. "I almost missed that, Maggie," she said in a choked voice. "That will become one of my fondest memories. Thanks to all of you."

Charles whistled to gain their attention, and the moment was gone.

"We have work to do, people. Ferg, you're up! But first, I have something to say. Today is going to be planning and details. All pretty much done here. Allison will stay with us, and Margie will take care of the children. We're good there. Tomorrow, we'll activate and put into action whatever we come up with today. We might even get some free time at some point. I have a huge turkey with all the trimmings ready to go into the oven since there are so many of us here today. And it's a way to say thanks. Corny as that may sound, I happen to like it."

"Hear, hear!" Jack said happily. He was more than ready for one of Charles's what he called soup-to-nuts wonderful meals.

"You have the floor, Ferg," Charles said.

Fergus stood up, opened a large manila envelope, and withdrew a one-of-a-kind, gorgeous invitation lined in champagne-colored satin. "I know how to do the date and the time on the computer, so it will look like it was all done in some top-of-the-line print shop."

Maggie and Allison were the only ones who oohed and aahed over the exquisite invitation. "Even the lining of the envelope is satin," Maggie said as she touched the soft envelope. The boys looked on, befuddled expressions on their faces. Maggie shrugged, guessing it was a girly thing guys simply weren't into.

"And this is Annie's stationery," Fergus said, holding up a quilted box that held engraved notepaper and envelopes. Again, only Maggie and Allison oohed and aahed over the engraved notepads. "Take note of the tiara on top and the crushed sparklers in the crown." The gang took note as Fergus requested, but there were no further comments.

"So, what's the plan?" Ted asked.

"That's why we're here, to come up with a plan," Charles said. "Who wants to go first?" No one wanted to go first. Cyrus let loose with a yip that meant nothing.

"I think we all agreed yesterday that we have to somehow get the Karas brothers out of the hotel to some neutral spot so no harm comes to anyone. It has to be somewhere that his army is comfortable with. Having said that, I was thinking, and it's just a thought, Annie's farmhouse. She has fifteen acres that back up to this farm. So, in essence, we're saying that adding our fifty acres to her fifteen brings the total to sixty-five acres with no busybodies to interfere or call the authorities. If you factor in mine and Nik's eleven acres, we're talking seventy-six acres altogether. No other neighbors. We could do a repeat of a shoot-out at the O.K. Corral, and no one would know or hear. Or care."

"So, we're talking about a personal, intimate luncheon. Let me see if I have this right," Maggie said. "First, I have to make sure we publish a picture of the actual invitation in tomorrow's edition. Along with a list of those invited with let's say three to maybe five open invitations. Last-minute invitees, so to speak. The Karas brothers are not on the print list. But the three or five or whatever number we decided who are on the open list still have a chance. Do I mention the private, personal, intimate luncheons for that list? Do I have all of this right, and do you all agree with me?"

"That works for me," Ted and Dennis said in unison. Espinosa's head bobbed up and down. The rest of the team was okay with it, too, even Allison.

"Okay then, here is the list. It's chock-full of politicians, star power, some media, dignitaries, and a few members of royalty who are virtually certain to decline. But it is Annie, so you never know. Personally speaking, I hate elitist lists like this one. Oh, one other thing, there will be three special guests of honor."

"Who?" everyone chorused at the same time.

Before Maggie could open her mouth to respond, Allison Bannon said, "Three survivors!"

"How did you know that?" Maggie asked in awe.

"Because it's the only thing that makes sense, and it's how I'd run it if I were in your place. How old are the survivors?"

"All are over eighteen. One just turned eighteen. Two are about to turn nineteen. They were taken when they were ten years old. They have been in intensive therapy, and all three have made remarkable progress. It's a given that their lives will never be the same, and their therapy will be ongoing.

Fortunately for them, they have an excellent support system in family and friends. I was stunned when I was told they agreed to attend. And, no, I cannot divulge my source, but the source came to me with the idea once they saw the article in the paper. At first I was reluctant, but the more I thought about it, the more I could see where maybe it would help the girls. Wouldn't it be great if they could actually stare down those bastards!

"Wait! Wait! It would be great if that were to happen and they were surrounded by Harry's Triad friends."

Every fist in the room shot high in the air.

"I'd give my last dollar to see that," Dennis said.

"Me too, and I'll even throw in my beachfront properties." Abner thought about what he'd just said for a second, then corrected his statement. "At least one property!"

"Are you going to mention the girls' names?" Charles asked.

"Only if they want me to. They're used to the notoriety and handled it pretty well when the news of their escape years ago first became public. In the end, it's up to them. If you are asking for my opinion then it's yes, they are not going to shrink or hide. They'll want to be right up front with their stories. It's how they're recovering, getting it out there, talking about it. I will say this, those young women are survivors.

"There is one more thing. My source came to me by way of Pearl Barnes. So we owe her a bit of thanks here for that. When it comes to Pearl, we all have to understand she would give up her life to protect the people of her underground railroad. Her . . . whatever you want to call it with Kathryn is personal, between the two of them."

"Now what?" Allison asked.

Charles looked at Harry, who was half asleep in his chair. "Harry, can you give us an update on your Triad friends? What's happening across the world?"

"So far nothing. I should be hearing from Ky in the next half hour or so. Is there something else you want me to do? If not, I'm going to take a nap."

The team talked it up, and there was nothing else that needed to be done.

"I did say there would be free time. Ferg and I will be cooking for our feast this afternoon. The rest of you can do whatever you want. Allison, I imagine you will want to go out to the barn to be with your children. Jack, that leaves you," Charles said.

"Cyrus and I will head back to the house. I need to check my roof and the downspouts with all the rain we've had the past few days. What time is dinner?"

"Six o'clock, and don't be late," Fergus said.

Within seconds, the room emptied out.

"It's just you and me, Ferg. What's your feeling on all of this? You getting any vibes of any kind?"

"Not the kind I want to talk about, mate. This whole thing is a conundrum wrapped up in an enigma."

"Avery is on his way over to the Sofitel to check things out. He's going to make one stop along the way to pick up a few of his operatives. He said he'd check in a bit later. With nothing else on our plates, no pun intended, I say we get on with our cooking. What's your thinking on home-made biscuits versus a dinner roll?"

"Biscuits. Fresh string beans or peas?"

"Peas, of course. Are you listening to the two of us? We're cooking or talking about cooking, and our chicks are out there doing all the work. What's wrong with this picture, Ferg?"

"We're just not used to all this waiting time. A mission in the past ran like clockwork; we worked by minutes and seconds. Here we're working in hours and days. Too much time in between. Wasted time. The other thing is we always had background. The Karas brothers appeared on the scene one day, as one of your chicks said, hatched from an egg. We can only work with the information that we have."

Charles lifted the heavy twenty-three-pound turkey, slid it into the oversize oven, then set the timer.

"Our mistake was not going after whoever it is who put the Karas brothers in business in the first place. That's who we want. We don't even have a clue as to who that might be. Shame on us, Ferg."

"I hate shelling peas. I'd rather snap green beans. It has to be some cartel. My guess would be El Salvador. We need to locate the hydra and kill it."

"Chop off one head and another one grows," Charles muttered.

"Then we torch it."

"First we have to find it. We have plenty of time to kill today, so let's go down to the war room and make war. I'll call all the people I know from our days in service, and you call yours. Something is bound to come up. For all we know, it did, and we missed it because we were concentrating on the Karas brothers."

Fergus washed his hands as Charles handed out treats to the dogs, accompanied by his usual warning: "Watch the house, Lady." The golden retriever took up her position in front of the door, her pups at her side. Pinewood was safe now.

On the way down the moss-covered stone steps, Fergus asked Charles if he thought a trip to El Salvador was on the horizon. Or some other godforsaken country.

"Not by either you or me, but possibly by Avery and his people if we manage to turn something up. There was a name, Ferg, that I heard a while back. Maybe a year or so in regard to drug cartels. It was a kind of . . . I know this sounds silly, but a singsong kind of name. Do you remember anything like that? The man supposedly is the head or was the head of something, and billions, that's with a *b*, go through his hands yearly."

"You think he's the hydra?"

"Right now it's all I can think of. The feds seem to be on top of all the other cartels and watch them for a misstep. I never heard anything about that particular name again. I forgot all about it until just now."

"Well, mate, maybe you need to go over there and sit down in Myra's chair, close your eyes, and *think* about it."

"You're a mind reader now, too? I was just thinking the same thing. If it looks like I have fallen asleep, wake me up."

"Righto, mate."

One hour and thirteen minutes later, Charles Martin bounded out of Myra's chair like he'd been shot from a cannon. "I've got it, Ferg. I've got it! Beteo Mezaluma! His people call him Beets. That's all I know, though, and I don't know if he hails from El Salvador or some other country. See what you can find out and check him out while I call Avery."

There was no sound in the war room except for the clicking of computer keys and soft, murmured questions for over two hours when Charles called for a coffee break and said he wanted to check the turkey.

Fergus made the coffee as he talked. "Afghanistan is the biggest opium producer in the world. They belong to the Golden Crescent. Burma is next. Some guy named Khun Sa, the leader, was called the Opium King. Some of the product comes from Vietnam, Laos, and Thailand. Three-quarters of the world's heroin supply comes from there. Khun Sa died in 2007, so now a bunch of other guys run the empire.

"Next is Mexico. Joaquín Guzmán, also called Shorty, actually made it to the *Forbes* list as one of the richest men in the world. We all know what happened to him. This is all part of the Sinaloa, Juarez, Medellin, and Cali Tijuana Gulf cartels.

"Then comes Colombia, where the Medellin Cali cartel operates, followed by Peru, which is the biggest producer of cocaine in the world. Last on my list is Bolivia, but I ruled them out. So take your pick. Where do we start?"

"Let me share all this with Avery and see what he says. Pour me a cup, will you, Ferg."

Charles hung up the phone with a strange expression on his face. "Avery recognized the name. Can you believe that? He thinks—he's not sure—but he thinks Beteo was with the Peruvian cartel but relocated to Mexico when Shorty was captured. He has some of his people on the way there already. And he knows of a guy who set up a security consulting firm in San Diego. He used to head up Special Forces when he was in the military. The kind of guy who can get the job done is what Avery said. He's reached out to him but warned me that if he agrees to help us, it will cost some big bucks. From what he said, this guy Beets is an okay guy to the people in the town where he resides. He takes care of them. He's their *patrone*. He walks about with no security, just like the rest of the residents. Knows all the kids by name, goes to christenings and weddings. Plays kickball with them in the open fields. Just a regular Joe. I'm having trouble wrapping my head around all of that, but if that's the story, then that's the story. Avery thinks a snatch and grab would be a piece of cake. Avery also said he doesn't know if Beets has the smarts to go into human trafficking. But he also said Beets might partner out and be involved anonymously. He said anything is possible.

"Now, if we could somehow find a tie between him and the Karas brothers, that would help. I think we should wake Abner to see what he can find out about our newest find. We need to know if Beets travels. And if he does, was he anywhere near where the Karas brothers were at specific times. I think we might be onto something, Ferg. I really do. Hold the fort while I go upstairs to wake Abner up."

"You've got it, mate."

Chapter Fifteen

Forty-eight angst-driven hours passed before Charles sent word to the team to meet at the farm.

The team grumbled as one, with Maggie and Jack being the loudest and the most outspoken as soon as they arrived. Charles shut them down with a withering stare. "Rome wasn't built in a day. When you all left here the other day, I said we needed to make this airtight. Nothing has changed in that regard, but now we have concrete proof of certain things, and, most importantly, the Karas brothers are still registered at the Sofitel. How many times do I have to tell you, it's all in the planning?

"Avery is not here, but I just spoke to him not ten minutes ago. He's in Chula Vista, California. As you all know, in our line of work you meet people who cross your path or someone will introduce you to someone else quite innocently that at the time you have no idea how pivotal they will be to you later on in life. That has just happened with Avery. Which is a good thing for us.

"There is a gentleman in Chula Vista, not that far from San Diego, who runs a security consulting placement service. He operates here and overseas. His roster of employees are all ex-military, like himself. Sterling, honorable personnel, unlike the people the Karas brothers surround themselves with. He himself is ex–Special Forces. When he retired, he formed the company, which, fortunately for him, took off like a rocket. He places his teams all over the world. He's got a triple-A, five-star rating as far as his company goes. He charges incredibly high dollar amounts, but Avery says he is worth every penny. Right now, money is not a problem for us. Or am I wrong about that?"

"No, you're right," Allison said before anyone else could say anything.

"Where is this guy in Mexico?" Abner asked.

"Tijuana. You just walk across the bridge from where Duke Callahan, that's his name, has his offices. When Beets is not traveling, he lives in a small village and blends in as one of the locals. He's mid- to late sixties. He's fit and trim, weathered to be sure. Strong like a bull, Avery said, because that's how the locals describe him, strong like a bull. A virile man, to be sure. He's married to a very pretty young woman, maybe late thirties, early forties. They have a small daughter. I'd say maybe seven or eight. There was a picture of her, which Avery said he found during his research, making her First Holy Communion, which tells us he's Catholic. Right now, we are waiting for Avery to call back. He's meeting up with Mr. Callahan to see if a snatch and grab is possible. Be patient."

Abner waved his arms about. "I've only been on this ten minutes, but the guy is not shy about hiding his money. I think he owns the banks where he keeps some of it. There are so many trails, it's going to take me a bit of time to give you any kind of total. That is what you want from me, right?"

"Yes," Charles said succinctly.

Abner went back to what he was doing, clicking furiously at the keys on his keyboard.

"So what we're saying is this Beteo Mezaluma is the hydra?" Jack said. "And just like that, we found him! And all because you suddenly remembered a name and ran with it. What are the chances of this actually panning out for us?" Jack asked, skepticism ringing in his voice.

"It happens that way sometimes. Everything points to Mezaluma. If we're wrong, then we're wrong, and we start looking again. Right now, it's all we have. With what Abner is digging up and with what Mr. Callahan knows, everything appears to point to Mr. Mezaluma. Waiting a few more hours for further confirmation is not going to break or build our case."

"You're right, Charles. As usual," Jack said grudgingly.

Charles shrugged and directed his next question to Maggie. "What was the reaction to the print list you published yesterday?"

"The switchboard crashed. We were down for hours. You would not believe the snippy and downright rude people who called in according to Terry, our switchboard operator. She said over two dozen people had called in before it went down to inquire what they would have to do to qualify for the five remaining open invitations. As far as I know, the Karas brothers did not call unless they tried after the switchboard went down."

"Maybe we're barking up the wrong tree where they're concerned," Dennis said. "And, yes, Maggie, I just used a hated cliché, but it damn well fits."

"Maybe they're waiting for orders from the hydra," Ted volunteered.

"Anything is possible," Charles said.

"Maggie, when are you going to deliver the handwritten invitation to the Karas brothers for the private luncheon with Annie that she won't be attending?" Harry asked.

"It's ready to go. I was just waiting for you all to tell me it was okay to call a messenger service to pick it up. Which means I have to go back into town. This is just my opinion, but I think once they get the invitation, they won't know what to do so they will have to make contact with the person who is behind all this to see if they should or should not attend. They're still at the hotel, so that almost has to mean they're waiting for *something*. If Avery is right, and it is that guy in Mexico, what's our game plan then?"

"I can't give you an answer to that until Avery gets back to me. Patience, people."

Under his breath, Charles repeated, over and over, "Come on, Avery, make this happen for us."

Avery Snowden looked around and was not impressed with his surroundings. He was standing in front of a plain glass door covered on the inside with a bamboo blind. He rang the bell and waited. CALLAHAN CONSULTING was the name on a small brass plaque that was weathered with age. The building was in a busy business complex of two-story buildings in an area called Triangle Square. Avery took a moment to wonder how the hell a triangle could be a square. These Americans were so strange sometimes. A voice squawked from the intercom next to the weathered plate, "Your name, please."

"Avery Snowden. I have an appointment with Mr. Callahan."

Avery heard the snick of the lock opening. He turned the handle and walked into a well-lit waiting room. It had colored plastic chairs, fake plastic trees, dog-eared magazines. The wall art was just that, pictures purchased at Target or Walmart for fifty bucks a pop. They were as colorful as the plastic chairs. The room looked just like his dentist's waiting room. Except for the crystal bowl of individually wrapped peppermint candies.

"Mr. Callahan will see you now, sir. Just follow me," an elderly lady with bluish hair said. Being the astute detective that he was, Avery deduced the lady was Callahan's mother. Duke Callahan's office was as shabby and barren as the front office. Obviously, this guy wasn't into appearances. Avery watched as Duke Callahan got up from behind an enormous desk and walked around to greet him. He was a bear of a man, with hair growing everywhere hair could grow. He also had a ponytail pulled back with a red bandana. Six-five at least, and he probably weighed in at about 275 pounds, give or take ten. All solidly ripped flesh. He was decked out in jeans that needed to go to Goodwill and a military olive-colored T-shirt that strained across his chest and upper arms. He held out a hand that was bigger than a catcher's mitt. Said hand, Avery thought, was attached to an oak-tree limb. This was one big hulking dude. The handshake was normal.

"Something to drink, coffee, tea?"

"No thanks."

"All right then, let's get down to it."

"I need some help. You come highly recommended."

"That's always nice to hear," Callahan said jovially. "Talk to me."

When Avery finished his tale, a full three minutes passed before Callahan spoke. "I've heard about Sir Charles Martin in today's time. I knew him personally back in the day, but his name wasn't Charles Martin then. Not that names are all that important. No, let me back up. What I said is not quite accurate, certainly not the whole story. I should say that not only did I meet him, but that he saved my life. He pulled me to safety, bandaged me up, told me I'd live to fight another day and not to whine about it. He left me lying where I was for someone to come and get me. I heard later that he went on that same day to save Prince Charles's life. It's true, it's documented and all. If you had more time, I could show you the scrapbook. I'm in. But I have to tell you, I only have one team of five available. Three men and two women. All superior in their fields. You say you have six men with you. If you count me and you, that makes thirteen, and please don't give me any crap about thirteen being an unlucky number. I don't see how we can fail."

"Murphy's law," Avery said sourly.

Callahan laughed, a great, booming sound. "That law doesn't apply to me or my people. Let's hear your ideas first, then I'll tell you mine. Remember now, I know this area. I know Mexico inside and out. Been there in the dead of night more times than I care to remember. Flash money, and you'll make so many new friends, you won't be able to count them all. But there are other ways, too, and I know them all. I do have a question. How the hell did you guys manage to snag the CIA's top rogue agent?"

Snowden laughed. He was about to give a flip answer but thought better about it. "She found us through a few mutual friends. Right now, she's not a rogue agent, or any kind of agent, for that matter. She's first and foremost a mother who is pissed off that those scumbags abducted her kids. Need I say more?"

"Hell no. You see that little lady out there when you got here? That's my mother. If she even thought you had evil thoughts where I'm concerned, you'd be dead right now, and I would be mopping up your blood. I know all about motherhood," Callahan drawled.

"Is it worth my asking how you got the Triad to agree to help you? That means they're coming to you. My sources tell me they don't leave their home base. Like never. I have a dossier on them six inches thick."

"Why not. All we had to do was promise them a mil

each and buy them a new Gulfstream. Oh, yeah, and a trip to Disney. That rogue agent is going to take them, along with her kids."

"Ya know, Snowden, for a Brit, you're okay. That's all it took, eh?" Then Callahan laughed so hard the room shook.

Snowden didn't know if he should be flattered or insulted. He decided to go with flattered and grinned, something he rarely did. Americans could be strange, but he liked Duke Callahan. Callahan was a man's man.

"What's your thinking on how best to take this guy? Yes, yes, he's just an ordinary peasant when he's in town. That doesn't mean there isn't security of some kind that's not visible. People can blend in easily. And then there's his cell phone," Snowden said, his voice edged in worry.

"Give me fifteen minutes, and my team will have all the information you need. Hey, Mom!" he bellowed. "Can you come here a minute?" He explained what he needed, and her response brought another grin from Snowden.

"I'm on it!" the little lady with the bluish hair said happily.

Callahan shrugged. "She needs to be needed. I get that. You want the real truth?" Not bothering to wait for Snowden to respond, he said, "The truth is that this place would fall apart without her. I hate goddamn paperwork. At any given moment, she can lay her hands on whatever we need. She's also a whizbang at coordinating all our stuff. She even knows how to hack," he said proudly.

"I hope you pay her well," Snowden quipped.

"See! That's another thing. She won't take any money. Not a red cent. She's everyone's mother around here. That's why I understand what you mean about that agent going rogue. Motherhood will win out every time."

"If you know about this guy, how is it you've never taken him out?"

"No one commissioned us to look into it. And the alphabet agencies hate me and my company. It's a constant battle with them. What really gooses the agencies is that I hired all their employees when they left. And I pay a damn sight better than the government does. We don't go looking for work. The long and short of it is that I turn down more cases than I take on. I have to. I do only high-quality work, and if you spread your team too far and wide, your results leave a lot to be desired. Any more questions?"

"That about covers it. Ah, excuse me, I have a call coming in that I've been waiting for. I'll put him on speaker so you can hear." Callahan nodded.

"What do you have for me, Tookus?"

Abner got right down to it. "The guy is rich as hell. He's got it stashed all over hell and creation. What do you want me to do now?"

"Steal it, of course. Transfer it to someplace safe. Then obliterate the accounts. How much are we talking about here?"

"Right now I'm up to $93 million, and there are, if I'm right, six more accounts to go. Phil helped me out, or I wouldn't be this far along."

"I need you to do something else. I need your pal, the one with the magic fingers, to shut down the cell-phone towers that service Tijuana, Mexico, when I call to give you the okay to do it. That means open lines on those phones I provided. Check and get right back to me. Just out of curiosity, where are you going to . . . transfer those monies?"

"Do you have clearance for me to tell you that? Not to worry, it will be safe," Tookus replied and then ended the call.

Callahan looked at Snowden. "Ninety-three million dollars! And he's just going to make it disappear! Who is that guy? I could use someone like him."

"Name's Abner Tookus, and he's good. Super good,

but the guy you really want, who you are never gonna get, is a dude named Philonias Needlemeyer. Right now, I can guarantee he heard everything you and I have just spoken about."

Callahan grimaced. "Yeah, right! This place is so bug tight, an ant couldn't make its way in here. Besides, Mom sweeps for listening devices three times a day."

Snowden's phone rang. He picked it up and it was all he could do not to laugh out loud. "Gentlemen, I want to thank you for the kind compliments. And, Mr. Callahan, tell your mother I compliment her, but she needs to update her equipment." The connection ended.

"What the holy hell!" Callahan exploded.

"Listen, man, don't even go there, just roll with it. The two of them are on our side, and that's all that's important. Ah . . . I wouldn't mention what just happened to your mother. Phil will be watching over you all from here on in."

"Uh-huh," Callahan said, rubbing at his whiskers. "Uh-huh."

Snowden looked at his watch.

"They have three more minutes," Callahan said, his eyes still dazed that someone had managed to infiltrate his organization. He was ticked off even though he knew it would never come to anything negative where his firm was concerned.

The door opened precisely at the fifteen-minute mark. Three men and one woman waited to be invited into the room.

Avery looked them over and liked what he was seeing. Three guys, all in their mid- to late fifties. Dressed in khaki pants, button-down white shirts rolled to the elbows, ties loosened, John Lobb shoes, military haircuts, clean shaven, papers and phones in hand. The woman was dressed almost identically, but her white blouse was silk. Her hair, the color of a sandy beach, was tied back in a bun. She wore little to no makeup because she didn't need it. Her eyes were big and brown as saucers. No jewelry except for a strap wristwatch. She wore high-top sneakers that were bright red. The shoelaces were white with little red lady-bugs crawling all over them. The lady had a sense of humor, Snowden decided.

Callahan made the introductions. "Drew Warner, Gary Jason, Roy Alabado, and this is Patty Molnar. Susy Jensen is out today taking her physical. She'll be back tomorrow."

Hands were shaken, guy shakes even from Patty Molnar. No one said anything, just nodding at the introduction.

"Whatta you got for us, and where did you get it?" Callahan asked.

"C'mon, boss, is that a joke?" Warner asked. "From the dark side, where else?"

"Give us the short version," Callahan said.

Gary Jason waved the wad of papers in his hands. "Believe it or not, there was not a whole lot of info out there, even on the dark side. He's married to a beautiful woman and has a child who is eight years old. The story is he was married two or three times prior to this marriage, and when the women couldn't produce a child, they were . . . disposed of. He lives and breathes for this little girl. Just loves her to death. Not much of a husband. He whores around. If the wife minds, she doesn't let it show. He travels a lot, at least once a month. We have his address and the shops that he patronizes. He lives at the end of a neighborhood street, the last house. We did a Google Earth search and have the printouts. Nothing out of the ordinary except he has a swimming pool. People in Tijuana do not have swimming pools, at least in the village where he lives.

"He's a creature of habit, has a routine. Which is good for us if this is a snatch and grab. As far as we can tell, he gets no company. But he's always on his cell phone. He leaves his house every day around eleven forty-five. Goes to Mass at the only church in town. He pays the priest to say a Mass at that time of the day because he doesn't want to go to an early morning Mass. He's the only attendee. After Mass, he heads down the street to a little café, where he eats lunch. He eats the same thing every day, tamales. The rumor is he taught the woman who does the cooking how to make them. He has two glasses of sangria followed by a cup of strong black coffee. He sits at his private table under an umbrella and smokes a Cuban cigar. No one goes near him except the woman who serves him his food. He waves to people, says hello to others while he watches what's going on on the busy street, which is usually nothing, just people going about their daily lives. When he's ready to leave, he hands out coins to any of the children who are around. Then he goes home and stays there. End of Beteo Mezaluma's day."

"He has a helicopter and a Learjet," Roy Alabado said. "He can fly both of them, but he has a pilot on standby he prefers to use for his travels."

Patty Molnar held up some pictures. "All of these are of the little girl, named Alicia. She's dressed in different out-fits, always dresses with ruffles and bows. In every picture, she's wearing shiny black patent leather shoes, Mary Janes they're called, and white socks with lace around the top. She has ribbons in her hair, which is quite long and curly, almost down to her waist. She looks like one of those an-gels you see on Christmas cards. And she wears a gold cross and chain around her neck. As you can see, she is a beautiful child. It's easy to see why the father dotes on her.

The mother, they say, is a real beauty, but there are no pictures. Her name is Elena."

"That's it?" Callahan asked.

"All we could dig up unless you want us to physically go across the border, but we all know no one is going to talk. No one, so what's the point?" Warner said.

Callahan looked at Snowden and shrugged.

"Thanks, guys. Get back to what you were doing. Don't leave the building, though, okay?"

Callahan said to Snowrden, "If I might make a suggestion."

"By all means."

"Liechtenstein is superb followed by the Antilles to stash money. Stay as far away as you can from the Caymans."

"I'll pass it on, thanks."

Snowden's cell phone rang. It was Abner.

Both men leaned closer to the table, where Snowden's cell phone was in speaker mode. "Phil says a piece of cake. All he needs is ten minutes' notice. Open lines all the way around. But he does want to know how long you want them to stay down. He said it's tricky. It's all about the satellites."

"Until we do the snatch and grab and make a clean getaway. Could be anywhere from an hour to maybe five or six. I'd like us back at Pinewood before they become operable again. There's no way I want him or his people getting in touch with the Karas brothers until we have Mezaluma under lock and key."

"You've got it. Call me." Snowden reached out, turned off his phone, and stuck it into one of the many pockets of his cargo pants.

Callahan dug at his beard. "From the sound of what I just heard, I'd say we're good to go. All we need is a time now. Work on that while I go talk to my team. We do what we call a ready drill before we even attempt something like this."

"I'll be right here. Thanks, Callahan."

"In the meantime if you need anything, call Mom. By the way, her name is Peg."

"Will do."

Chapter Sixteen

Charles looked around at the team assembled in his kitchen. Everything was neat and tidy, and the coffeepot was working at full speed as he watched the members of his disgruntled team mumble and mutter to one another about downtime, wasted time, the need for action, then let loose on the incredible rainfall of the past few days. "I'm just glad I don't live out here," Maggie complained. "No matter where you step, it's ankle-deep mud. The good news is the weatherman said it's going to stop raining by noon, and the sun will be out. It will take weeks for the ground to dry out."

"Thank you, Maggie Spritzer, for the weather tutorial. If you're done complaining, let's hear what happened during the night. With the time difference between here and California, where Snowden is, and in China, where Harry's friends are, there must be some kind of news. It's nine o'clock here, so it's six in the morning where Avery is. What do we know about him, and what's going on?" Ted asked.

Dennis chirped up that he would like an update on Harry's Triad friends.

"I can tell you what I know about Avery, but Harry will have to talk to you about the Triad. Right now, Avery and his new colleague, Duke Callahan, are inside a bodega in

Tijuana. Attached to the bodega is a little café where Beteo Mezaluma goes for his daily meal of tamales. They broke into the bodega around four this morning and are waiting for the little lady who owns it and cooks the tamales.

"Their plan is to stay there until Mezaluma shows up for his daily lunch. They'll add a few extra ingredients to his food and his sangria. Just enough to make him a little woozy but still able to walk on his own. Mr. Callahan's team of five will be helping to move things along. His team consists of three men and two women who just came off an assignment and were on a five-day hiatus but agreed to help out. The men will be doing the surveillance outside, and the two women will head to his home to . . . ah . . . discuss things with his wife.

"As I told you earlier, Mezaluma has his own Learjet and a helicopter, which he knows how to fly but rarely does. He has a pilot on standby twenty-four/seven. Avery's plan is to get him to the airfield where the plane and helicopter are in their hangars. Callahan can fly both. The plan is to . . . um . . . dispose of the pilot somehow. Avery didn't go into detail on that. If they manage to actually get airborne, the plan is to fly here with Senor Mezaluma. Callahan thinks he can get clearance and get him through customs. I say he *thinks* he can do it. It is not a given. The landing will be at a private airport at which he has connections. Avery has made arrangements to be picked up by his people and will bring us a new guest for our chamber down below. Sometime late this evening."

"Sounds like a lot of *ifs*," Jack said.

"Yes, it is," Charles said solemnly.

"What do the two women operatives hope to gain by going to the house where he lives?" Maggie asked.

"A woman-to-woman kind of thing, mother to mother possibly. Avery said the rumor is that it is not, by any means, a happy marriage. Mezaluma plucked her out from her family and said he was going to make her his bride so she could give him an heir. His other two or three wives were unable to do that. What that means is there is no love there. But we already discussed this. Their thinking is she will help and hand over whatever it is they want from her with the promise that her husband will never return. That's assuming she has access to whatever it is the boys want. There have to be records somewhere. Timing is everything."

At the word *timing*, everyone in the room looked at Abner.

Abner threw his hands in the air. "How many times do I have to tell you all that taking down a cell tower is not easy. You don't just wave a magic wand, and poof it goes down. You have to wait for the satellite to be in the right position. Once it is overhead, it's a piece of cake. Like I said, ten minutes." He sighed. "That means that Phil, who is on this, has to wait for just the right moment. You want it to go down at noon. That might not be possible. It might have to go down . . . say . . . at ten o'clock. You have to prepare, or, I should say, Avery and that guy Callahan have to be ready. I have an open line with Phil right now. He's thinking at the moment it might be one twenty-seven. Somebody needs to call Avery and apprise him of that. Like now would be a good time."

Charles had his cell in his hand and was tapping out a code that would allow him to speak with Avery no matter where he was in the world. His first words were, "From here on in we need to keep this line open. Abner seems to think Phil can shut down the tower around one twenty-seven our time, ten twenty-seven your time. Possibly sooner. Are you following me here, Avery?"

"I am, Sir Charles. Callahan and I are in place. The little lady who owns this bodega is being very helpful. Very. It's as we thought—there is no love here in this town for that bastard. Yes, he is the *patrone*, but he rules by fear. In public, they sing his praises, and in private, they curse him and his very existence. Even the priest is afraid of him. There is not a soul in this place who will be sorry to see him go and never come back."

"Have you been able to find out if the man has any kind of security, given the way he walks out and about so freely?" Charles asked.

"Only locals, whom he pays a few pesos to be his eyes. There is no muscle there, if that's what you're asking. At least according to Senora Santos, who owns this bodega. She said if she puts the word out, no one will hassle us. She seems to be the real thing, Sir Charles. Callahan agrees. Everyone around here is related in some way. She has a helper who comes in around the middle of the morning, a young girl, someone's third cousin of another cousin, that kind of thing. She will tell her to leave and spread the word. I didn't want to take on that responsibility without checking with you first. Bear in mind that we will be parading this guy through town and out to the airfield."

"Do it," Charles said. "Keep this line open."

Charles turned to the group. "You all heard that, so no sense in repeating it. Abner, inform your friend of these developments."

"I wish I were out there with them," Allison Bannon said wistfully. "I live for the day I can get my hands around that man's neck, so I can personally choke the life out of him."

There didn't seem to be any answer to that declaration, so the room went as silent as a tomb.

Harry suddenly jumped up. "Sorry, folks, I gotta go! My guys will be arriving in a little over an hour." Jack and Cyrus jumped up, ready to leave. "*No!* You stay here. These guys spook too easy. I work better alone. Remember, we don't even know how they managed to get here. There's going to be a lot of back-and-forth going on with the authorities. China . . . well, they're the bad guys. I'll bring them here the minute we clear customs. Be ready for us. I need your car keys, Jack. I came on the Ducati." Jack tossed him the keys.

"Now what?" Maggie asked. "When do we send the personal note inviting the Karas brothers to the private luncheon? I'm thinking now would be a good time. Or as close to when the tower goes down, so they can't contact Mezaluma. What that means is I have to go back to town, get the personal note I wrote that I left at the house, contact a messenger, and have him pick it up and take it to the hotel. Tell me what you want me to do."

Charles weighed her words. "Go, but take Ted or Dennis with you. No one goes alone anywhere from here on out. Except Harry. When you get to your house, call here, leave the line open but have your messenger in place in the lobby of the Sofitel so he can turn it over to the Karas brothers' security team. Tell the messenger his orders are to wait fifteen minutes for a response. If there is no response, he is to leave, and the invitation is null and void. Word it however you like, but just be sure they understand there is a deadline for the luncheon *tomorrow*."

Maggie and Ted were up and out the door within moments. She called over her shoulder, "Rain stopped. I can see some sun out toward the highway!"

"There doesn't seem to be anything for me to do here, so if you all don't mind, I'm going out to the barn to see my kids. When it's time for us to leave, they are going to miss all the animals. Andy formed a real attachment to one of the cats, and he calls him Baby Boo. He carries him everywhere and asked for a basket because sometimes he gets heavy. That's another memory I might have missed if I weren't here. I don't know how to thank all of you. I know, I know, I keep saying that, but I feel like I have to say it."

"Go see your children," Charles said gently. "Take this tray of brownies for them and let me whisk up a container of juice."

Allison stood by the door, straining to see the ray of sunlight Maggie said she saw. It wasn't visible to her eyes, but then she saw a glimmer. She smiled just as Charles handed her two shopping bags. "I put their lunch in there, too. I don't think it's a good idea for them to be here in the house right now, with so much getting ready to go down. Call me from time to time so I can update you. You'll be able to hear when Harry arrives with our guests and when Maggie returns. Then you join us."

Jack poured himself a cup of coffee as soon as the door closed behind Allison. Cyrus got up and went to the door, Lady right behind him with her pups. All exited in an orderly procession. They were back ten minutes later, their paws muddy and wet.

"I'll clean them up. It will give me something to do while we wait, and yes, Charles, I will then wash the towels," Dennis said. At Cyrus's bark, he hastened to add that he would also fold them when they were dry.

"I don't think I've ever been so bored in my entire life," Jack groused. "If I drink any more coffee, I'll be bouncing off the ceiling. Ask Snowden what's going on out there."

"It's breakfast time out there, as you well know, while we're approaching the lunch hour. This is simply dead time. Accept it, there are no other options at this time."

Jack continued to grumble, much to Cyrus's dismay. He growled and shifted position. Translation: *Either do something or keep quiet.* Jack opted for the latter as he let his mind wander to Harry's meeting with the Triad. He looked at his watch. If the Chinese flight was on time, it should have landed or be about to land. He envied Harry right at that moment.

*   *   *

Harry stood off at a distance as he waited for the sleek new Gulfstream to land at the international terminal. The sun, which was now out in full force, shone down on the aircraft skin, making it sparkle like a huge diamond. Harry wondered how much it had cost. Not that he cared, but he was curious. He knew he had a good fifteen minutes until the aircraft came to a complete stop, and the passengers were permitted to disembark. Then he had to escort said passengers to customs unless Ky had somehow made other arrangements.

Harry Wong was good at waiting. He simply withdrew into his inner core and let peace reign through his body. He could stand in his present position for hours on end and not move a muscle. While he *could* do that, he elected not to. He wanted to see what he called the grand finale, the Triad tripping off the plane to step onto American soil.

Harry ticked off the minutes in his head until the sound of powerful engines whined down to pure silence. Five more minutes passed before the shiny new doors opened, and a staircase was wheeled to the open door by airport workers. Two burly Chinese men, who looked like Sumo wrestlers, descended the steps, carrying portable wheelchairs. A third man followed. He watched as the chairs were unfolded and set in place. The three men looked at the approaching group of men, three Chinese and three American, the Americans dressed in airport security outfits. Customs, he thought. Or people with authority who could direct the newcomers to a safe haven. The burly men bowed respectfully before they headed back up the staircase.

Five minutes later, the three men who had carried the wheelchairs down the stairs appeared in the open doorway. Each man carried a frail, elderly Chinese man. Harry, who did his best not to laugh, thought they looked like

Chinese mummies with their long, straggly gray hair and mustaches that reached to midchest. All wore thick glasses, thicker than the proverbial Coke bottle glasses so often referred to.

The three ancients wore colorful kimonos festooned with gold-embroidered dragons on the sleeves and lapels. Their heads were lowered to avoid the glare of the sun. Harry did notice that their hands were not visible but tucked into the wide sleeves of their kimonos. He giggled to himself. That Ky, he was such a prankster.

The three men settled the ancients in the wheelchairs, then handed over all the required documentation to the three American officials while the three Chinese men bowed and chanted something that sounded like pure bullshit to Harry's ears.

No one moved, there was no dialogue. One of the Americans pulled a rubber stamp out of an envelope he had carried in his pocket. He stamped and stamped and then stamped some more. Or else, Harry thought, the stamp ran out of ink. Regardless, the three ancients were free to go but not before there were more bows, more head bobbing.

Harry raced over to the van that would take the Triad to the ring road that would lead them out to the highway. He slid open the panel door, yelled to the driver that he would meet them three miles down the road at the Mobile gas station.

"What! What!" Ky screeched. "What happened to 'Great performance, you could have fooled me, man, you are one crafty son of a bitch'?"

Harry gave an airy wave as he sprinted off to the parking area, where he had left Jack's BMW. He almost choked on his own laughter.

Seventeen minutes passed before the panel van careened into the Mobile station. Harry got out of Jack's car, which he had parked next to a Dumpster.

To Harry's surprise, it was a boisterous, warm-and-fuzzy greeting, with lots of back clapping, cheek kissing, and high fives. "What happened to bowing to my superiority?" Harry asked.

"We don't do that shit anymore, bro. Only the ancients hold to the old ways. We do it in their presence to show respect. We walk and talk just like you do over here in this wilderness. We're the new breed, or haven't you heard? Is that your car?" Ky asked, pointing to Jack's BMW. "I was expecting a Bentley," he cackled.

"Where's your gear?" Harry asked.

"What gear? You think because we're Chinese we travel with that crap we make for your people. You're looking at it," he said, touching a nylon backpack that looked fully loaded to Harry's eyes. "Now that we're rich, we can buy whatever we want when we need it. By the way, I'd appreciate some walking-around money. Free and trust goes a long way, but when you need clean underwear, you need money to buy it. It's a deal breaker, Harry. And you more than anyone should know it pays to travel light."

"So what are we waiting for, a bus, a train, or are we leaving in this kiddy car?" Ling asked.

"Another comedian. Just what I need. Get your asses in there, and we can be on our way," Harry growled.

Inside the car, the Triad turned serious, the fun and guy talk over. Now it was down to business. "Talk to us. Tell us where we're going, what we can expect, and what you want the outcome to be. We like to think about things a bit, you know, run them up the flagpole to see if we think they will fly. You got your side down pat?"

"Pretty much." Harry explained about Snowden and the California connection with Duke Callahan and his global security business. "With the three-hour time difference, it confuses things. Reaching the Karas brothers can't be done until the cell tower goes down. Time. Everything takes time."

"I've heard of him and his company. He's got a sterling reputation. Harry, were you bullshitting me when you told me you guys were the ones who took down the Internet? How the hell did you do that? I thought only a terrorist organization or something like that could actually do it. You must travel these days with some mighty powerful dudes. How'd that happen, Harry? Seriously, I want to know."

"If I told you, I'd have to kill you."

"Don't you mean *try* to kill me?"

"No. I meant what I said. Knowledge isn't always a good thing. Old Confucius saying," Harry said, and laughed.

"You're such a dick, Harry. I don't want to know anyway because if I did know, I might lose sleep over it, and I sleep pretty good as it is."

"You should get married and have some kids," Harry said. "Give some thought to who is going to take care of you when you become one of the ancient ones. Paying someone to take care of you is a lot different from a family member who does it because they love you. You guys are rich now; save that money for down the road. Just between us, I heard some talk about if we're successful, they're willing to throw in a *bonus*."

"Okay, Dad," Ky drawled. "*Bonus* is a word. A word I happen to love, but it does need clarification. We need to hear a dollar amount. Seriously, Harry, I hear you. We all hear you. We talked about it on the plane nonstop. We have a plan for when we get back home. Don't worry about us. We're just yakking here for fun."

Harry wasn't sure if he believed his old friend or not. Maybe it was better that he didn't know, but he did respond to the question: "Another million each. Good old U.S. currency. No taxes. No paper trail. Clean as a whistle. Think about *that*. What that means is don't go pissing off my people.

"We're almost there. Another five miles, and you get to meet everyone."

The minute Harry approached the gates, he could hear all the dogs barking. The gates opened wide, and he roared through, blasting the horn three sharp blasts. The kitchen door opened, and everyone inside the house piled out to greet the newcomers.

Introductions were made. Hands were shaken. Eye contact was made. Out of the corner of his eye, Jack could see Allison Bannon sprinting toward them from the barn. Harry introduced her.

Lady and her pups decided they weren't needed, so they moved off to their special places to take care of business. Not so Cyrus, who stood glued to Jack's side. Jack could feel the big dog quivering. It was clear to him that Cyrus didn't know what to make of the strange newcomers who had just arrived.

"So this is our team?" Ky said.

Harry pointed to Jack, then Allison, then tapped his own chest. A yip from Cyrus made him grin. "And our canine friend here. His name is Cyrus. All told, we are a seven-man team. I told you that on the phone."

"You didn't tell us the seventh member was a damn dog," Ling said.

"Well, I'm telling you now," Harry shot back.

"No dogs!" Momo said. "They get in the way. No dogs!"

Cyrus literally started to vibrate. *Oh, shit*, Jack thought. *Here we go.*

Harry eyeballed Ky, the undisputed leader of the Triad, who was looking back at him, a strange expression on his face. "Well! Is there a problem? The dog goes, or we scratch the deal. That means no dollars, and you'll have to give back the plane. It's a no-brainer."

"Prove he's a warrior," Ling snarled, stepping forward.

Harry let loose with a loud sigh. "Oh, man, you really don't want to go there, do you? Correct me if I'm wrong here. You want to go up against this dog. Is that what you're saying?" He looked at Ky for confirmation. Ky simply rolled his eyes and shrugged.

Ling stepped into the middle of the courtyard and waited. Jack walked Cyrus to the dueling position. He leaned down and whispered in the big dog's ears, "This isn't shits and giggles, Cyrus. I know you know this, but it never hurts to hear it again. It's the eyes. *Never* take your eyes off your adversary. Never. And remember this, he only has two legs, you have four. Buck-ass naked, the guy weighs maybe one-forty. You have the edge, and you have those beautiful teeth I brush every day. Remember the eyes. I'm going to stand back now. Make me proud, big guy."

Team Cyrus moved to be closer to Jack. Eyes wide, they watched as Ling approached Cyrus. Cyrus didn't move. He waited, stone still. They could all hear Ling muttering some gobbledygook that didn't faze Cyrus at all. He just stood stiff and tall.

A blue jay took that moment to swoop across the courtyard, and it was all Cyrus needed. Team Cyrus watched a black streak hit the air as though it were going to chase the blue jay. Instead, powerful jaws locked on Ling's neck in less than a nanosecond. The two Triad members let loose with a shrill "Eiowww!" Team Cyrus clapped, whistled, and stamped their feet.

"Release!" Jack said. Cyrus obeyed and sprinted to stand next to his master. Ling dropped to the ground, stunned.

"Beautiful, buddy, just beautiful!" Jack said loud enough for everyone to hear.

Team Cyrus waited. Would the Triad feel shame? Would they walk away?

Ling got up off the ground. He massaged his neck. Not a drop of blood. A smile tugged at the corner of his lips. He trotted over to Cyrus and dropped to his knees, so he could be eye level. "You are a true warrior. I bow to you in respect. You have my admiration." He bowed low a second time.

Cyrus dipped his head and accepted the accolade. Then he nudged Ling to get up. He held out one of his massive paws. Translation: *This is the U.S. We shake hands here.* Ling held out his hand.

"And he understands Greek, and he can bark in Greek, too. And, he can fold towels," Dennis said as proudly as if he were the one who had trained the dog.

"This is true, Harry? I get the Greek part, but folding towels!" Ky said, awe and admiration ringing in his voice.

"Hell yes! I told you this was no Mickey Mouse production."

"Speaking of Mickey Mouse, is Disney still on the table?" Ky laughed.

Harry just rolled his eyes. That Ky was such a card sometimes.

The gang moved then to return to the house. Jack lagged behind with Cyrus. "Buddy, you made me feel so proud today. I don't have the words to tell you what a great job you did, and you didn't even break the skin." Jack dropped to his knees and looked Cyrus in the eye. "That guy Ling, he's really good. They're all good. When he said you were a true warrior, he meant it. Now when we go back to see Dr. Pappas, we'll have a story to tell him. He's going to love the compliment Ling gave you. We won't mention the blue jay. Then again, any diversion is a plus for our side."

Cyrus nuzzled Jack under the chin. He let loose with a

series of soft yips that could have meant anything. Whatever it was, Jack knew that his dog loved him. That was all
that mattered. As they strolled back to the house side by
side, Jack said, "It's the eyes. The window to the soul. The
eyes tell us everything."

Cyrus entered the kitchen ahead of Jack to celebrity sta-
tus as the three Chinese wanted to know everything there
was to know about him. He allowed himself to be petted,
scratched, and belly rubbed along with taking a few offered treats until he had had enough. He took his place
under the table and waited for Charles to serve lunch.

He dropped off to sleep, knowing he was a true warrior.

Chapter Seventeen

Avery Snowden, Duke Callahan at his side, strolled
down the broken and cracked sidewalk or what had
once been a sidewalk. They stopped from time to time to
look at the various stalls full of junk being peddled.

Avery suddenly yanked Duke into a dark-looking alley-
way that smelled of things better not spoken of. "It's
Charles. He says another five minutes, and the cell tower
will be going down. We should head back." The time was
11:20.

"If Senora Santos is being truthful with us, then Mezaluma should be leaving his house about now for the
twenty-five-minute walk to the church. We need to be in
place long before he gets there for lunch. Did she say how
long the Mass is?" Callahan asked.

"Thirty minutes. She said he arrives around twelve-
forty and has his first glass of sangria while he waits for
her to bring his tamales. Along with his second glass of
sangria. We need to move, chop chop," Snowden said, his
gaze sweeping the street for anything out of the ordinary.
Everything looked the same as it had yesterday and an
hour ago.

The two men were traveling the back alleys so that they
could enter the bodega by the back entrance. They opened

the door quietly and stepped into the kitchen. Senora Santos looked up but said nothing as she worked on the tamales she was making. A huge pitcher of sangria sat on a small table near the doorway, a glass next to it.

Avery reached into one of the pockets in his cargo pants and brought out a vial. He emptied it into the pitcher. He looked around for something to stir it with but couldn't see anything so he dipped his entire hand in the pitcher and swirled the pink-looking liquid around and around, liking the sound of the clinking ice cubes.

"Not that it matters, but when was the last time you washed your hands?" Callahan grinned.

"Probably sometime yesterday, seeing as how we were up all night and neither one of us showered. You worried about germs or something?"

"Nah, just making conversation."

Snowden put his index finger to his lips for Callahan to be quiet, and held up the phone so both could hear Charles say, "Tower will go down in precisely eighty-six seconds."

Snowden started mouthing the numbers, his eyes on Senora Santos's cell phone, which he had turned on minutes ago and was lying in plain view on a butcher-block table. He almost let loose with a loud whistle when he saw the face turn gray. "Done!" he hissed to Callahan.

"Our boy just arrived," Snowden added. "It's just the way Senora Santos said. The man is truly a creature of habit."

Both men watched and waited. Mezaluma looked up and snapped his fingers, the signal that Senora Santos was to bring his first glass of sangria. Both men were stunned at how calm she was, how her hands were totally steady, with no tremors at all.

When Senora Santos returned to the kitchen, she whispered, "I truly hope this is the last time I will ever have to serve that evil creature." Both men assured her that they would make her wish come true.

"By now, the whole town knows not to interfere. When you leave here with him, no one will accost you, and if they do it is for . . . display only. No harm will come to either of you. This I promise." Both men nodded at the woman's bravery.

Snowden and Callahan waited for another snap of the fingers. Time for the tamales and another glass of the man's favorite beverage.

"My agents should be at Senor Mezaluma's house by now," Callahan said as he looked at his watch.

"His movements are sluggish," Snowden whispered from his position on the kitchen side of the curtain that separated the eating area from the kitchen. "I don't even think he's chewing, just swallowing and washing it down with the sangria. Oops, looks like he's done, he's snapping his fingers."

"Yes, senor," Senora Santos said as she bustled through the doorway. "Are you not well, senor? You did not finish your lunch. Do you want your coffee now?"

Snowden and Callahan were both surprised at how gruff and guttural the man's voice sounded when he spoke. "I am well, have no fear. I will pass on the coffee and go home now. The padre's short sermon made me tired." Senora Santos scampered back to her kitchen.

Snowden came up to the table from the left and Callahan from the right. Both men reached down at the same time to lift Mezaluma from his chair. He started to sputter indignantly, but his heart wasn't in it. "Who are you? Take your hands off me."

"We're your new best friends. If we take our hands off you, you will fall flat on your face. We're simply helping you along. Or would you like us to call someone to take you home?"

"My phone isn't working," Mezaluma said, slurring his words. "The damn thing never works."

"We'll take you home?" Callahan said.

"Why?"

"Weren't you listening? Because we are your new best friends, and you have no one else to call because your phone isn't working," Snowden said.

"Where is the airport where you keep your plane?" Callahan asked.

"Why do you want to know that?"

"Because we are going to fly you home. Tell us how to get there," Snowden said, cheerfulness ringing in his voice.

"A taxi. The driver knows where it is. Fly me home?" Mezaluma stopped in his tracks and eyed both men suspiciously. "No." His knees buckled just as a rickety taxi stopped in the middle of the road. Both men shoved Mezaluma into the backseat, where he fell over in a fat lump.

"Take us to his airfield. You know who he is, right?" Callahan barked.

"Si, senor, I know where it is. I thank all the gods in heaven that you are taking him away. It is not far, a mile or so. There is a pilot there who is very loyal to . . . to that devil. Be very careful, senor."

Mezaluma started to snore in the backseat as the rusty old taxi chugged down the rutted road. "There, just ahead, is the airfield. What do you want me to do?"

"Take us as close as you can, so we don't have to drag him too far. Where is the pilot, do you know?"

"He will come out to greet you. This is as far as I am permitted to go. I have been here before many times, so I know this. Plus, I am the only taxi in town."

Snowden reached into his pocket and withdrew a wad of U.S. money. He handed it over to the taxi driver.

"If this money is for my silence, keep it. I will not breathe a word of this to anyone. I am doing this for free."

Snowden nodded but insisted the taxi driver take the money. In the end, he did, with a wide smile just as a man emerged from a small shack off to the left of the plane and helicopter. He let loose with a long stream of Spanish that the driver returned in kind.

"He said we cannot come here; we must go back because he did not get a call we were coming. I told him the cell phones are not working and that Senor Mezaluma is asleep in the backseat and to help you put him on the plane. He says he will not do that."

"Really!" Callahan drawled. He walked six short steps to the pilot and hit him square in the jaw. He dropped to the ground and went still. To the driver, he said, "Vamoose. We can take it from here. We'll tie him up and put him in the shack. Tell someone to cut him loose in six or seven hours. Not a minute before. *Comprende?*"

"*Si. Si.*"

It took every bit of muscle both men had to drag the drugged man in the backseat out of the taxi. They let him fall to the ground. They then dragged the surly pilot, not caring if he got road burn on his body, over to the shack. They pushed him in, duct-taped him with tape from Callahan's backpack, and shut the door. They sprinted back across the rutted tarmac to where Mezaluma was still out cold.

"Man, would you look at that!" Callahan said, pointing to the helicopter. "I'd give my eye teeth for one of those babies. It's a Black Hawk. Where in the hell did that guy get one of those? And it's new!" he said, his voice betraying his outrage.

"You want one of those?" Snowden asked.

"I'd kill for one of those. Even I, with all my government and military connections, can't get one."

"So let's take it instead of the plane, assuming you can

fly it. When we get to your place, we leave it behind and take one of your planes to D.C. That works for me."

"Just like that, we steal a Black Hawk?"

"Yeah, just like that. Who is going to complain? Not that guy in the shack—it happened on his watch, and besides, no one in this jerkwater town cares about the man's helicopter. You *can* fly it, right?"

"I can fly anything that has wings. Okay, let's get this guy aboard and hit the clouds. We shouldn't have any trouble getting clearance from here since he's who he is. I'll call a guy I know on the U.S. side letting him know I'm the pilot of this rig. Haven't you figured out yet that it's not what you know, it's who you know?"

Snowden laughed as he helped pull, drag, and push the overweight devil onto the helicopter. When they had him secure, Callahan checked everything, and within minutes, they were airborne. He set the Black Hawk down fifteen minutes later on U.S. soil. The two men high-fived one another as they eyed the sleeping man strapped into his seat.

"We have at least another fifteen minutes for my people to get here to transport him to my plane. Then I want to park this baby in my space. Snowden, are you sure I can keep this bird?"

"Sure as I'm standing here. The paperwork is on you, though. I do know a few . . . forgers who can help you through the process." Snowden cackled at his own wit.

"Probably the same ones I know," Callahan said gleefully.

While they waited, they tried to reach Callahan's agents, but there was no response. Snowden looked worried. "My people do not fail. If they aren't answering their sat phones, that means they are otherwise occupied. I had no idea you Brits were such worrywarts."

"And I had no idea you Americans are such cocky sons of bitches."

"Trust me, okay, my people will deliver. By the time we're ready to head to D.C., we'll know what they know and the information will be in Sir Charles's hands."

Back in the Tijuana neighborhood, where Beteo Mezaluma resided with his beautiful wife and pretty little daughter, things were going well, indeed. Elena Mezaluma was showing Patty and Susy where her husband kept his records. "He does not trust computers. He writes everything down. All his devil work is chronicled in these four ledgers. What else do you need from me or need me to do?"

Susy explained about her daughter and the dress-up outfits she wanted the little girl to try on so they could take pictures. Patty pulled out a long blond wig made especially for young cancer victims and explained in detail what she wanted and hoped to gain with her and her daughter's cooperation. Elena reluctantly agreed.

"What's going to happen to us now?" Elena asked fearfully.

"Nothing. Other than you are free of him. You can stay in this house, or you can return to your family. Everything here now belongs to you. You also inherit whichever aircraft my confederates did not take, so I'd sell that first thing before someone confiscates it," Susy said as she neatly aligned all the costumes she'd brought for the little girl. "I got these at a shop that makes costumes for little girls who enter beauty pageants. I'll leave them with you so your daughter and her friends can play dress-up. Fetch your daughter, please; we're in a bit of a hurry."

Five hours later, when Duke Callahan shut down his private plane, all the information his operatives had gathered was in Sir Charles's hands, and his team was safely back in the Chula Vista office, congratulating themselves on a job well done. All of them knew there would be a generous bonus in their next paycheck because Duke Callahan was a generous, fair-minded boss.

"There's our ride," Snowden said.

"Where?" Callahan said, straining to see through the foggy glass. "Ah, the ambulance!"

"That devil is going to wake up in about twenty minutes. We need to be on our way out to the farm. The ambulance will follow, with siren screaming, and we'll be going a hundred miles an hour. Be prepared."

"I gotta say, Snowden, I like your style. You can come work for me anytime."

"How about you come work for me?" Snowden shot back.

"You can't afford me." Callahan grinned.

"You sure about that?" Snowden inquired slyly.

"Where's *our* ride?" Callahan asked as four of Snowden's men loaded the gurney into the back of the ambulance. "What about the paperwork?"

"All taken care of. Our ride is over there," Snowden said, pointing to a sleek silver Maserati.

The messenger from Quick Fast Service entered the Sofitel hotel right on schedule. In his right hand he carried an elegant embossed envelope. He was dressed impeccably, in a crisp blue company uniform. He walked over to the registration desk and said, "Can you please tell me who is in charge of the Messrs. Karas? I want to deliver this envelope to him or her, as the case may be."

The clerk pointed to the far side of the lobby. "I believe it is the man seated in the burgundy chair nearest the elevator. If it isn't he, I'm sure he can tell you who it is," she said politely.

The messenger made his way to the burgundy chair and said, "Excuse me, sir. The clerk at the desk said you are in charge of security for the Messrs. Karas. I have a letter here from Countess Anna de Silva. I was told to deliver it and to wait fifteen minutes for a response. Can you please deliver it? I'll wait over there on the gray chair. I cannot wait longer than fifteen minutes. We need to be clear on that, sir."

The man, whose name was Adolpho, reached for the envelope, sniffed it, shook it, and nodded. He walked over to the elevator and pressed the button that would take him to the floor where the Karas brothers were. After leaving the elevator, he didn't bother to knock but simply opened the door and walked into a lavish suite of rooms. Ryland looked up from where he was sitting, annoyed that the symphony he was listening to was being interrupted.

His head of security handed over the envelope. "The messenger said that his instructions were to wait fifteen minutes and leave if you don't respond. What do you want me to do?"

Roland held up his hand, which meant wait.

"What is it?" Roland asked.

"A luncheon invitation for tomorrow at the countess's country estate. There's a map giving directions. Quick, Roland, call our benefactor and find out what he wants us to do."

"It went to voice mail."

"Keep trying. I'm not sure we should be making this decision on our own, and the clock is ticking," Ryland said, his eyes on his Rolex watch.

"Still no answer. It's not unusual. Just say yes, and if we have to cancel, then we cancel. Assuming we are able to reach our benefactor. He still isn't answering. Go with yes."

Ryland looked down at the invitation and bit down on his lower lip. This was a coup of sorts. Yes, it was short notice, but the countess was known for being eccentric. Finally, with five minutes to spare, he nodded to the security man and said, "Tell the messenger we will be delighted to attend tomorrow's luncheon."

The security man left the room and literally ran down the hall to the stairway, which he took because the elevator was too slow. He took the steps three at a time. He made it to the lobby just as the messenger was getting out of his chair and preparing to leave. Breathless, he said, "The Messrs. Karas will be delighted to attend the countess's luncheon tomorrow."

The messenger simply nodded and left the hotel. The moment he was outside, he called Maggie and said, "He said yes, and they will be delighted to attend." He could not keep himself from laughing at Maggie's whoop of joy.

Maggie clicked on her phone, and before Charles could even say hello, she announced, "It's a go. They will attend. Anything going on that I missed?"

"Not a thing, dear."

"Okay, then, Ted and I are on our way back to the farm. See ya."

It was a hair-raising ride out to Pinewood, one Duke Callahan said he would never forget. Nor would he forget the people he met, the two strange dogs whom he later swore knew what he was thinking before he knew it himself, the dungeons, the war room, and the cell where Beteo Mezaluma now slept and the Triad from China that stared at him stone faced.

"A package arrived by . . . mysterious means about fifteen minutes before you arrived. It's addressed to you, Mr. Callahan. I think it was flown here by a military jet. Is that possible?" Charles queried.

Callahan laughed. "You know that old saying, it's not what you know, it's who you know. It's your new guest's records in ledger form. It's all in there except for one thing. The names of the freighters, the boats, the ships that transport the children." He handed it over with a wild flourish. "You got any cold beer around here? Anything but Mexican beer will be fine."

Dennis rushed to the refrigerator and reached for a bottle of good old American beer, Budweiser, even if the company that made it had its headquarters in Belgium. Callahan downed it in one gulp and asked for another. Dennis happily obliged. He liked this big bear of a man.

"Oh, and a cuppa tea for my British friend here."

"Now what?" Jack asked.

"We head for the war room, talk to our new guest, and show him how we do things here at the farm. Not to be confused with the farm otherwise known as the CIA," Charles said, menace ringing in his voice.

Chapter Eighteen

The parade to the living room and the secret panel that would lead them down to the war room was made in silence. Almost.

"What the hell, Harry!" Ky hissed.

"You ain't seen nothing yet. I keep telling you, Ky, this is *not* a Mickey Mouse operation. Just go with the flow here, okay?"

As always, the gang saluted Lady Justice the minute Charles turned on all the lights. The Triad whistled softly as they looked around at the renovations Isabelle had done to this particular section of the dungeon.

"I saw a program on TV once of NORAD. This kind of looks like it," Ling said in awe, as he and his two colleagues looked on, their mouths open, their eyes glazed at what they were seeing.

"No one knows of this place?" Momo asked.

"Only those we want to know," Jack said. "And now you know."

"How long have you been doing this, Harry?" Ky whispered.

"What? You writing a book or something? The short answer is a long time. Now be quiet and observe the object of this mission. The hydra."

Beteo Mezaluma sat on the narrow bed in the oversize cell, looking dazed and miserable. He was also filthy dirty from being dragged across the courtyard, his clothing ripped. He was barefoot; his leather sandals were somewhere outside. His fat feet were as dirty as the rest of him, his toenails like claws. "When we couldn't decide how to get him down the moss-covered steps because of his girth, we put him on his already bruised back, gave him a shove, and he slid down to the bottom to land in a heap," Jack said.

"Where is this place? You kidnapped me! I will have you killed and not shed a tear over your deaths," Mezaluma snarled.

"Now, that's pretty funny seeing as how you're in a cell, and we're out here. But to answer your question, you are in Virginia in the United States. We flew you here earlier today." Pointing to Snowden and Callahan, Jack said, "These two gentlemen, your two new best friends, brought you here. After they stole your Black Hawk helicopter. I think by now your Learjet is in San Diego. Your wife said she didn't want it. Waste not, want not."

"Bastards!" A string of Spanish profanity followed.

"Speak English, or I'll knock your teeth out," Snowden said.

"Takes one to know one." Callahan grinned.

"What we have here are all your records." Charles held up the four thick ledgers that had just arrived. "You are the scum of the earth, Senor Mezaluma. What is not recorded in these ledgers are the names of the freighters, the ships, the boats, along with their routes and dates for the transportation of the children you kidnap. That's what we want from you now."

"I don't know what you're talking about. I deliver produce. Nothing more."

Jack whipped around and asked who had Mezaluma's

cell phone. Callahan handed it over. "This is your cell phone, you fat toad. We took down the cell tower so you wouldn't be able to use it. We listened to the messages and you have seventeen calls from the Karas brothers. You do know who they are, don't you? They are the two stooges who do your dirty work, along with a whole army of perverts like yourself. Now this is what you are going to do. I am going to write down on paper what you are to say when you call them back. Do you understand what I just said?"

Another string of fast and furious Spanish ripped from Mezaluma's mouth.

Callahan opened the cell door and punched the fat little man square in the mouth. Teeth flew in all directions. The fat little man howled as blood filled his mouth. "I told you to speak English. I warned you what I would do. There is a lady present, so do not do it again. Do you understand what I just said? Nod yes if you do."

Mezaluma's head bobbed up and down.

Dennis moved off to return with a roll of paper towels. He handed them to Callahan, who in turn ripped off several sheets and handed them to their guest, who tried to staunch the flow of blood from his mouth with shaking hands. "Barbarians!" he spat.

Jack stepped forward with a sheet of yellow paper torn from a legal tablet. He had used a black grease pencil and printed what he wanted Mezaluma's responses to be once the call was made to the Karas brothers. "Here's the drill, you fat pig. We dial the number, and you say only what is on this paper."

"Don't trust him," Allison snarled.

Harry looked at the Triad. "What's your thought on a four-way?"

The Triad pondered the question. "Seems like a viable solution." Ky grinned.

"Everyone out of the cell but our guest," Harry said as he stepped forward, followed by the Triad. Ky and Ling jerked both of Mezaluma's arms as far back as they could. Harry and Momo each grabbed a thigh and jerked backward. Mezaluma's dirty feet left the ground, leaving him suspended in midair. "Now, this is how it's going to work. You say what is on the paper, nothing else. You even try to say something other than that and we will snap every joint in your body and leave you here to die. Nod if you are willing to do what my colleague asks of you." Mezaluma's head bobbed.

Jack pressed the digits to the Karas brothers' cell phone. It was picked up on the first ring. "Speak!"

"This is Ryland, sir. We have been trying to reach you all day."

"Cell tower went down," Mezaluma lisped.

"You sound . . . different, sir."

"I was at the dentist. Why did you call me?"

"We got a luncheon invitation for tomorrow from Countess de Silva. We wanted to know if we should attend or not. This is what will decide if we are put on the list that I told you about. When we couldn't reach you, and the messenger was waiting for a response, I said yes. But we can cancel if you say so."

"Yes, attend and apprise me of what went on when you return."

"Yes, sir. Anything else?"

Harry gave Mezaluma's arm a good hard yank, and Ky did the same thing.

"No." Short and sweet. Jack disconnected the call.

Harry and the Triad dropped Mezaluma, who was now openly crying and still spitting blood. Everyone tiptoed around the mess on the floor to return to the corridor outside the cell.

Charles stepped forward, the ledgers in his hands. "We

know these belong to you. Your wife gave them to us. I commend you on your meticulous record keeping. Everything you recorded will go a long way with the authorities to prove you are the head of the human-trafficking and drug ring that has so successfully worked for you for many years. The head count, the dollar amounts paid for the children, the number of pounds and crates of drugs. We knew about the funeral homes and the nail salons, and these ledgers confirm it all. It's over now. Except for one thing. We need the names of the freighters, the boats, the ships, the cargo-transportation methods. We need their sailing records."

"I do not know what you are talking about. Those are not my ledgers. I sell and transport produce," Mezaluma snarled.

"Bullshit!" Callahan said.

"Maybe this will help you to remember," Charles said as he withdrew eight-by-ten glossy colored pictures of Mezaluma's daughter, Alicia, wearing a curly blond wig. He showed him six different provocative pictures. "Tell us what we want to know, or she goes on the auction block. None of the bidders will know her hair isn't blond until they take possession of her. You know what will happen then, don't you? They will send her out on the circuit. She'll be dead in a year, two at the most. And then the people you do business with won't want to trade with you anymore because you are a dishonest man. What's it going to be, Senor Mezaluma?"

The fat little toad sitting on the bed started to blubber.

"Oh, dear, I forgot something. We stole all your money. Abner, show Senor Mezaluma his various accounts. We did get them all, didn't we? As a reminder, we now own your Black Hawk, and the Learjet has almost certainly been sold by your wife to provide for her and your daughter," Charles said.

"Yes, indeedy, we got them all. He's a pauper. He couldn't buy an all-day sucker if he wanted to," Abner said proudly.

Abner stepped into the cell and held up his laptop. "Read it and weep, you filthy, perverted, disgusting son of a bitch!"

The gang watched as disbelief at what Mezaluma was seeing registered, followed at first by anger, then outrage. He started to curse and shake at the same time.

"Imagine making all that money selling produce!" Abner chortled. "We're all in the wrong business."

Charles waved the pictures of Mezaluma's daughter in front of him, waiting for a response.

"If I tell you what you want to know, will you let me go, so I can return to my wife and daughter?"

"Of course we will. We are not the barbarians you think we are," Jack said.

"How do I know I can trust you? Look what you did to me. You threatened to take my daughter."

"Well, when you put it like that, I guess I see your point. But, you have no other options," Jack said.

"I might as well be dead," Mezaluma whined.

"Well, that is an option, of course. The choice, of course, is yours. Do not cooperate with us, and we can have you killed or worse. Cooperate with us, and we can release you to return to your wife and daughter. Enough already, you want to play ball or not?"

"I don't believe this," Allison said. "That bastard is actually thinking about it!"

"I don't trust you. Take me back to Tijuana; then I will tell you everything you want to know."

"It doesn't work that way, senor. Last chance, or those four guys who had you suspended in the air for the phone call get you all to themselves," Jack said as he held out the yellow legal tablet and pen. "We're going to leave you here for an hour. When we return, if that tablet doesn't have the information we need, Alicia is on her way to the auction block, and it will be courtesy of the Karas brothers, who are being picked up as we speak."

"That will never happen. They have a forty-eight-man security team in place."

"And we have the FBI, Homeland Security, the CIA, and every other agency in our nation's capital at the ready. What are the odds of forty-eight trigger-happy goons surviving an onslaught like that?" Jack demanded.

Mezaluma folded into himself and curled up in a fetal position.

"One hour, you son of a bitch. If that tablet isn't filled up when we come back here, you are a dead man or worse."

After Jack locked the cell door, the team turned and returned to the kitchen. No one said a word. All they did was stare off into space, wondering what would happen an hour from now.

"Tea and coffee coming up," Charles said cheerfully.

"This next hour is going to be as long as eternity," Allison mumbled to no one in particular.

"C'mon, Cyrus, let's go for a walk," Jack said, opening the kitchen door. Cyrus scampered outside, followed by Lady and her pups. While the dogs romped, Jack sat down on Charles's favorite stone bench under the three-hundred-year-old oak tree that provided shade from the hot sun. It was quiet and peaceful, so he relaxed and let his mind race. So many children who would never be returned to their parents. While the ledgers recorded the sale of the girls, there was no mention of anyone who bought them or where they were taken after being purchased. Each child was given a number. There were no names. The buyers were designated with letters. Numbers and letters. How in the name of God could they track them down? He seriously doubted even Mezaluma knew the buyers' names. In the end, all they would be able to do was alert the proper authorities to put the various sailing vessels on their watch list. Possibly the captains of the ships might be of help, with life sentences in prison staring them in the face.

Jack knew he was being naive to think his team or any agency could stop the human trafficking. Maybe stop it for a little while until a new hydra took over. If there was any good to come out of this, it was that Abner had con-fiscated all of Mezaluma's money, which they could use to fight the bastards, so they never got a strong foothold again.

And if they put their best people on it, perhaps they could identify the parents of the lost children and anony-mously send them some money. Not that money would compensate or even come close to taking away their pain at their loss. He had to give that some serious thought. Somehow it didn't sound right, money for the loss of a child. Maybe a bucket of blood from one of the bad guys handed over to a grieving parent.

Jack didn't like where his thoughts were taking him. De-cisions that would be made would have to be made by professionals.

Cyrus ambled over to the stone bench and looked up at Jack as much as to say, *We'll get it done, and in the end, it will be what it will be. All we can do is our best.* Jack stroked the big dog's head with gentle hands. He looked toward the barn, where Allison's kids were happily doing school-type work and learning about farm animals. He smiled, knowing they were safe and sound and would now have their mother in their lives much more than before.

Jack looked down at his watch. Fifteen minutes to go. "You know what, Cyrus? Until those three kids came to us, I never thought I would or could kill anyone. If some-one asked for a volunteer list to pop that Mezaluma guy,

I'd be first in line. I mean that." Cyrus just stared up at his master. He tugged at his trouser leg. Time to go in.

Jack whistled sharply, and Lady and her pups raced up to them, panting.

"Time to go in, Cyrus."

Things were no different in the kitchen than before he had left. Jack looked pointedly at the clock, then at the gang. "I think it's time to go down to the war room. It's showtime!"

No one was more surprised than Jack when he saw Mezaluma scribbling furiously on the pad. He looked up and stopped writing. He waited for Charles to approach the cell he was in. Charles didn't open the door, just stood and waited for the man to hobble over to him and hand the legal tablet to him through the bars. He said nothing as he made his way back to the bed against the wall.

The gang retreated to the war room, where they all sat down at the table. "It's all here, the names of the ships, the names of the captains, their points of origin. Where the ships sailed to. The number of passengers disembarking at particular ports. It's not as detailed as I would like, but I doubt anyone could remember all those details. What is here will be more than enough for the proper authorities to do what they have to do. Now, the question is, where do we send it and to whom? After I make a dozen or so copies for safety reasons."

"Is there a way to fax it or send through an e-mail from here that won't show up anywhere?" Allison asked. "If you can do that, then I can tell you whom to send it to."

"I can do that," Abner said.

Charles looked at Allison. "Are you sure?"

"Yes, I'm sure."

"All right then, I'll make copies, and Abner, you do what you have to do."

"Since the CIA can only deal with matters that have a foreign dimension, I assume you want this information sent from a foreign country so that it can be used by the CIA, and they're given the credit, opposed to the FBI. Am I right on that, Allison?" She nodded to indicate Abner was right. "Okay, then. Whom do I send it to?"

"Luka Casselli. He trained me and was my section chief and my handler. When you send it, it has to look like it came from me. I have to use a code." She scribbled some numbers and letters on the yellow legal pad. "That's it."

"Do you . . . ah . . . want to send a personal message with this information?"

Allison grimaced. "You mean like, thanks for all the memories? No. Just send the information and tell him the . . . wait a minute. How are we going to get the ledgers to him?"

"How else but messenger?" Dennis said. "Plain brown paper tied with string. The messenger can leave them at the guardhouse. I guess that's the personal message."

Instead of wrapping the ledgers, Jack pulled on a pair of plastic gloves and wiped down the outside of all the ledgers before he slipped them into an oversize manila envelope. It was a snug fit, but he managed to get them all in. Then he taped the envelope shut.

Allison reached for the black permanent marker and started to write on the envelope. She addressed it to Luka Casselli and in the corner wrote Allison Bannon along with her identity code. "Done! It won't matter if my fingerprints are on the envelope or not."

"Who wants to take this into the village messenger shop?"

Espinosa volunteered. Charles handed him three one hundred–dollar bills. "That's for rush delivery, which means *now*. Wear gloves. Say you have psoriasis or something on your hands. Keep your head down, your ball cap low on your face. Those places have security cameras, and don't forget the sunglasses. Take the farm truck."

Charles looked over at Abner. "Let's say that in an hour from now, you can go ahead and e-mail Casselli, which will be as close to when the ledgers are delivered as we can get."

"Absolutely," Abner said, a wicked grin on his face.

Duke Callahan stood up. "Well, people, it was nice meeting you all, but I have a business to run, so I'm going to be heading on out. Nice working with you, Snowden. Like I said, for a Brit, you're okay in my book. Call me if you need me. I can find my way out. Take care, everyone."

Hands were shaken, a few back slaps were exchanged, but it was Allison who hugged the big man. "You take care and fly with the angels."

Even though the war room was full, it seemed empty once Duke Callahan left.

"What are we going to do with the hydra?" Allison asked, hatred ringing in her voice.

Abner raised his hands like a schoolboy. "As we all know, there is the dark side to the Internet, the underbelly. The sick and depraved live there in the darkness. Believe it or not, there is a circuit there for people like Mezaluma. That's how they get their kicks. I'd show you, but then it would be in your heads forever. It's better you don't see. I can get in touch and tell them where to pick him up. Of course, you have to dump him somewhere."

"Then what happens?" Allison asked, a bite in her words.

"The same thing that happens to all those children he stole from their parents. It's anyone's guess how long he'll last. The man has no conscience. He'll get whatever he deserves, and our hands are clean. In a manner of speaking. At least, we do not kill him, torture him, etcetera. Before you do that, take a vote. If the ayes have it, then we go for it."

Every voice in the room said, "Aye."

"Okay, I'll make contact. Avery, you're up. You and

your people will have to transport him to whatever location they give me."

Harry looked over at the Triad to see how they were reacting to what they'd just heard.

"What? You think that doesn't happen in China? More so than here. It's so common, no one pays attention anymore. Couldn't happen to a nicer guy," Momo said flippantly.

"Is there anything else to be done today? If not, we're on for ten tomorrow to prepare for a luncheon that won't take place, tomorrow or any other day, right?" Jack asked.

Everyone agreed.

"I'm going to take these guys back to the dojo so we can do some practice trials. We'll be here by ten in the morning. I forget, whose car am I driving?"

"Go ahead, take mine. I'll walk home," Jack said. "Cyrus loves the run through the fields."

The others followed Jack out the door, Allison, who was headed for the barn, the last. Jack couldn't help but notice her stiff shoulders, the set of her jaw. She wanted Senor Beteo Mezaluma dead, and she wanted to be the one to kill him.

"Allison, killing someone is quick and easy, then it's over. You don't do that anymore, remember? What's going to happen to that human piece of trash is far worse than killing him. He will die, but it will be slow. I can almost guarantee that very soon after it begins he will be praying for death."

"I know. I know. Jack, how do I get rid of the pictures I have inside my head of the thousands of children I couldn't save? Children he put out there. Tell me how," she whispered.

"I don't have the answer, Allison. You're going to get on

with your life with your kids. Time will help. A new life. You can start a club or an organization that will help kids. Stay involved. The rest of us will keep up the fight."

"Thanks, Jack. I'm glad I got to meet all of you. See ya in the morning."

"Yeah, see you in the morning," Jack said softly.

Chapter Nineteen

The day! At least that's how Charles and the gang thought of it.

The gang was seated around the dining-room table with breakfast on the sideboard. Something for everyone. Eggs, bacon, sausage, pancakes and waffles with soft butter and warm syrup, sweet melon. Unlimited coffee, tea, and juice. A feast.

The time was eight-thirty in the morning. The sun was out, and it looked like *the day* was going to be a beautiful one.

"Eat hearty, children," Charles joked. "It's going to be a very long day." They obeyed, even the Triad, who, to Harry's dismay, professed a love of all American food.

"I am going to violate my rule of not talking business at the table. We need to go through our plan one more time before you all leave for Annie's place. Fergus and I will follow after we square things away here." He looked at Allison and said, "Margie took the children to a location in the District that Avery provided earlier. One cannot be too careful." Allison merely nodded.

"I sure hope you guys are as good as Harry says you are," Dennis said as he reached for a crisp strip of bacon and crunched down on it after putting it in his mouth.

"Forty-eight guys is a serious obstacle to overcome. I can pitch in if you need me. I only have a brown belt, but I can hold my own." He shrugged when no one commented on his offer.

"There is a question of vehicles," Maggie said. "Ted, Espinosa, Dennis, and I will be in the van. Where do we park it?"

"In the back. It won't be visible from the front driveway, but I do expect the security team will do a walkabout," Fergus replied.

"Annie's car and Jack's BMW will be in front. Jack is the one who will open the door for the Karas brothers on their arrival. He's going to pose as Annie's secretary, so his car being in the front won't cause alarm. I'm sure they have a way to run the plates but will find nothing out of the ordinary. The first thing they will do will be to set up a perimeter. We need to figure out which way they're going to do that," Charles said.

"So we're all going to be inside at the outset, is that right?" Abner asked.

"Correct," Charles responded.

"What's the plan if the brothers want to bring some of the security inside?" Allison asked.

"A flat-out no. With a clarifying statement they are free to leave if they make it an issue," Charles said. "I think since this is a more or less one-on-one, the brothers will agree. If I'm wrong, we'll improvise and suggest a picnic on the veranda. Although I doubt that the Karas brothers even know what a picnic is."

"When we left here yesterday, I took the boys over to Annie's farm to show them the layout," Harry said. "We did a few practice exercises all over the grounds before we went to the dojo and worked out. When we get out there, we'll show you what we call our plan."

Cyrus moved, nudged Jack's leg. The food was all gone. "Let's get this show on the road."

Avery Snowden pushed back his chair. "And I'm going to be where? I understand I'm here strictly for mop-up work, but where do you want me stationed? Where do we park our SUV?"

Fergus held up his hand. "I think it's a mistake to try to hide all of our vehicles. Annie's farm is a working farm. Supposedly. What that means is there would be all kinds of cars, trucks, vans, farm equipment scattered about. Don't you all think it will keep that little army busy trying to keep track of everything if we leave it all out to be seen?"

"Good point," Ky said. "I vote for everything out in the open."

There was some muttering among the gang, but in the end, everyone agreed with Fergus's suggestion.

Cyrus raced to the door.

Annie's farm was two miles down the road, as the crow flies, from Pinewood. The caravan arrived in short order. Snowden got out, walked around, then strategically pointed to various spots for everyone to park their vehicles.

"Looks like there's a party going on. We should have bought some balloons," Ted said, laughing out loud. "I don't think we're going to pose a problem to the brothers. Meaning, Joe, Maggie, Dennis, and me. Annie does own the *Post*, after all, and she would want pictures for tomorrow's edition along with a write-up. The brothers are used to being celebrities in their own right. It's that little army that will be the problem."

Annie's courtyard was three times as big as the one at Pinewood, so there was no problem doing a mock drill.

"Eight suburbans parked here might be a problem," Jack said as he shaded his eyes from the sun. "Let's route them back toward the barn. Avery, the first chance your people get, disable those SUVs." Avery nodded his agreement.

Charles and Fergus arrived just as the group scattered.

The time was eleven-thirty.

Inside, the gang milled around as they checked out all the first-floor rooms, vantage points, window views, and the time as measured in seconds that it would take to get from one vantage point to the next.

The time was twelve noon when the gang assembled in Annie's kitchen.

"An hour to go. I suppose the Karas brothers might be fashionably late, but I doubt it since the messenger who delivered the invitation was firm on his wait time. If anything, I think they will be about ten minutes early. Their army will use those ten minutes for surveillance; then they'll troop on up to the veranda," Jack said.

"Espinosa, Ted, Dennis, and I will be in the sunroom," Maggie said.

"Fergus and I will be in the kitchen," Charles said.

"I'm not sure why I'm even here, but I'll be upstairs in the first room on the left," Abner said.

"You're here to show them we have all of Mezaluma's money. And to tell them their free ride is over," Charles said. "And, of course, to show them your picture gallery."

"The Triad, Harry, and Allison will be in the library, where they will be waiting for Jack once he opens the door, impersonating Annie's secretary," Charles said.

"You still want me and my people in the greenhouse? We will be visible, bear that in mind," Snowden said.

"I wonder if . . . I wonder if the brothers will send out an advance guard, so to speak. Say four of the SUVs, which would mean twenty-four guards," Snowden mused half to himself and half to the others. "We need to take that into consideration. They might even want to check the inside of the house. That is a real possibility, now that I think of it."

"That's not going to happen. The part about their coming into the house," Jack said. Cyrus threw back his head and howled, which meant he was in total agreement.

Allison Bannon threw her hands high in the air, a disgusted expression on her face. "I just remembered something I read about the brothers. Damn it, I can't remember if it's that they are allergic to dogs and cats or they're afraid of them. When I read it, I must have glossed over it, thinking it wasn't relevant to the case. But yeah, it's one or the other."

Jack burst out laughing. "Ferg, how many barn cats you got out there in yonder barn?" he drawled.

"I know the answer. Nine!" Allison shouted.

"Snowden, go scoop them all up and bring them in here. That should liven things up a bit," Jack said, still laughing.

The time was 12:40 when Snowden and his people set down all nine hissing, snarling cats that didn't seem to know what to do.

"They'll figure it out," Charles said. "Okay, everyone, go to your stations and stay sharp."

That left Charles, Fergus, Jack, and Cyrus, along with the nine squalling cats that still didn't know what to do. Cyrus barked incessantly as he tried to shoo them off in different directions. When the cats stayed clustered, he gave one of them a gentle swat with one of his big paws. That did the trick, and the cats hightailed it in different directions.

The time was 12:50 when they heard the sound of the first vehicle approaching the house. The sound increased as seven more SUVs followed suit. "Sounds like a supersonic jet," Jack said, and grinned. "How do I look?"

"Like a slob," Fergus replied, laughing. "Annie would never let you work for her dressed in cutoff shorts, sandals, and a T-shirt that . . . well, it's better left unsaid. Our guests will get the tone of the message."

Cyrus was quivering from head to toe in excitement. The cats were back circling the kitchen at a dazzling speed.

The moment the doorbell rang, Jack smoothed down his hair and walked out of the kitchen, Cyrus at his side. He opened the door with a wide flourish, a questioning expression on his face as he stared at two men who towered over him. "I'm the countess's personal secretary. Today is my day off, but I agreed to stay on to help with her luncheon. And you are?"

"The Messrs. Karas's security team. We'd like to inspect the premises before they enter. It's standard protocol for our employer."

"Well, now, you see, that's not possible. No one crosses this threshold unless they are invited. That's one of the countess's pet rules. You can fetch your employers, but you may not come in. It's just the way it is. Kind of take it or leave it, if you get my drift," Jack, in the guise of the put-upon secretary, said breezily.

"The dog has to go."

"Where?" Jack pretended not to understand just as two of the barn cats streaked across the foyer. It was all he could do to stifle his laughter. "Sorry again, the dog stays."

"Cats! There are cats here, too!" both security men said in unison.

"Yep. Nine in total. The countess loves them; they all have royal names, too. So, what's it going to be? We going to stand here in the doorway talking about animals or is your boss, as in plural, coming for lunch? Like I said, this is my day off, and I've already wasted half of it on this pissant luncheon."

Both security men backed off. "We will, as you suggest, speak with our boss to see what they, as in plural, want to do."

"Looks like an army out there," Jack said, craning his neck to see where the SUVs were positioned. "You'd better snap to it, guys, the countess is hell on wheels when it comes to punctuality. It's five minutes past the hour now. You have maybe seven minutes, or else you can head on out."

The two guards raced to the cluster of SUVs and yanked open the door of the car containing the Karas brothers. "You have seven minutes to decide to go in or not. No security is permitted inside. And . . . there are cats and one massive dog inside. What do you want to do?"

"I knew this was a mistake," Ryland said as he climbed out, shook his jacket into place, and strode forward. Roland followed. "Since we're here already, we might as well suffer through what is sure to be a beastly luncheon. Stay close."

"They say the countess is eccentric," Roland said.

"We follow orders," Ryland snapped.

The door opened before Ryland could ring the bell. Jack stretched his neck to see if anyone had followed the two brothers. He swallowed hard as he saw the solid flank of men surrounding the eight SUVs.

"James Emerson, the countess's private secretary," Jack said, extending his hand. He noted the brothers's buffed and polished nails. "The countess is running a tad behind today. She asked me to escort you to the solarium. She said you are both avid connoisseurs of fine art. You can view her art gallery, which I must say is quite impressive. She has several original Monets and two original Rembrandts."

Mystified at this strange behavior, the brothers had no other choice but to follow Jack, who was apologizing profusely, babbling actually, about his day off and his casual dress. "The countess should be done polishing her tiara by now. I will advise her that you're waiting for her. Enjoy your luncheon, sirs." He couldn't help but notice the two men sniffing for cooking aromas, which were, of course, nonexistent.

Jack suddenly moved sideways to avoid stepping on one of the cruising barn cats. Cyrus barked. The cat hissed and snarled.

"Good God, is that a cat?"

"I believe it is. Ah, yes, that's Smokey Joe. He's the countess's favorite. Ah, here comes Yogi Bear, and the third one is Fred. They're the ordinary cats. I have no idea where the royal ones are. Enjoy the artwork, sirs."

Not to be outdone, and just for fun, Cyrus ambled over to the brothers, who appeared to be clutching at one another, and showed them his pearly whites. Then he growled, after which he let loose with a mighty howl that scared the three cats so badly, they ran for cover.

"You just had to do that, didn't you. Show-off." Jack laughed as he headed for the library to meet up with the Triad and the others.

"Ah, just in time," Harry said. "We were just about to get dressed."

"Dressed for what?" Jack asked.

Harry tossed him a lump of some black material. "What is it?"

"Your ninja outfit!" Allison snapped. "It's for shock and awe, and one size fits all."

"Whatever," Jack said as he donned his new black garb. Cyrus prowled and growled at these strange goings-on. Jack's assessment when everyone was fully dressed was, "If I look half as scary as the rest of you, this should be a win-win for us." He looked down at Cyrus. "Remember what I told you the other day—it's all about the eyes. See, all that is visible on the six of us is our eyes." Cyrus stopped growling as he watched Ky hand out seven metal pointed stars and small cylinders.

Even though Jack knew what he was stuffing in his pockets, Ky said, "I hope your pitching arm is good. Use all your upper-body strength when you throw it. Aim for the upper arm, and it will paralyze it. The minute we hit the courtyard, set off your smoke bomb. Then drop to the ground so you are Cyrus's height. He has the advantage. The smoke will be waist high, giving us the edge. We go for the legs, and we have to move fast. The smoke will last about four to five minutes, then we set off a second round. The minute we step outside, we have maybe thirty to forty seconds of shocked surprise. That's enough time for them to pull their guns. We need to throw the stars in the first five seconds. Don't worry about Cyrus. To them, he's just a dog. They have no idea what a warrior he is, but they will find out soon enough. Any questions?"

No one had any questions.

"Let's do it!" Harry said.

Ky took the lead, followed by Ling and Momo. Then Harry, Jack, and Cyrus. And last was Allison, who was speaking softly to Jack.

"Jack, if anything happens to me, get in touch with Lizzie and . . ."

Jack reached out and gave her arm a hard tug. "If you're going into this with a negative mind-set, then you need to stay behind. Decide right now!"

"I'm good, Jack," Allison whispered.

Ky opened the door and all six ninjas stepped onto the porch.

It all happened just the way Ky said it would. The only thing he left out was the shrill Chinese shrieks of warriors going into battle and Cyrus's bloodcurdling barking. He also left out the cursing that resonated in the air from the Karas brothers' private army.

"Game on," Harry said as he threw out the first star with deadly accuracy. The others followed suit, the sun bathing the stars in liquid silver. The smoke bombs went off in tandem as the ninjas leaped from the porch, then dropped low to the ground, Cyrus leading the way.

The ninjas rolled and tucked, leaped in midair, legs spread, taking out two of the security team at once. Guns came into play, shots were fired randomly, the shooters hoping to hit unseen targets.

The second wave of smoke bombs went off. Grunts and curses, along with Cyrus's insane barking, rivaled the noise level of a rock concert in full swing.

Suddenly, automatic fire erupted. Cyrus raced off. Jack heard a loud thump, a crazy squeal of pain, another thump, then a triumphant bark, just as he heard Allison cry out. On his hands and knees, Jack crawled to the sound just as Cyrus appeared out of the fog. "I'm hit, Jack," Allison gasped as she struggled to breathe.

"Man down!" Jack roared. "Snowden!" he roared again so loud he thought he had burst his own eardrums. "Easy, stay with me, kiddo," Jack said as he tried to assess the damage to Allison Bannon. She was gut shot and was bleeding out. "*No!*" he roared a third time.

"Lizzie . . ."

"Shut up! I promised you nothing would happen. Just shut up. Do you hear me? Stay with me—we're going to fix this." Jack moaned as Avery Snowden pushed him out of the way. Harry yanked him to his feet. He tottered, but Harry held tight.

The Triad appeared out of the smoke, which was almost gone. They all watched as Avery and his people scooped up Allison and raced for the closest vehicle.

"Goddamn it to hell!" Jack cried.

There didn't seem to be anything to say to that comment, so the group remained silent.

"There's work still to be done; then we have to depart these premises," Ling said. Jack shook his head to clear his thoughts, knowing the mission wasn't over yet. There would be time enough later to deal with his guilt.

"I'm good," Jack said.

"We need to tether these guys," Ky said, as the Triad rummaged in their many pockets for what they needed. "Hand to ankle," he barked. "Count the stars, make sure we have them all, along with the smoke casings. Sooner or later, your authorities will figure out it was us. This is our MO. No evidence equals no proof we were ever here."

It took barely twenty minutes to gather all the evidence, stockpile the guns in one massive pile, and drag the bound private army to where the dismantled SUVs were parked.

To a man, they each looked around, satisfied that they had policed the area to perfection. "They'll talk to the authorities to save their own skin, but none of them saw our faces," Ling pointed out.

Harry looked at Jack for instructions. "I told you, I'm okay. Time to head inside to take care of the Karas brothers." On the veranda, Jack didn't bother to open the door, he just kicked it open. Everyone came running from all directions, even the Karas brothers.

Seeing the black-clad ninjas, the brothers tried to shrink against the wall, cowering together like five-year-olds in the dark.

"Your army is all tied up in a pile out there," Jack said. "There's no way out for you two. We need some information from you, and we need it now. We are going to ask you once and once only."

Jack looked around at his team. "Everyone out, head to Pinewood. Harry and I will take care of this. I know you want out of here, Ky, so go. We'll meet you back there once we take care of business. Oh, yeah, someone needs to take the cats back to the barn before they go crazy. Dennis, Ted, Espinosa, get on it."

Maggie lagged behind. "Where . . . what . . . ?" Tears filled her eyes.

"Go!" Jack barked as he patted her back. "Just go, Maggie," he said gently.

Jack ripped at his headgear, as did Harry. They tossed them to the floor and advanced on the Karas brothers, with Cyrus following close behind them.

"This is as good a place as any," Jack said, "especially since it's already a mess."

"We do not know anything. We can't help you. We came here in good faith to a luncheon to help the countess's cause with children," Ryland bleated.

"Bullshit!" Jack said as he rifled through the folder Charles had handed him on the way out. "See this picture! It's your boss, Senor Beteo Mezaluma. He's on his way to the death circuit. Your army is all tied up outside, waiting for the authorities to come for them. You tell us what we want to know, and you can walk out of here." He looked over at Harry and said, "Get Abner back in here!"

Harry stepped to the door and bellowed for Abner, who stopped in midsprint and returned to the house. "What?"

"Show these two gentlemen all those fancy bank accounts they *used* to have."

Abner happily obliged. "What you are seeing on this screen means you are broke. You have no money anywhere in the world, just as Senor Mezaluma has no money. We have it all! Billions. With a *b*. Take as long as you want to study what you see on the screen."

"Things are looking pretty bleak for you right now, guys," Jack said. "Just about as bleak as what Abner just told you about your old boss, who is no one's boss any longer, and his financial situation and future prospects in life. Would you like to place bets on how long he lasts on the death circuit?" Jack said.

"No more designer suits, no more silk underwear or

gourmet food, no more six hundred–dollar hairstyles, no more manicures and pedicures, no more fine wine and first-class travel. The only place you will be traveling to is on a bus to a federal prison, where you will be wearing an orange jump suit with *no* underwear, cardboard sandals, and your hair will be in a ponytail. No reading material, and certainly, there will be no classical music. Well, maybe some rap now and then. Now make nice and tell my colleague what he needs to hear," Harry said.

Jack held up his hand. "Remember, I will ask only once. What is the name of the ship that sailed with the last load of children? When did it leave, and what is its destination? And, of course, the date of arrival. We know you two are the ones who coordinate all the travel transfer of the kids."

Ryland blustered, "You obviously have us mixed up with two other people."

Jack looked at Harry. "I'm taking that as a no, they aren't interested in helping us. What's your take?"

"I agree," Harry snarled.

"Okay. We know you're lying, so . . ." Jack turned to Abner and told him to leave because what was about to go down wasn't fit for his eyes or ears. Abner didn't need to be told twice. He ran as if the hounds of hell were on his trail.

"As I was saying, you, Ryland, love to listen to classical music. Actually, I was told you live for music when you aren't engaged in coordinating the abduction of helpless children. Now that's a fact. Roland, I'm told you live to read. Ryland, we're going to make sure you never hear the sound of music again because we're going to rupture your eardrums. Harry, do his right ear."

"Done!" Harry said. Ryland roared in pain.

"You're up, Roland. You will never read another word." Before Roland could take a breath, Jack dug out one of his eyeballs. Jack could feel Cyrus's warm breath on his leg. He was panting heavily.

"No!" Roland screeched. Jack stuffed the eyeball into the palm of his hand. "I suppose you could stick it back in, but it won't work."

"What's the name of the ship, the destination, the arrival time, and how many children on board?"

"For God's sake, tell him or I will," Roland screeched.

"The *Golden Angel*. It sailed out of Charleston, South Carolina, bound for . . . for Saudi Arabia. There are 240 children on board."

Harry did what he had to do just as Jack did what he had to do.

Afterward, they walked out of Annie's foyer, leaving one man with no eyeballs and a man deaf as a stone. Jack called over his shoulder, "I'd stay put if I were you. Someone will come for you. Or not."

The short ride back to Pinewood was made in total silence.

The huge coffee urn was on, but no one seemed interested. No one seemed interested in talking, either.

"Jack, you need . . . what . . . to go upstairs and take a shower. You're covered in blood," Maggie said.

Jack nodded and headed for the back staircase. Cyrus stayed behind, to everyone's surprise. He took up his position by the sink.

"Where is Mr. Snowden?" Dennis asked.

"I don't know, son," Charles said.

"We have to call . . . someone to . . . come for those . . . creatures."

"Yes, we need to do that. And we will. Just as soon as we get ourselves all situated. We need to wait for Jack."

Ted walked over to the coffeepot, poured coffee into cups, then handed them out.

When Jack returned to the kitchen, he reached out for the cup of coffee Ted handed him.

"The boys and I need to return to the dojo," Jack said. "They can't be within a mile of here when the authorities show up." Charles nodded as he watched the Triad remove all their ninja apparel. "We'll take it all with us."

The Triad made the rounds, shaking hands and bowing. Ky spoke for the others. "While the mission was a success, we . . . we lost a valiant warrior. When we return to China, we will designate a shrine in her name. Thank you again for your hospitality."

The Triad walked over to Cyrus, who stood at attention. "Warrior Cyrus, you have our deepest admiration and thanks for taking the lead on our mission. We will also designate a shrine in your name on our return home."

Cyrus yipped and held out his paw to be shaken.

"That's pretty strong stuff, Cyrus," Jack said. "Dr. Pappas is going to turn himself inside out when we report in next time." Cyrus barked happily.

"I guess we need to clear out, too," Ted said.

"Yes. Once I call this in to the name we sent the ledgers to, every alphabet agency in the District will be out here, and they will find their way here to Pinewood, and to you, too, Jack, if those inhuman sons of bitches can describe you to them, so you also need to leave.

"This way, when the authorities show up, it's business as usual. Let them prove otherwise. You sure now that you policed the area, and nothing was left behind to tie us or the Triad into what went down at Annie's farm?"

"We're sure," Jack said.

"Abner will stay behind here with us," Charles said. "We need him to bounce the call to Mr. Casselli off a satellite."

Fergus made fresh coffee while Abner worked his phone and computer in tandem. "Okay, Phil, make it happen," he said to the person on the other end of the open line. He handed the phone to Charles.

"Mr. Casselli, Allison Bannon asked me to call you should she get in harm's way. I'm doing just that. She said to tell you she left something for you at Countess de Silva's country estate. The countess, by the way, is out of the country at present. She said you would be able to put two and two together. It is also my sad duty to tell you that Agent Bannon was shot and killed a short while ago." Charles listened, then said, "It's not important who I am or what my name is. Ms. Bannon said you were one of the few good guys left and to speak with no one but you, which is what I am doing."

Abner ran his finger across his throat to show that Charles had to cut the call or it would be traced. "Goodbye, Mr. Casselli."

Fergus waited until Abner left before he poured fresh coffee for himself and Charles. "I feel terrible, Charles."

"I know."

"What should we do?"

"Nothing. Would you like to play a game of chess?"

"Might as well."

With things back to normal and the house quiet, Lady took up her position by the kitchen door, her pups alongside her after Charles locked the door.

Just another day at Pinewood.

The mourners were few in number, just the gang and one man standing off to the side under a tree. A light, misty rain was falling. There were two dozen chairs set up under the blue canopy. But they weren't all filled. The gang had taken a vote as to what kind of ceremony would be proper. In the end, they decided to forgo a funeral home and a service, opting instead for a nondenominational minister, who said the proper words for the benefit of the three small children sitting in the front row at the grave site.

The service was somber and short.

Maggie eyed the Springfield casket. Polished bronze. Top of the line. She looked over at Jack, who simply stared ahead. She wondered what he was seeing, if anything. More than likely he was remembering Allison Bannon and his promise to her that nothing was going to happen. Tears rolled down her cheeks as the minister finished his eulogy. One by one, the mourners walked past the casket and laid a white rose on top.

Maggie looked over at the kids, who appeared dazed. She remembered someone's saying that they were full of Benadyrl. To keep them calm. After the service, they were being transported to Las Vegas, where Lizzie would take over. She made a mental note to call Lizzie. Like Jack, she had made a promise to Allison.

Maggie and Ted were the last to leave the grave site. "Hold on, Ted. I want to talk to that man over there." Before Ted could stop her, Maggie sprinted to where a very tall, kind-looking man stood. "Maggie Spritzer. I'm a reporter for the *Post*," she said, holding out her hand. "I think you might be Luka Casselli. Am I right?" The man nodded. "Allison said you were an honorable man. She trusted you. She confided in me."

"Your point?" the big man said.

"Who paid for this funeral? That's a pretty pricey casket. You issued an STK on her, and yet I didn't see anything in any paper except our own about what she did for your agency."

"I refused to issue the STK. I quit on the spot. I paid for this funeral out of my retirement fund. Any more questions?"

"Not a question. A statement. I damn well hate you and your people."

"Totally understandable," the man said, walking away. After taking two steps, he turned around and said, "Everything isn't always black or white, miss. Please remember that. Perhaps someday we can talk about this."

"C'mon, Maggie, let's go home," Ted said.

"I don't want to go home. Let's go get something to eat. I want to come back here after . . . after they . . . lower the casket into the ground."

"Why? Do you think someone is going to run off with the casket?"

"No. I just want to see it *finished*."

"Then let's just wait in the car. I'm not hungry."

"That works for me," Maggie said, heading for the car.

An hour later, Allison Bannon's grave was filled in. The workers and their equipment had been loaded onto a pickup truck. The awning and folding chairs went into another truck, with a tarp over them. Other than the fresh earthy mound of dirt that would eventually sink, it looked like there never had been a funeral.

Maggie ran as fast as she could through the rain with Ted following close behind. She dropped to her knees in the soft earth at the base of the headstone. She traced the carved letters of Allison's name with her index finger. "This is not her real birth date. The death date is correct. Mother of Carrie, Emily, and Andy. That's correct, too. It doesn't say wife. And do you see what these two letters are at the base of the stone? *A.T.* What does that mean to you, Ted?"

"I don't have the faintest clue. I suppose you do. We're getting soaked here, so spit it out, and let's go home."

"*A.T*, Ted. *A.T* means Agnes Twitt. Allison Bannon isn't buried here. I thought there was something funny about that Springfield casket. Allison Bannon is alive somewhere, and I betcha Avery Snowden is behind it all. He spirited her away. No one was supposed to know. No one. Even Jack, who is taking the blame for her death."

Ted's eyes almost popped out of his head as he stared at the initials *A.T.* "Are you sure?"

"Damn straight I'm sure. Why else would that guy Casselli show up here? To make us all think this is for real. I bet he helped Snowden spirit her away. I know I'm right. I just know it."

Ted knew it, too. He put his arm around her shoulder and led her back to the car.

"Do you think they fixed her pearls, Ted? You know, they were askew. 'Askew,' who uses words like that nowadays? Why didn't I say 'crooked' or use some word other than 'askew'?" Maggie babbled.

"Let's go get a steak and a cold pitcher of beer. We can toast Agnes since no one else is here to do it. Does that sound like a plan?"

"Okay. Let's get drunk, Ted, and call an Uber to take us home, where we can do other things."

"Now that is the best and nicest thing you have said all day. I. Am. Your. Man."

The private airport in Orlando was quiet, with no planes taking off or arriving. There was only Ky Moon's Gulfstream, which was being readied for takeoff.

Boxes and colorful shopping bags littered the tarmac as the Triad approached the plane. The portable stairway was already in place, and the pilot and copilot were on board for the long trip back to China.

Seven days had passed since their arrival, and as with all good things, they had to end at some point. The Triad jibber jabbered on about how they had reverted to the age of ten and been kids again. Ky turned to the young woman standing next to Momo. "Thank you for sharing your children with us to enjoy this magical place. You were a wonderful tour guide, Allison."

"I had as much fun as you did. We still have some hours left before you drop me off in Boise, Idaho, to start my new life. I'm a pretty wicked chess player. It's I who should be thanking you."

"Ladies first," Ling said, motioning to the stairs. Allison Bannon scampered up the steps like a sleek panther. She stood in the open doorway, her gaze searching for a certain face. When she saw it, she shot off a stiff salute.

The man who was the recipient of the stiff salute offered up one in return.

"Have a good life, Tea Pope. You've earned it."

Epilogue

Months later.

Cyrus let loose with a loud bark, then another. The mail had just been dropped through the mail slot on the front door. "I hear it, Cyrus," Jack said, getting up from his chair at the conference room table. "I'll get it; you welcome our guests."

Today was the day the gang was having their Christmas luncheon. It was early in the month, but they had all voted for this day because this year, finally, they were getting to take a vacation. It had taken months of planning between the girls and themselves, but finally they had managed to come up with a viable two-week period that was perfect for everyone.

"I cannot wait to get to the islands," Maggie said, her teeth chattering. "I've been looking forward to this since October. What's for lunch?"

"It was delivered right before the mail. Something for everyone: Chinese, Italian, ribs, veggies, and cheesecake. We have beer, wine, and soda, and, of course, coffee," Jack said. "Before we dig in, we need to thank Dennis for the Christmas tree he set up and all the decorations we've been privy to these past few weeks. He also volunteered to take it all down before we leave, so a round of applause to our youngest and richest colleague, Dennis!" Jack said.

The gang hooted, hollered, whistled, and stamped their feet, to Dennis's delight.

Maggie proceeded to hand out plates and silverware along with napkins. Ted poured the drinks.

"Anything in the mail besides bills?" Abner asked.

"I don't know, let me look. Are you expecting something?" Jack asked.

"No. But we don't usually get bulky yellow packages like the one you just got," Abner responded.

Jack frowned. It was true. He should have noticed that, but his thoughts were on his and Nikki's trip to Paris.

Jack ripped open the envelope. "Whoa! What have we here!"

"What? What? What?" the gang chorused.

"It's from Tea Pope. No return address, and the stamp is so blurred I can't see where it was sent from."

"Well, what is it?" Maggie demanded.

"Pictures! The kids. Boy, they've grown in eight months. Allison looks happier than a pig in a mud slide. Look at the little guy. The back of the picture says the cat he's holding is Baby Boo, but Baby Boo turned out to be Baby Booette, and they now have six kittens that Andy takes care of. Emily has two rabbits, and she named them Maggie and Dennis. Carrie has two springer spaniels named Jack and Harry."

"They look so happy," Maggie said, tears rolling down her cheeks.

There wasn't a dry eye in the room when Jack read the short note, which the kids had signed, along with Tea.

Abner was the last at the table to handle the pictures, which he returned to the mailing envelope. "I do have a question, guys. Don't go getting uppity at the term *guys*, Maggie. You are one of the guys, and you know it. Phil wants to know what you guys want him to do with all that money he squirreled away for all of us."

"To be decided," Charles said. "We did do what Allison wanted us to do with Lizzie's help, which is to help in the war to save and work for missing and exploited children. We donated every cent. It won't eliminate what's going on, but it will put a serious dent in the operation. A new hydra will rear up sooner rather than later. That's when we can delve into all that other money and make it work.

"Lizzie told me that, on Allison's instructions, she sent a bucket load of money to Luka Casselli. Anonymously, of course. She told him where it came from, and he didn't have a bit of trouble accepting it. He's retired on some island that has no phones and no electricity. He lives with candles and propane. Fishes for his food, has a garden, and has learned how to cook," Charles said.

"Who should we toast?" Fergus asked as he poured champagne into funny-looking paper cups.

"I know! I know!" Maggie squealed.

"Who?"

"Now who do you think? Agnes Twitt, Alfred Saddlebury, Chester Mason, Sasha Yakodowsky, and Benjamin Franks!"

There was no laughter, no jocularity but there were wet eyes as the funny paper cups were raised high in the air. Instead, Dennis said simply:

"Rest in peace."